Don't You Want Me?

INDIA KNIGHT

D0177246

PENGUIN BOOKS

PENGUIN BOOKS

Published by the Penguin Group
Penguin Books Ltd, 80 Strand, London WC2R 0RL, England
Penguin Group (USA) Inc., 375 Hudson Street, New York, New York 10014, USA
Penguin Group (Canada), 90 Eglinton Avenue East, Suite 700, Toronto, Ontario, Canada M4P 2Y3
(a division of Pearson Penguin Canada Inc.)
Penguin Ireland, 25 St Stephen's Green, Dublin 2, Ireland (a division of Penguin Books Ltd)
Penguin Group (Australia), 250 Camberwell Road, Camberwell, Victoria 3124, Australia
(a division of Pearson Australia Group Pty Ltd)
Penguin Books India Pvt Ltd, 11 Community Centre, Panchsheel Park,
New Delhi – 110 017, India
Penguin Group (NZ), 67 Apollo Drive, Rosedale, Auckland 0632, New Zealand
(a division of Pearson New Zealand Ltd)
Penguin Books (South Africa) (Pty) Ltd, 24 Sturdee Avenue, Rosebank, Johannesburg 2196,
South Africa

Penguin Books Ltd, Registered Offices: 80 Strand, London WC2R 0RL, England

www.penguin.com

First published 2002
Reissued in this edition 2011

1

Copyright © India Knight, 2002

The permissions on p.261 constitute an extension of this copyright page

The moral right of the author has been asserted

Printed in Great Britain by Clays Ltd, St Ives plc

A CIP catalogue record for this book is available from the British Library

ISBN: 978–0–241–95178–1

www.greenpenguin.co.uk

MIX
Paper from
responsible sources
FSC
www.fsc.org
FSC™ C018179

Penguin Books is committed to a sustainable
future for our business, our readers and our
planet. This book is made from paper certified
by the Forest Stewardship Council.

In memory of my father,
Michel Aertsens,
1927–2001

Where is the life that late I led?
Where is it now? Totally dead.
Where is the fun I used to find?
Where has it gone? Gone with the wind.
A married life may all be well,
But raising an heir
Could never compare
With raising a bit of hell
So I repeat what first I said:
Where is the life that late I led?

– Cole Porter

I

I am lying in my bed, listening to Frank having sex again. 'Gur-runt, gur-runt, gur-runt, gur-runt, gur-runt' is what it sounds like: coitus as iambic pentameter, which you must admit is unusual. His is the only voice I can hear: is he having the sex with himself, I wonder? Because he's being unnecessarily vocal for a solo performance: if you have a quick Barclays, you hardly need to provide your own running commentary. What can he possibly be saying to himself? 'You're hot, Frank, mate. You make me hard, know what I mean? Does this feel good, Frankie, baby?' God, how creepy. How deeply, deeply creepy. The *freak*!

I do not deserve my life, I really don't. I've never deliberately hurt anybody, I pay my taxes, I love my child, and what do I get? An absolute pervo smut-freak of a house-mate: a man who lies there dirty-talking himself. Oh, yuck. Oh, blee. I might have to switch the light on and pace up and down for a bit.

Still, makes a change, the solo business. It's usually a duet.

But I spoke too soon, for lo, here's tonight's ladyfriend, who's been silent as the tomb until now: 'Eee,' she's saying – perhaps she's from Yorkshire. Very high-pitched, at any rate. 'Eee.' Oh, I see: 'Frank-eeee.'

I suppose that makes it marginally better. But still . . . I am really, really happy for Frank that he's having so much sex – someone in this house has to, and it sure as pants isn't me. But I'd rather not be listening. Not that that's what I'm doing – listening. I am *overhearing* by accident. You couldn't not. Oh, I wish I was earless and had lots of elegant turbans, like my great-aunt, who of course *had* ears, but you get the gist.

On and inexorably on it goes: 'Gur-runt, gur-runt . . .' (Frankie's sexual technique is quite impressive: it's been at least twenty-five minutes. Dominic took about half this time, including foreplay. Still, he was English, so what can you expect? I'm lucky I got away with my bottom intact.)

I know what you're thinking: that it's all very well for me to sit, or rather lie, here complaining, and that if I don't like it then I should stop listening like some depraved voyeur, or rather *écouteur*, and maybe put some music on, or get into the shower, or just *go somewhere else*. But I can't. It's two a.m.: the creak of floorboards, let alone a sudden blast of either water or Puccini, would simply make it perfectly clear to Romeo and Juliet that I can hear everything. Besides, I'm cosy in my bed: I don't want to go out anywhere. And it's raining. It always rains here.

Christ, I wish he'd hurry up. Why are the walls so bloody thin, anyway? There's a whole bathroom between us: I really shouldn't be able to hear a thing. This is a big fat square Victorian house: you'd think the walls were as thick as tree trunks. They probably made them thin on purpose, so that Mr Unwholesome Victorian could hear the maids being shagged. Bloody pervy, weird English (I must stop saying that, actually, or even thinking it: I'm half English myself).

Thank God Honey is tucked up two floors away. Brahms's Lullaby this ain't, *comme on dit à New York*.

'Woah, God,' Frank suddenly shouts, sounding agonized. 'Woah, God.'

'Eee,' she says. 'Aaaa. Aaaa.' And then, sounding oddly tribal, 'Oa. Oa. Oa. Oa.' Exactly like that: four times. She likes the simple vowel sounds, clearly.

And then she screams.

Clear as a bell, she screams, 'In my face. Yurgh. Yurgh. Hooooooo yes. Hoooooo yes. RAAAAH.'

And then, finally, there is quiet.

So obviously it's a teeny bit awkward at breakfast the next morning. I wasn't going to say anything – I tend not to – but I wake up both knackered and in a furious bad mood. I didn't get to sleep until after three, and Honey woke up at six, as toddlers will. Mary, her baby-sitter-cum-occasional child-minder, has finally arrived to look after her for a few hours, and the two of them have gone off into the living room armed with puzzles, board books and a vast collection of dollies.

Honey looks as fresh as a daisy. I look like a gnarled old oak, especially under the eyes. It's just before nine, and here we are in the kitchen. Frank's wearing his favourite battered tartan dressing gown and is squeezing oranges. The oranges match his hair (body, head and, presumably, pubis). So if you think this is one of those 'And there the love of my life was all along, *right under my nose*' stories, you are very much mistaken.

Frank has a lot going for him: he's charming, he's clever, he's funny, he's kind, and he is extraordinarily professionally successful – my ex-husband Dominic now sells his paintings for tens of thousands of dollars. His face is nice too: stern jaw, flinty grey eyes and a mouth that looks potentially cruel (very sexy, I always think) until he smiles his lovely, faintly goofy disarming smile. Great body, too: lanky yet broad but not overdeveloped, and marvellous sinewy arms from all that painting.

So on paper, yes, foxy in the extreme. On paper, I'd read about him and shout, 'Go on, my son,' to myself. On paper, I'd be the one having sex with him, and teaching him the beauty of consonants. But this isn't paper, and while all of the above are true, there is one insurmountable problem.

If I got desperate enough, I could just about go with light strawberry blond. Or pale Titian, maybe, or whatever lying excuses for 'ginger' people come up with. But Frank isn't merely ginger. He is, as I said, as orange as the fruits he is squeezing: not merely ginger, but practically fluorescent. He makes the average carrot look pretty peaky.

The problem isn't just his head hair. The problem, for me, with gingers – and yes, I happily admit I have a problem, so you don't need to bore me with 'What would it sound like if you substituted "black people" for "gingers"?' because I *know*, I know how bad it sounds – lies in the secondary hair. (Black people, cleverly, never have ginger hair.)

If it was just the head, I could make my ginger lover wear a hat at all times, or I could just shave it off. There would still be a faint marmalade shadow, but if I kept my contact lenses out, I probably would barely notice. No, it's the other hairs. It's the ginger chest hair, and the ginger arm and leg hair and – here's the crux of it – the *ginger armpit hair*, all damp and curlicued after lovemaking . . . and the pubic hair. The orang-utan-orange pubic hair of someone

4

like Frank. I simply can't countenance it: for some people it's hairy backs that make them dry-heave, or men with pronounced female buttocks (never, I'll grant you, a good look), or the old weeny peeny problem. Or – God – man-boobs. For me, it's orange pubes: *no pasarán*.

That's not all, unfortunately. And I can't dismiss the other stuff as easily – as facetiously – as the orange body-wool, either. The fact is that Frank is casually promiscuous in a way that stuns and fascinates me in equal measure: joyfully, guiltlessly, permanently up for it. Which is fine, of course, but one wouldn't necessarily want to go there: every woman Frank sleeps with becomes a notch – an instantly forgettable, inconsequential little notch – on his bedpost.

He's forgetful in other respects too. I happen to know that Frank has a child up in Newcastle, where he comes from (Frank never wears coats). A child – a daughter – whom he never sees and never mentions. And the child presumably has a mother, of whom Frank has never spoken. And I have a problem with that, I really do: such a problem, in fact, that I can't even bring the subject up with him. I am silenced by my own disgust. So let's just say Frank is not my dream date, and leave it at that.

But I digress.

'Morning, Stella,' Frank beams, handing me a glass of orange – natch – juice. 'Sleep well?'

I raise one eyebrow and give him a slow, deliberate look. He understands it, and a hot blush starts creeping up his Celtically pale face.

'Maybe you could very sweetly buy me a present,' I tell him sternly.

'What, like a bunch of flowers? It'd feel a bit like apologizing to the landlady,' he smiles.

'I was thinking more of earplugs.'

'Oh, God,' says Frank, covering his face with his hands in the usual way. 'Oh, God. I'm really, really sorry.'

'It's OK,' I tell him. 'But honestly, Frank, you do this all the time, and if you're going to be quite so, um, vocal, then earplugs really might be an idea.'

'Yeah,' says Frank, staring at his bare toes, which are scrunched with horror. 'Honestly, Stella – I didn't even know it was going to happen, otherwise, you know . . .'

'What? Otherwise what?'

'Well, we could have gone to hers, or whatever.'

'You never do, though, do you? Are they all homeless? Anyway, I hope it was worth it. Was it good?' I've gulped down my juice and am standing by the coffee machine. 'Coffee?'

'Yes, please. Was what good?'

'The sex, Frank.'

Frank, I am pleased to notice, has gone scarlet. What with the tangerine above the red face, he looks like the kind of cardigan women wore in the late Nineties.

'Stella, honey, you can't ask things like that,' he says, trying not to stammer. He shakes his head. He is scrabbling for something to say. 'I'm a good Catholic boy,' is what he comes out with, absurdly.

'Yuck! Don't talk to me as if I were your mummy. Firstly, you're not a boy: you were a thirty-five-year-old man, last time I looked. Secondly, Catholic doesn't come into it, frankly.'

'Stella,' Frank interrupts.

'Thirdly,' I interrupt him back, 'thirdly, Frank-eee, there

6

is nothing good or Catholic or even boyish about *coming on women's faces*. Classy number, was she? Known her long?'

Frank slams his juice down on the counter, spilling it.

'For fuck's sake, Stella! Have some respect!'

'What, like you respect the female form?'

'Stella! Stop it!'

We stand in uneasy silence, glaring at each other. I might have gone too far, I think to myself. On the other hand, it gets really on my nerves when people – English men – are all uptight about something you've actually heard them do. I'll just go a little further: test his mettle.

'Oa. Oa. Oa,' I shout, right into his face. 'Oa, Frankie, baby.'

Frank looks truly appalled. He runs his hand through his hair, which is standing up in soft peaks, like egg whites would if egg whites were orange. And then he smiles, and I smile, and then we giggle.

'You're an appalling human being,' he says. 'You do terrible things.'

'Pot,' I reply. 'I don't believe you've ever met kettle.'

He rolls his eyes.

'Really, Frankie. I know it's none of my business, but "oa, oa"?'

Frank is trying to look severe, and failing. He laughs through his nose, and then properly, out loud. When he laughs, his eyes start watering, which always sets me off. He does it now. We laugh, and then he snorts, and then we're friends again.

I expect you're wondering how I come to be sharing a house with a sex-obsessed ginger man. It's a bit of a long story, but I'd better tell it, and that way we'll have got the boring explanatory bit out of the way and can go on with the rest.

My name, as you will have noticed, is Stella. It's really Estelle, but I got so tired of the mispronunciation I had to put up with daily – 'Ee-stell', 'Eh-stelley', 'Es-tewell', even 'Esther' – and with people asking me to spell it for them, that I anglicized it some years ago. I am, as I mentioned, partly English, on my mother's side. My father is French (and, I think, possibly gay, though I can't be quite sure; certainly, he's the campest man on earth, as you will see). I was brought up in Paris, speaking French, although Mummy, being one of those tenaciously snobbish Englishwomen who spend twenty years abroad and deliberately don't quite master the basic gist of the language, always spoke English to me at home.

So I was brought up bilingual, although obviously living in Paris meant that all my day-to-day business – school, friends, shops, restaurants – was conducted in French. We spent summer holidays in England every year, staying with my maternal grandparents at their house in East Sussex, and this, combined with my mother's descending like a ton of bricks the second her immaculate ear discerned anything approaching a French accent in me – 'Darling, don't be *froggy*' – means that I speak English like, well, a native.

(Odd of my mother to marry a Frenchman and then be embarrassed by Frenchness, isn't it? If she imitates someone French, she literally says, 'Nee nor nee nor'. But it often happens when English people marry 'foreigners', I notice: blissfully exotic for thirty seconds, and then an albatross of shame for the next twenty years.)

I spent a couple of years at a boarding school in the

shires when Mummy and Papa separated, when I was fourteen. That was when I realized, on a daily basis, that I could sound as English as Judi Dench, but that, like it or not, in the middle-class world which I inhabited, I was hopelessly, helplessly foreign: I liked my family better than I liked horses, I couldn't eat grey mince, I'd done snogging, I liked cigarettes and was allowed to smoke one a day at home, I refused to play lacrosse on the grounds that it would ruin my calves (I know: terrible of me – true, though), and so on and so inexcusably foreignly forth. Still, I made some nice horse-faced friends and became good at tennis, so it wasn't entirely wasted.

I shan't bore you with my days at university – two years at the Sorbonne, one at Cambridge, reading Romance Languages. All you need to know is that I didn't work particularly hard, went to a lot of parties and generally had a lovely time. After Cambridge, I got married to the boy I'd been going out with in the summer term: we were only twenty-two and, really, it was doomed to failure. In the event, it lasted two silly, giggly years and the split was entirely friendly: Rupert is even Honey's god-father.

Unfortunately for lonely old me – I could do with an extra friend right now – Rupert, having lived the post-marital life of an eligible west Londoner to the full – shag-pad in Ladbroke Grove and so on – decided six months ago to grow a beard, up sticks and move to the Hebrides, where he studies birds, eats crabs, wears itchy sweaters and is, by his own account, blissfully happy. Funny how people always revert to type: I remember his mother telling me that he spent his entire childhood collecting feathers and climbing up trees to find nests.

I moved around Europe for a while and then, aged twenty-seven, I went home to Paris and started working as a translator. I had a wonderful life: a flat in the Marais, good friends, a fantastic bistro right underneath my apartment – they'd send up old-fashioned *soupe à l'oignon* when I had a cold or a hangover. The only fly in the ointment was work: there's a limit to how excited you can get translating endless documents about petrochemical companies' plans for expansion. Still, it seemed that the more boring and technical the job, the better you got paid, so I pottered along happily. The odd love affair along the way kept things zinging nicely; I was, with the luxury of retrospect, perfectly content.

I met Dominic Midhurst when I was thirty-four, through my poofy father, who has always had a fondness for contemporary art (at one stage during my childhood – this would have been the late Sixties – he decided we should live in a bare white house with white rubber flooring and huge disturbing, nightmare-inducing canvases of what I remember to be carcasses, though surely they can't all have been, adorning the double-height walls. We also had a small, graphically realistic painting in the downstairs loo of an erect, perfectly pink penis called, not unreasonably, *Le Penis*, artist unknown, though I always suspected Papa had sketched it).

When we met, Dominic, who was a couple of years younger than me, was just beginning to create his empire: he understood the importance of PR and publicity before anyone else did, and had a stable of young conceptual artists (what does this *mean*? Don't all artists have a concept? It's like the houses you see advertised for sale, proclaiming themselves to be 'architect-designed'); artists who could all be relied on to grace the gossip pages of the tabloids on a regular basis with some outrage or other.

My father bought some works – you could hardly call them paintings – for his XVIième apartment, and after a few months it turned out that Dominic needed someone to translate his increasingly hefty, wordy catalogues for him. Oddly, since he's never claimed to actually like Dominic much, Papa volunteered me, and although neither the idea of my daddy getting me a job, nor the art, nor the pale, blond, effete Dominic was exactly my cup of tea, the alternative career-wise would eventually have involved something like moving to Brussels to translate at the European Commission. Working for Dominic meant I could keep my beloved flat, keep taking the onion soup, and continue my affair with a Parisian bookshop owner with a foot fetish (inexplicable, as fetishes go. I mean, *feet*). So I took the job and started translating the quasi-nonsensical catalogues.

Eventually Dominic decided it would be easier for everyone concerned if I worked from his Paris gallery rather than from home (there were then two galleries, one in Paris and one in London: he divided his time between them) with, in many cases, the art hanging in front of me, for clarification purposes. As well as translating the catalogues, in which ludicrously pseudy sentiments were expressed in award-winningly ludicrous pseudy sentences, I began involving myself with the general day-to-day life of the gallery; this occasionally involved going to lunch with Dominic and some potential buyers.

Dominic, like my mother and Jane Birkin, spoke only the most rudimentary, heavily accented French: very charming, boldly fast, but not quite up to a serious discussion of the various merits of our various artists. After the clients had left, we'd sit and drink a cognac companionably, and slowly came to realize we quite enjoyed each other's company. 'You make me laugh, Stella,' he once said, with the sense of shocked, not entirely delighted wonder one might use if saying, 'You make me poo.'

So yes, obviously, we started dating, but it took two years: hardly the old *coup de foudre*. Sitting in the back room of the gallery, I'd noticed he had a predilection for vacant-seeming leggy blondes with artfully striped hair: the kinds of women who look best in sports cars (Dom had two, both red: if big car = small dick, I thought to myself, does big car × 2 = 'Is it in yet?' proportions?).

I had the legs, but that was about it: in every other respect, I was the physical antithesis of what he usually went for. I'm tall, have shoulder-length dark brown hair, once poetically described by Dominic as being the colour of bitter chocolate, and matching eyes. I'm OK – I really like my eyelashes – but you wouldn't necessarily think 'polo and champagne' if you looked at me, and polo and champagne were very much what Dominic seemed to be about deep down: he was about those women who you think must have micro-manicurists, invisible to the naked eye, permanently welded to their immaculate fingernails. My fingernails were bitten and, at the time, I wore no make-up and no heels: I dressed out of (French) thrift shops, in fourth-hand old dresses by Dior and Balenciaga. I looked remarkable, I'd always tell myself, but in the capital of style, I must have also looked pretty peculiar.

He was hardly my type either: he was like my school friends' brothers. You know the look: sort of Bleached English, complete with floppy former public schoolboy hair and a pronounced liking for scuffed Chelsea boots and frayed pale pink shirts from Turnbull & Asser. Being an art dealer, though, this look was accessorized with a perfect mockney accent and a selection of sharp black Prada coats that deliberately confused the issue class-wise: his artists, it seemed to me, appeared to believe that Dom was a geezer done good. He didn't disabuse them.

But then, two years after I'd first met him and six months or so into those lunches, Dominic lunged (the English always lunge, as if they want to pin you down before you run away). It was easy not to resist. The amount of time he spent in Paris convinced me that he was not problematically English, especially when it came to sex: he didn't want to spank me, or be spanked, for instance. Dominic was charming, witty, spoke French fearlessly badly and was always whisking me off to some *m'as-tu-vu* new restaurant where, very occasionally, people would recognize him. How could I resist him?

We got Not Married, which is to say official cohabitation began, in 1999, which was also the year we moved to London. I was thirty-six and hadn't spent time in the capital for over a decade. In my heart, I knew even then that he was hardly the love of my life; but then surely that was the point of getting Not Married: you could always walk away without too much debris. In theory, at any rate. Even then, though, the theory seemed a bit half-arsed: I mean, either love someone and marry them, or don't, and keep your own apartment. (I didn't, sadly: my Marais flat went up for sale, and all my stuff got packed into boxes and shipped to London.)

To his credit, Dom didn't claim that I was the love of his life either: what he said was, 'We'll have such good fun,

Stella. We'll have everything we want. You're the only woman I know who doesn't bore me.' I was *charmed* by this last sentence, as you would be. And then, even though we were from the generation that didn't get married – too bourgeois, which is a laugh, considering our circs – he clicked open an old box from Cartier and presented me with a Thirties emerald, when I'd expected either nothing or a 'contemporary' number with metal spikes and stones that looked like ploppety pellets. So that, conclusively, was that.

He was right: we did have fun, we liked each other, and if the bed-action quickly became unremarkable, we never discussed it. He kept his promise, too: our life by then was, I suppose, really quite glamorous from the outside: dinner invitations arrived by their dozen every week at our big, leafy Primrose Hill house; there were two or three parties a night; and Dominic's growing fame meant that, although we still hung out with his posse of artists, our social circle grew increasingly large, with all sorts of creative types lounging about our drawing room, as well as the odd promising young MP, media tycoon or on-the-up actor.

By the time Honey was born – a year later, making me, as my obstetrician kindly pointed out, an 'elderly' first-time mother – it would not be an exaggeration to say that we knew what passes for 'everyone'. The world, or at least London, was our oyster, and if every now and then I wondered why the oyster had no pearl – well, that was just me being spoiled. And if a part of me wondered why pregnancy hadn't spurred us on to tie the knot – it seems incredibly *rude* to me not to marry someone when they've gone to the trouble of carrying your child and pushing it out of their poor vagina – well, ditto.

I was never entirely comfortable with the boho notion of Not Married: it seemed a bit of a swizz from the female standpoint, and once Honey came along the feeling just got exacerbated. It's all very well to lie about how 'It's only a piece of paper' and to make jokes about balls and chains, but really – who, given the choice, wouldn't swish around Mayfair with a twenty-foot train? But having done it once, I told myself that wanting to do it again was just greedy. I told myself a lot of things in those days.

The real problems started occurring shortly after Honey's birth, when I finally pointed out to Dominic what had become painfully obvious to me over the past year: namely that the social circles we moved in may have been glittering, but the people in them were fantastically dull. Most of his artists were what Dom, in his nastier moments, freely described as 'barely literate oiks' (secretly despised) who believed their own publicity so much that they found their own unintelligent boorishness potently, dizzyingly charming. They all drank like fishes and would end many an evening vomiting and exposing their cocks, like unattractive adolescents with an interest in being 'outrageous'. The problem was that some of these Bright Young People were by now in their forties, and you just *died* of embarrassment on their behalf, or at least I did. Dominic pretended to look amused, and then rang the gossip columns.

I never got on especially well with them once I knew them properly (which took seconds: there often wasn't anything *to* know). Sometimes I'd wish someone would point out that this particular Emperor or that had no clothes. Hard to do, though, when you're the agent's wife: instead, you had to smile and say things like, 'I adored *ShitMan*. So clever of you to create beauty out of your own, er, waste,' and then look enthralled as Artist A or B haltingly, as if translating simultaneously from Xhosa, explained the (literal) ins and outs of the creative/lavatorial process. That was when I started developing internal Tourette's: the words that came out of my mouth were perfectly reasonable; but the words galloping around my head were dementedly not.

There wasn't much more luck elsewhere. Dominic's handful of old school friends, now MPs and journalists, seemed oddly ingratiating: I think it's fair to say that, residual fondness aside, they only really liked Dominic and me because of our so-called friends. 'One meets the most extraordinary people at your house,' the Member for Acton's wife once told me, with the kind of sniff, familiar from my mother, that meant, 'It may very well be fun, but it isn't quite cricket.' My own school friends were now married women running large households in the Home Counties: sweet, but hardly soul-mates, banging on about Pony Club, pressing jam recipes on one and moaning about their lack of sex lives. They, too, considered me a curiosity: having thought of me for years as bad French Claudine from *Mallory Towers*, they were interested enough in the superficial gloss of my life to remain in touch, but the gloss, such as it was, was so alien to them that any conversation would end with them faux-shuddering and saying, 'Oh, Stella. What a funny life! I don't know how you do it.' I wanted them to envy me; it was clear they didn't.

I suppose what I am trying to say is that I was lonely. Not pitiably lonely, certainly, and the old thing about making your bed and lying in it certainly applied. But once my darling little Honey came along, I started asking myself what kind of a household she was being brought up in. Our five-bedroomed Primrose Hill house was a sort of upmarket dossing place for Dominic's clients, friends and assorted hangers-on, even when Dom wasn't there (he still spent half his time in Paris): I'd come down with her for the early-morning feed, nightied and leaky-breasted, and find strangers lying across the brutal and frankly ugly designer furniture. I was too old for this, I kept telling myself, and besides had never had any kind of yearning for this rock 'n' roll lifestyle: I wanted hardcore domestic, in the way that you always want the opposite of your own childhood. Something, it became clear, had to give, and since Dom was either unwilling or unable to abandon – well, his life, it made sense to remove myself from it. We separated a year ago, when Honey was eight months old. I wasn't sorry: disliking Dominic's life was one thing, but I'd also begun to dislike him.

Dominic, who is so freakily controlling professionally, was pretty much exemplary about the split, which is more than I can say about our friends. Not Marriage notwithstanding, he gave me the house, a decent amount of alimony – which I supplement with the odd translating job – and moved, conveniently, to Tokyo, where gallery number four was about to open (number three's in Los Angeles), his Japanese girlfriend in tow. Dom surfaces for a few days once a month. It's not ideal as far as Honey is concerned – her main contact with her father is via Hello Kitty parcels from Japan, faxed drawings and little notes – but he claims to be devoted to her and I see no reason to disbelieve him. On the other hand, the house is now a haven of blessed peace and calm, there are no horrible surprises in human form when we come down to breakfast, there is no dirt, and Honey is the cheeriest, chirpiest eighteen-month-old imaginable, so we must be doing something right.

I've completely redecorated the house, funding myself from the sale of a couple of the more hideous art works which Dominic had given me during our marriage: a giant sculpture of a seven-foot-tall man that looks just like Morph's spastic brother, excreting the world while screaming with bottom-ache (*This Hurts Me More Than It Hurts You*, plaster and cigarette ash, 1996, sold on by me for – seriously – £20,000); and a drawing by Kevin Autan, who may or may not have limbs – I'd guess he held the pen in his mouth – of a woman with the face of a mosquito (*Stung*, crayon and biro, 1998, £8,000).

So where there were concrete floors and stainless steel, there's now reclaimed oak flooring and cherry-red cup-boards (the kitchen); where there were hideous Seventies love-seats, hard lines and pale grey walls, there's fresh yellow paint, squishy sofas, flowers and faded patchwork throws (the living room); and our bedroom, formerly an angular minimalist nightmare, is a softly lit, hot-pink den of sin: I took my inspiration from the New Orleans bordello look. Except, of course, that I have no one to sin with.

I didn't like many of the people Dominic and I hung out with, but I never let them know it: I fed them, watered them, gave them beds to sleep in and cooked them eggs in the morning. I went to their boring dinners and spent weekends in their country houses, I talked to them. I was as gracious as I am capable of being. I bought their children presents, even though most of their children behaved like monsters and were so plain that really the best present would have been a brown paper bag. I even went on holiday with a few of them, an experience reminiscent of finding oneself in a Victorian freak show, sandwiched between the Pinhead and the Bearded Lady, with their child the Torso, writhing about on the floor, making subhuman noises: it would always take me weeks to recover.

Now, I'm not saying these friends of Dominic's should have sworn eternal allegiance to me when Dom and I split up. But they vanished, proving that some clichés only endure because they are so true. Sure, a few of the men took me out to dinner, were affronted when I wouldn't weep prettily, bemoaning my fate, let alone bitch about Dominic, and lunged just before pudding, with varying degrees of crudity. And yes, a couple of the women rang me to see whether I was 'all right', and seemed disappointed to hear that I was (just as a few women became oddly watchful of their husbands when I was around, as though their portly, balding partners were all Brad Pitt, and as such irresistible to me). But that was all.

I can't say I miss them, exactly, but you'd think that in 2001 people would understand that an amicable separation doesn't necessarily mean that the whole world has to take sides. But take sides they have: Dominic is rich, successful, knows everyone and throws great parties. I'm a non-working housewife of sorts, left in my big house, barely knowing anyone really – not properly – and although the invitations haven't quite dried up, I sometimes feel like a horrible kept thing, rattling about my cage, beholden.

Frank, bless him, was the only one who really stuck by me. I met him a couple of years ago in Paris: Dominic had meetings all day and Frank, already a star client, needed to be entertained (he paints giant, twelve-foot-plus canvases of cows: not quite my thing, but at least he can draw – the cows do look like they're about to come up to you and moo). I took him to lunch at L'Ami Louis, where we ate perfect roast chicken and drank perfect white Burgundy well into the afternoon, and then we went shopping for candles at Diptyque on the Boulevard St-Germain, and then we went to look at Marie Antoinette's sad cell at the Conciergerie. 'Don't start,' I said as we ascended the dark, narrow stairs. 'What?' asked Frank. 'I know the revolution was a good thing et cetera et cetera,' I said, 'but I won't have you making jokes about nobs all deserving to have been dragged to the guillotine. Not while we're actually looking at her things.'

He didn't, and later he said he'd like to see Versailles, and this seemed so unlikely, so improbable – Francis Keane, artist as pop star, wearing his working-class credentials like a badge of honour, wanting to see the prettiest, richest, most glittering thing he could see in Paris – that I was enchanted.

We became firm friends, and when Frank needed somewhere to live upon coming back from Berlin, where he'd been working for the past six months as a consultant to some German museum of modern arse, I offered him a room in my house. He's been here three months and is, in many respects, a marvel: he's a domestic god, and not only on the cooking front – within two weeks of arriving, he secured the services of Mary O'Connor, an old friend of his mother, to look after Honey. There's clearly something not quite right with Frank in the commitment department – the number of women who have been up my stairs are testament to that. Still, so what, really? Each to his own: I don't see that it's actually any of my business. I just wish that I could view his slapperiness with the amused detachment I would probably muster up if I were with someone myself. But I'm single, and the amount of sex Frank gets is getting me down, and if I'm not careful it'll make me bitter. I must find some of my own.

2

I know I bang on about the English being strange, but clearly a little part of me isn't quite convinced, since I've sort of married two of them. I must make more of an effort, I resolve, and be less condemning, and here, in this morning's post, is my chance: a postcard from Isabella Howard, one of the former friends, not sighted for months, asking me to dinner on Friday. Which is tomorrow – rather impolitely short notice, but I am not in a position to mind. Surely Frank or Mary could baby-sit.

Human company! New people! I practically skip upstairs to get dressed – little vest, green cardigan with brown fur collar, violet tweed skirt and my favourite shoes, pea-green slingbacks. It's October, but I can never quite manage tights. I stuff my hair into a rubber band, slick some Vaseline on to my lips *et voilà*: hardly glamorama, but ready to face the day.

Frank must have gone to his studio; there's no sign of him. I scoop Honey out of Mary's lap, because today we're off to playgroup. Felicity, one of our neighbours, recently noticed I had a child roughly the same age as hers and asked me along to Happy Bunnies, a parent-run playgroup a couple of streets away. It's on Tuesdays and Thursdays and two of you take it in turn to do shifts, reading the children stories and changing their nappies and so on. The other mothers are there too, keeping an eye on things, so it shouldn't be too difficult. Today is our first time, and I'll be tailing Felicity as Helper Number 2 and sort of learning the ropes.

I'm really rather looking forward to it. I know hardly anyone locally, let alone anyone with small children, and I sometimes feel leprously alone as I wheel Honey along Primrose Hill or up Hampstead Heath, wishing desperately that I had someone to chat to, and then to go for coffee with afterwards. After today, God willing, I may have. I let out an absurd little squeak of excitement, which Honey copies all the way to the front door.

'We are mice,' I tell her happily. 'We are squeaky mice.'

'Mama,' says Honey, who doesn't say much.

It's going to be a good day, I feel, as I push the buggy on to the damp pavement.

The church hall that Happy Bunnies is in is incredibly dirty. The lino is smeared and dusty, the equipment covered in smudges and fingermarks and sticky patches. Why haven't the Happy Bunny parents got busy with the Domestos Wipes? And why are certain kinds of middle-class people so weirdly keen on dirt? I think it's because they think it's bohemian and anti-bourgeois, but really, my God. A tousled beauty with a perfect complexion and faint traces of mud under her fingernails is one thing, but this is quite another; and anyway, the dirt thing is a dead giveaway that you're in a place where every woman has been privately educated, has a name that ends in 'a' and sees herself as not a run of the mill member of the bourgeoisie but as something gayer, less predictable, freer: a bohemian. And Primrose Hill, where we live, is boho central. Sometimes I really yearn for the scrubbed surfaces and disinfected floors of somewhere less apologetically middle class, like Balham.

God, the dirt. Why, for instance, do all of these children have runny noses which no one is wiping? And there's a powerful smell of nappy. Still, best to pretend there is nothing peculiar about this (though clearly there is: if your child has a dirty nappy, change it, for God's sake – there's nothing bohemian about shit).

I beam hopefully at the assorted mothers – half a dozen or so of them – sitting on child-sized chairs watching their offsprings' nasal dribble with pride, and my heart sinks. They're a dull-looking lot, and then there's the person directly to my left. She is an elephantine woman wearing – can this be possible in 2001? – a tightly belted pastel-blue jump suit. Her toenails are gnarled and filthy. One enormous, veiny breast is out, being suckled voraciously by a malevolent-looking child with little avian eyes. He must be at least four years old. Christ. It makes my nipples hurt just to look at her. I turn away, but not, I think, quickly enough. The woman, the creature – she reminds me of a cow: perhaps Frank could paint her – shoots me a dark look, having presumably registered the sheer horror on my face. She has the same eyes as her son: they rather suggest their owner would like nothing better than to peck at your corpse.

'Everyone!' Felicity says, clapping her hands. 'Everyone!'

Everyone looks up.

'This is Stella,' Felicity says, pointing at me.

Everyone stares a slow, up-and-down stare, and I feel like it's my first day at primary school. Maybe the slingbacks weren't such a good idea: this looks very much more like Birkenstock and unvarnished toes territory.

'And this little bundle – ' Felicity points at my arms – 'is Honey. How old is Honey, Stella?'

'Honey is eighteen months, Felicity,' I answer in kind, making myself want to laugh, but not daring.

'Aah,' says Felicity, sweetly but pointlessly. 'Eighteen months.' She raises her voice: 'Honey is eighteen months, everyone.' This doesn't elicit much of a response from the crowd, who keep on staring uninterestedly.

'Right,' says Felicity, crazily brightly. (Is she on Prozac? I don't feel I know her well enough to ask.) She looks around her somewhat wildly. 'Now. Introductions. This is Marjorie – she's Play Leader – and little Euan,' she says, pointing at the woman with the udders. 'I'll work my way around the group clockwise, Stella. So, at one o'clock: Emma and Rainbow, Amelia and Perdita, Venetia and China, Kate and Ichabod, Susannah and Mango, Julia with the triplets – ' IVF, I think to myself – 'Hector, Castor and little Polly – that's Pollux, he's a boy, but we don't believe in gender stereotypes here, do we, everyone? No, we don't. Oh, and Louisa with Alexander,' she adds, almost as an afterthought: name shame, clearly.

I give Louisa-with-Alexander a broad grin, which she returns; I feel myself about to become hysterical. Ichabod? Mango? And call me an O-level Classics swot, but Hector? Hector, whose mutilated body was dragged behind a chariot until his face fell off? And Perdita, meaning 'the lost one'? What do people think of when they name their children? I know 'Honey' is hardly conventional, but we only called her it because we optimistically thought that it would force everyone to be kind to her all the time. How could you snarl at a Honey?

'Righty-ho,' says Felicity in her jolly Sloane tones. 'That's the intros over and done with. Make yourself at home, Stella. There's a kettle over there if you fancy – ' and here she puts on an amusing cleaning-lady voice – '*a nice cup of char*, and then we'll get on with the activities.' She raises her voice again and claps her hands: 'Free time, everyone, free time.'

Oh, dear Lord, what an unprepossessing little group. I put Honey down by a pile of manky-looking Duplo and wander off towards the kettle, but am immediately pulled back by Honey screaming, and then crying broken-heartedly. A small but oddly corpulent boy has pushed her on to the floor and is standing on her hand, stamping his grubby trainer down on it again and again.

'Oi!' I shout, like a fishwife. 'Don't bloody do that.' I shove him away – his arm is sticky – and pick Honey up.

'Ow,' says Honey. 'Ow me.' She starts crying.

The fat child is glaring at me, nasal leakage crusting his upper lip. His skin is the colour of greying underwear. He's about three years old.

'Don't do it again,' I tell him, showing only a fraction of the anger I feel. 'You can't go round hurting people, and look, she's so much smaller than you.' I kiss Honey and put her down again.

'My Duplo,' the child says, kicking it and narrowly missing Honey.

'It's everyone's Duplo,' I say, 'and you weren't even playing with it.'

The child crouches down by Honey so that they are the

same height. Before I can do anything to stop him, he's put his face right next to hers and bitten her little cheek, hard.

'Ow!' screams Honey.

I can't very well spend my first morning at Happy Bunnies beating children up, but my goodness, I am sorely tempted.

'I said, behave yourself,' I hiss. I can feel the poison in my voice, reminding me that I am not one of those nice women who unilaterally like all children. 'Now go and play somewhere else. Go on, scram.' Piss off, blob, I want to add, but don't, obviously.

'Icky, darling,' says a voice behind me. 'Oh, Icky. Were you a little bit silly?'

'Waaaah,' wails Ichabod – not a cry, more of a demented roar. 'WAAAH.' He kicks his mother right in the shins as she approaches. I see her wince with pain.

'Silly? Hardly. He stood on my daughter's hand and then he bit her face,' I tell the woman – Ichabod's mother, Kate, it turns out, a harassed-looking woman with badly dyed hair cut like an old lady's, with weird clumps above the ears – above Honey's screams. 'It seems a bit much in the space of five minutes.'

'Oh, Icky,' Kate says. 'Oh, Ick.' Can't she say anything else, like 'Sorry'? Why isn't she metaphorically walloping him around the head for being such a little shit? She turns to me, looking none too pleased. 'I do hope you didn't tell him off?' she asks accusingly.

'Well, I did, actually. Look.' I show her Honey's hand, on which the imprint of a trainer sole is coming up in angry welts. There are bite marks on her cheek.

'We never tell Icky off,' Kate says. 'We don't believe in

telling off. He is expressing his anger as best he knows and, being a child, that means physically.'

Zoom, goes my temper. Zoom, and whoosh. 'I am expressing *my* anger in the only way I know how,' I tell her, making a gigantic effort to keep my voice pleasant. 'And being an adult, that means verbally. Though I'm sure I could muster up something a little more *physical* if you insisted.'

'Icky's just tired,' Kate says. All the bulgy veins in her neck are showing and she is looking at me with pure hatred. 'You're a tired boy, aren't you? Yes, you are,' she says, adopting the tone we used to use with our dog.

'Then I suggest you take him home,' I say, in the same even tone, 'and put him to bed.'

'Felicity obviously hasn't explained the playgroup's Basic Rules to you. Telling children off is very old-fashioned. These days – ' she looks me up and down: that phrase was a reference to my age, I expect, though she can only be a couple of years younger than me – 'we don't believe in disciplining children. They just grow and evolve organic-ally, like, like *herbs*.' Kate shoots me another filthy look, sniffs furiously and, ignoring my flabbergasted face, stomps away, Ichabod wobbling in her wake.

Herbs? And the vile nappy smell, I register, is coming from him. Tired, my arse. The absolute mantra of crap, middle-class parenting is He's Just Tired. Hand grenade lobbed right into your face? Excrement smeared over your walls? Setting fire to hair? Walking up and down the dining table kicking glasses on to the floor? Murdering the baby with a kitchen knife? Aah, He's Just Tired. Which always begs the question, never satisfactorily answered, *If he's so fucking tired, why isn't he in bed?*

I want to scream; ridiculously, my hands are shaking. Honey has calmed down and I put her on the floor again: I really need that cup of tea.

'Hi, I'm Louisa.' The pretty blonde whose eye I caught earlier has appeared by my side. She pats my arm and smiles as she hands me the milk. 'Don't worry about her. She has some fairly peculiar notions about child-rearing. Ichabod isn't potty-trained, for instance – Kate doesn't believe in it,' she says, rolling her eyes.

'I'm Stella.' We smile at each other. 'Horrible little fucker.'

Louisa, to her immense credit, giggles. 'Isn't he?' she asks rhetorically. 'Absolute nightmare. Not the only one, unfortunately. As you'll no doubt discover – you're doing the activities this morning, aren't you? I'd better let you get off, then. I just wanted to say hello and, you know, don't worry.'

'Well, thanks for coming over,' I say, feeling immeasurably better. 'See you later.'

'I hope so,' Louisa says shyly. 'I sometimes feel like I'm in a madhouse when I come here. You – ' she smiles – 'have the virtue of seeming reasonably sane.'

'That's what you think,' I clumsily joke back, but I am delighted: a friend! Well, a potential friend, anyway: a counterpoint to Udderella in the corner, who's finally put away her giant breast and is proudly watching little Euan, who has the springy, hunched walk of a teenager, scamper up the indoor climbing frame, a pleased, satisfied, and – yeurch – *bucolic* look spreading across her bovine features.

OK. Perhaps it's me. Perhaps it's just me, and I am weird and have strange foreign ideas, and prehistorically believe that children ought to have some vague notion of what does and what doesn't constitute normal, decent behaviour. If it's me – and it does seem to be – then I apologize. But Jesus Christ almighty, that was surreally horrible. Just after I'd led the children into a sing-song – we'd just got to 'Hey, Diddle Diddle' – Euan, son of Marjorie, pulled down his blue corduroys, squatted, grunted and did a poo right by Book Corner. No one said anything. The poo stayed there for minutes, with us all staring at it, until his mother languidly said, 'Just a little accident,' picked the poo up in her bare hand and walked over to the bin. Not the lavatory, which is situated just around the corner: no, the kitchen bin. Euan then lay on the floor, his enormous boy's legs up in the air, while his mother wiped ineffectually at his bottom with a tiny, Economy nappy wipe.

Then, as we were making worm spaghetti out of red Play-Doh, Ichabod punched Mango right in the face. 'Never mind. Icky has issues with anger,' Mango's mother said, in the manner of one attempting self-hypnosis, though I could see she was pretty pissed off. 'Oh, he's just tired,' said Kate, Ichabod's mother, at which, I am sorry to say, I sniggered out loud – me and this Ichabod are going to have a problem, I'm afraid – and earned myself another black look.

Polly, which is to say the unfortunate boy Pollux, delighted everyone by leapfrogging over gender stereo-types and choosing to dress as a ballerina for the duration of the games; his mother told him he looked very pretty, darling, and I tried not to think about Dr Freud. Polly's brother Castor didn't speak once, despite being two and a half, and played obsessively with the same train engine for two hours, screaming like a wild animal whenever anybody approached him, so then I tried not to think of articles I'd read about autism.

Rainbow, Perdita and China, all about four years old, seemed entirely preoccupied with showing each other their knickers; Perdita taught the other two that her mummy called her vagina her 'pussy'. 'Miaow, miaow, pussy,' they chorused for half an hour: one step to the left, one to the right and UP with the skirt. 'Miaow, miaow, *pussy.*'

And sweet little Alexander, aged two and a half, sat quietly on the floor by a bewildered Honey and pretended to read her a book about bears.

Louisa and I did go for a coffee, and what do you know? She's a single parent too. Although I always feel a bit fraudulent when I include myself in this category, a single mother is what I am: a single mother living in a big house, with childcare whenever I need it, which I do see isn't the same thing as being a single mother on income support on the seventeenth floor of a tower block, but still. Louisa's husband traded her in 'for a younger model', she told me, which is pretty tragic considering that Louisa is thirty-four. She lives in a flat above the organic bakery on Regent's Park Road and works part-time as a hat maker. Over coffee and hot raisin toast, we had the kind of shy, delighted conversation two lonely people have when they discover they like the same things. Anyway, Louisa and Alexander are going to come over and play next week, and she says we should go for walks to the park together. So there was a silver lining to my gigantic cloud: Happy Bunnies turned out all right in the end.

'See you on Tuesday!' Felicity had called out as we left. 'Marjorie is going to teach the children yoga!'

'Yoga?' I'd asked Louisa.

'That's what she does – she's a yoga teacher,' she'd answered.

'Why does she weigh twenty stone, then? I mean, she's hardly toned and sinewy, is she?'

'Maybe she's twenty stone and *very bendy*,' Louisa had replied, and we'd laughed all the way up the hill. Yes, things are definitely looking up.

3

We go to Sainsbury's after Honey's afternoon nap, and when we come back at about six o'clock, exhausted (toddler in the trolley: total nightmare) the living room has Casablanca lilies on every available surface: in vases, in jugs, in the tiny Sèvres teapot my father gave me on my eighteenth birthday, and crammed into glasses and jam jars. There's a delicious smell of lemon and rosemary permeating the house. Bang on cue, Frank appears, wearing my rose-patterned Cath Kidston apron. 'Amends,' he says, smiling his goofy smile. 'I am making amends. Flowers, and then roast chicken, roast potatoes, glazed carrots and chocolate tart.'

'You shouldn't have,' I say, beaming, as I bend down to undo the clasps on Honey's buggy. 'But I'm glad you did.'

'The way to your heart is through your stomach, I know. And I'm really sorry about last night,' Frank says, holding Honey while I scrabble underneath the pushchair to fish the three squashed bags of shopping out. 'Hello, Honey.'

'Oi here,' Honey says, smiling at him. I don't know why she talks like a simple yokel. It's one of the mysteries: why does my daughter speak like Pam Ayres?

'There's no need to be. You're a grown man – you're allowed to have sex.' Though so much sex with so many different people isn't ideal, I think to myself. 'Anyway, I'll just whisk miss upstairs for her bath, read her a quick story, and then I'll be all yours.'

'Cool,' says Frank. 'It'll be ready at eight. Oh, and by the way, your dad phoned.'

Oh, God. 'What did he say?'

'Something about coming to stay for a couple of days – he's ringing back later.'

'Do you know,' Frank says at dinner, 'you've been in every night since I moved in.'

'Not quite every night – I've been out a *few* times, Frank. And anyway, I've got another bloody translation hanging over my head, and I can only work in the evenings. Besides, you've been out enough for both of us. Pour me some wine, will you?'

'Here, pass your glass. Well, pretty much every night, then. You should get out more. You know I'd be happy to baby-sit, or you could always ask Mary.'

'Well, yes,' I say, spearing a carrot. 'I could. Did you do these with thyme? They're delicious. The thing is, where would I go? I don't really fancy taking myself off to the cinema, like a saddo. What am I supposed to do – roam the streets? Go down the station for an hour or two in the Photo-Me booth?'

'Surely there are people you could go and see?' He actually looks concerned, bless him, which makes me feel embarrassed and burdensome.

'That reminds me. I'm going out to dinner at Isabella Howard's tomorrow night. See? Ha! I'm not so tragic after all.'

'I'll watch Honey, then. And I wasn't saying you were tragic. But what about the other nights? You can't just stay in all the time. You're in your prime, Stella – I mean, what about, you know, dates?'

'Well, I yearn for them, obviously. But who with, Frank? Seriously.'

Frank laughs. 'Come on, Stella. It can't be that bad. You're an attractive woman. Interesting face. I wouldn't mind sketching you some time.'

'I am not a cow. Though a woman at playgroup this morning is. Do you want her number? She's completely bovine. She's a manimal.'

'I don't just do cows, you know,' he says, sounding affronted. 'I mean, I can actually wield a pencil, believe it or not. I do portraits – it's just I don't show them.'

'I know, I know. Sketch me, then,' I answer, speaking with my mouth full. 'It'd be fun. So if I'm attractive and presumably not absolutely monstrous on the personality front, where's the talent, Frank? Show me the talent.'

Frank laughs again. 'Well, the talent isn't to know by telepathy that you exist. It's not going to find you pottering about at home in Primrose Hill. You might have to actually leave the house, Stella. Venture a little further.'

'Don't make me sound agoraphobic. I'm perfectly happy to leave the house. Could you pass the potatoes?'

He does. They are heaven, these potatoes: crispy, sticky round the edges with chicken juice, and scented with rosemary.

'You eat very Frenchly,' Frank observes.

'What do you mean?'

'Well, you eat like you're hungry.'

'That's because I am, idiot-boy. It's supper time. Would you prefer me to push the food around and only have one tiny half-carrot?'

'No, no,' says Frank. 'It makes a nice change, that's all. English girls don't eat like they like it, especially the southern ones. You, on the other hand, often have thirds.'

'Which Irish people often pronounce as "turds", have you noticed? Me, I like fourths, if I can help it. Especially if someone's gone to the trouble of cooking me a delicious dinner, which this is. Could I have some more chicken?'

We masticate happily for a minute or two. 'Where do you find your dates?' I ask him. 'Are they art groupies?'

'Sometimes. They were in Berlin. But at other times I just meet people, you know, by being out and about. At parties and things. Shall I take you with me next time?'

I don't think he is being entirely serious, but he does nevertheless have a point: I can't just sit here gathering cobwebs.

'Yes, please,' I say. 'How about next Friday? You could teach me how to pull, I've forgotten how. It'll be fascinating.'

'OK,' says Frank. 'There's a party next Friday, as it happens, and we can go for drinks first. And you would pull, you know, Stella, if you wanted to.'

'Can't wait. What happened to the screamer from the other night, by the way? Miss Face Pack. Have you rung her?'

'That was just a shag.' Frank shrugs.

'Is that what you're proposing for me? Because I'm a bit past the old one-night stands. It's too squalid. I am a mother, you know.' I say this rather as though I were, in fact, the Blessed Virgin.

'You,' says Frank, pointing his knife at me, 'have never made any bones about being a woman who likes sex.'

'And?'

'And if you like sex, then go out and get some. It doesn't have to be squalid, you know.'

'No?'

'No.'

'I don't believe you. I'm not up to speed on current sex etiquette either. Probably these days everyone comes on everyone else's face, and it's considered perfectly normal, or even rather sweetly old-fashioned. And I couldn't bear it. Plus, you forget: I haven't had sex with anyone since Dominic. It would be weird, not having sex with my husband. Surreal, actually.'

'He's not your husband.'

'He never was, if you're going to be technical about it. The fact remains, it's got to be pretty damned strange doing it with someone new after all this time.'

'I guess so,' Frank concedes. 'But you'll have to do it some time, so you may as well get cracking. No point beating about the bush.'

'Nice choice of phrase, Frankie.'

'I know,' says Frank, beginning to snigger. 'I chose it especially. Ready for pudding?'

My father rings in the middle of all this. He's coming to London to do some shopping, he says.

'Aren't there any shops in Paris, Papa?'

'*Non, chérie,*' he croaks in his nicotine-stained voice. 'The shops are for old men and I am feeling very vital these days. My sap is rising and I need to see my tailor. Could you put me up for a couple of days? I was thinking of coming next Friday.'

'Of course. I'm out Friday night, though.'

'I will amuse myself.'

'You could chat to the baby-sitter.'

'Baby-sitter?' he roars. 'I'll baby-sit. We can have drinks and watch a movie.'

'Honey's only eighteen months old, Papa,' I say, wanting to laugh: I have a mental picture of my father, wearing a Noël Cowardesque dressing gown, smoking a cigarette, pouring Honey a beaker of gin and it, and settling down to explain the finer points of Truffaut to her.

'Is she really?' he asks, sounding surprised. Then he sighs. 'Goodness, babies grow slowly, don't they? Compared to the other mammals. If she were a dog, she'd be an adolescent by now. Oh, well, perhaps a cartoon, then. Bugs Rabbit or something.'

And then he says the words that have struck dread into my heart since I was thirteen: 'I've bought you the most fabulous outfit, Estelle.'

My father loves buying me clothes. The problem is, he doesn't buy outfits, he buys costumes. Aged thirteen, I once had to spend a week dressed as Carmen, in a big red flouncy number, to satisfy his then fixation with flamenco (my mother had to wear a mantilla around the house and kept bumping into things; they separated shortly afterwards). The Carmen outfit wasn't too bad, in retrospect. My father has also, over the years, bought me the clothes of Brünnhilde (complete with wig), Ophelia (trailing green tissue-paper weeds), Boadicea ('to honour Mummy's roots'), a cowboy (inexplicable, this one, but as I say, I think he's gay), and so on and on and on.

He buys the clothes, and then hangs around so that I have to try them on, and then he insists on taking me out to lunch or dinner, during which he screams with pleasure at the beauty of whatever costume he's forced me into.

He's quite eccentric, I suppose, but a dear sweet man, and I couldn't hurt him by refusing to slip into whatever little number he's picked for me.

My father is chuckling happily. 'Have you got anywhere to go, Stella? Because you'll wow them if you wear my present. You'll knock 'em dead.' He is fond of these weirdly Seventies expressions, bless him.

'We'll see. What time will you be here?'

'Four-ish, I expect. I'll get a cab from Waterloo. See you then, *mon ange*.'

'*A bientôt*, Papa.'

I turn to Frank, feeling giggly with wine. 'We may have to go pulling in fancy dress,' I tell him. 'My dad's coming over and he always brings me a costume.'

'Fine by me,' Frank laughs. What I like about Frank is that you never need to explain anything to him: he just rolls with the idea.

I creak upstairs, feeling rather well oiled, and reflect that it's been a great day. I've made a potential new friend and so has Honey, lovely Frank's made me dinner, and I'm really looking forward to seeing my father, gifts notwithstanding. Plus, I'm going out tomorrow and next Friday: why, it's almost beginning to sound like a normal life.

4

We have a massive garden, by London standards – I suppose it's about 100 feet long. As I'm having my morning coffee, I realize that the grass really looks like it needs a haircut: I must mow it, probably for the last time until the spring. I take a last sip of coffee, push away the newspaper (I increasingly ask myself what the point of papers is: giving you that extra little nudge towards the ledge if you're feeling suicidal?) and put on the wellies which stand by the door.

The lawn mower's in the shed and the shed is full of spiders. I shoo them away, eyes closed, and hoick out the massive machine. I know you're supposed to raise the blades, or possibly lower them, so I lug the machine on to the grass and push it upside down, in order to examine its undercarriage. The blades look very rusty. The garden's lovely though: a sort of damp overgrown wilderness.

'Hello there,' says a somewhat reedy voice.

I look around. I can't see anyone.

'Over here,' says the voice. 'By the bush.'

I look in the direction of the sound and, sure enough, there is a human face right by the holly bush. It's the face of Tim, my next-door neighbour. He and his family moved in about six months ago and, this being London, aside from the odd 'Good morning', I've never had much of a conversation with them.

There's something marsupial about him, I think this

morning, possibly because the light is falling in such a way as to make his eyes glint out in a most unusual fashion. There's also something weedy about the man, and although he looks perfectly normal – no lips to speak of, though – there is something that powerfully suggests he got daily wedgies at school and hasn't quite recovered.

'Oh, hi, er, Tim, is it?' I smile in his direction.

Quantity surveyor, if I remember rightly. Wife stays at home. Why isn't he at work?

'Just mowing the lawn,' I say. 'You don't know anything about moving the blades up or down, do you?'

Why isn't he budging from the bush, I ask myself? He looks crazy, peering through the spiky leaves like a bushbaby. But now he does, slowly, walking along the side of the brick wall which separates our two gardens and reappearing just above the hostas.

'Timothy Barker,' he says, in a slightly nasal comedy voice. 'At your service.'

'Stella de la Croix. Bit of a mouthful,' I say from habit. 'Just "Stella" will do. Hello,' I say again, now that I can see him properly. He's wearing a blue checked shirt and faded brown corduroys.

'Janice has taken the boys to Majorca,' Tim volunteers.

Janice is presumably the wife – red hair and lots of gold jewellery. The boys are about ten and twelve.

'That's nice,' I say. 'Is it half-term?'

'Indeedy,' Tim says, nodding solemnly. 'Indeedy.'

I can tell he's about to say it a third time, so I nip in with a cheery, 'So, do you know anything about moving these blades? I'd be really grateful if you did.'

'*Raising* the blades,' Tim chuckles. '*Raising*, not

"moving". French, aren't you? How come you don't speeek like zis?'

'I just don't,' I shrug. 'How do I do it? With the blades?'

'Ahaa,' says Tim. 'Ahaa.'

I'm getting a bit bored of this, so I smile vaguely in his direction and then turn my back, applying myself to the lawn mower.

'Hubby not about?' Tim bellows from about six feet away, making me jump.

'We're separated,' I say, facing him again.

'I knew that,' Tim says, thwacking himself unnecessarily forcefully on the forehead. 'I knew that. I meant your new bloke.'

'Excuse me?'

'Ginger fella,' Tim says, suddenly speaking like my grandfather. 'Tall strapping lad.'

'That's my house-mate,' I say. 'His name's Frank.'

'Call it what you will,' smirks Tim. 'Takes all sorts, madame, or should I say mademoiselle.'

He's beginning to annoy me now, so I walk over to the wall.

'I call him my house-mate because that's what he is. We share the house. He's sort of the todger.'

'Heeeeeeee!' Tim laughs, clasping his hand to his mouth like a pixie. I wonder if he's quite all there.

'Lodger. Lodger,' I shout, correcting myself. 'He's the lodger, and he's out at the moment, and I really need to be getting on, so if you don't mind – ' I gesture at the lawn mower, smile a goodbye and go back to inspecting the blades.

'Coming over,' Tim bellows efficiently, moving from the spastic to the businesslike. 'Won't be a tick.'

Turns out that raising – or, in this case, lowering – the blades simply involves turning a large plastic button around and then flicking a little lever. I don't quite see why Tim couldn't have just told me: we've been out here for ten minutes and I could have done it myself by now. He has very capable hands, though: big, square hands with long fingers and clean, pink-and-white fingernails.

'All done,' he says after a nanosecond.

'Thank you very much,' I say.

He doesn't move, or stand up, but remains on his haunches, smiling at me friendlily. I'm sure he's a quantity surveyor, which means he can't actually be half-witted, or else he couldn't work, surveying quantities or whatever it is he actually does. But then he's not working, is he? He's at home on a Friday. It's all a bit bewildering: is Tim retarded, or is he not?

'No work today?' I ask. I've got up, at least, but unfortunately this means that his squatting form is level with my crotch.

'Day off,' Tim says, finally getting up.

We stand in silence – a sort of *loaded* silence, utterly inexplicably: how on earth did this come to pass?

'Anyway,' I say, 'I really must mow the lawn now.'

'I'll do that for you,' Tim says, suddenly on the ball again, stretching out the pockets of his cords. 'Hand it here.'

'There's really no need . . .'

'It'd be a pleasure. Where's the extension lead?' At least he is speaking like a normal human being again.

'Over there, by the table. It's very kind of you. Can I get you anything? Tea? A cup of coffee?'

'Afterwards,' he says.

Either I'm imagining it, or the way he's saying it makes the word sound heavy with promise. And although I can't quite see properly because of the light, I could swear he winked.

'All in good time,' he chuckles. 'All in good time.'

In the event, Frank decided to come back for lunch because he'd forgotten some cow photographs that he needed to work from. The sight of him clearly alarmed Tim, who came over all marsupial again, declined the cup of coffee and scarpered back over the wall crying, '*Au revoir.*' What an odd little man. Still, as he so rightly pointed out, it does (indeedy) take all sorts.

Frank, Honey and I shared some smoked mackerel pâté and half a loaf of sourdough bread, washed down with elderflower cordial, after which he went back to the studio, Honey went for a nap and I was left to try and decide upon an outfit for tonight: my first dinner party in ages.

When you're part of a couple and you turn up at dinner, things are simple. You've made a bit of an effort, obviously, but basically you go as you. No longer: I genuinely have no idea of what I should wear in my newly separated circumstances. Clothes maketh the man and all that: I don't know how to advertise myself.

What look do I go for? Slightly widowish, to make it clear that my life as a sexual being is now over, and that I know my place, which is by the fire, embroidering blankets for Oxfam babies? Hair in a chignon, no make-up, an ankle-length dress in a dark colour, say chestnut or plum, and something white, to suggest unsullied virtue, or at least virginity regained – would a kerchief be too much? A wimple? Probably. And anyway, I'm not at all sure I could muster up the requisite facial expression: sorrow mingled with sweetness mingled with resignation, like Olivia de Havilland in *Gone with the Wind*.

Or there's always the schoolmarmy look, so very popular with the modern divorcée: it says, 'I have reinvented myself as *une femme sérieuse* now that I am free of my silly partner. I'm doing an Open University degree in Applied Sociology, you know.' I could wear my spectacles instead of contact lenses, use the correct pronunciation for any foreign food-stuff – 'Pass the *parmigiano*'; 'Wonderful Rioja'; '*Café au lait*, please' – and breathe excitedly through my mouth if anyone mentioned cats or self-help books (funny how women who claim to Run with the Wolves are always Women Who Stagger with the Stoats). Not really a crowd-pleaser, this look – which requires man-made fabrics and bad hair – but it goes down very well with the women, I've noticed, especially if you were fun-loving and easy on the eye before.

But it doesn't quite float my boat either. What to wear, what to wear? There's always the Hello Boys option. You know: the newly single woman of a certain age (though let's not forget I am thirty-eight, not sixty-two) who appears with full war paint on, frock slashed to the navel, heels that dwarf every man in the room, glossy highlit hair, carmine lips, and flutter flutter with the old eyelashes. Lock up your husbands! This one, I feel, has distinct comedy possibilities, though obviously one doesn't want to look too much as though one actually *charges*. Unfortunately, I may have to leave it this time, since the look involves a degree of cosmetic surgery: you need massive rigid breasts that start just under your neck at the very least, and an orangey tan is essential. Also, maybe lessons in tantric sex (perhaps Marjorie from playgroup could help me out?), so that you can sit next to strange men and thrillingly whisper, 'I come for hours.'

Oh, the gloom. Seriously, what am I supposed to wear? I'd be clearer on this subject if I knew what capacity I had been invited in: am I just a punter, an ordinary guest, or has some single man kindly been earmarked for me by our helpful hostess? Am I simply making up numbers – I was, after all, invited at late notice – or is there a plan at work here? If so, surely I should be let in on the details: assuming there's a single man designated for single sad me, then what kind of single man is he? Do I dress up or down? Smart, or – horrible word – casual? Hair? Make-up? Shoes? Feather boa? Crotchless pants? It would be terrible to wear heels if Single Man were short, for instance. Should I show I'm still on the case by wearing something trendy? Last time I looked, this involved an Eighties revival: should I wear a Kajagoogoo T-shirt and fingerless gloves?

Perhaps I should ring Isabella up and ask her directly. Hi, Isabella. You know dinner? Well, do you foresee rampant sex for me? What do you reckon, Issy – will I pull? Shall I wear tassels on my nipples? A burka? What?

In the end, I ring Louisa from playgroup. She's clearly been here before, because she is adamant in her advice. 'Go as yourself,' she says. 'Wear exactly what you would normally wear. Don't be shy or self-conscious, and behave exactly as you would normally behave. And have fun, more to the point. It's only dinner. Will you ring me tomorrow and tell me how it was?'

I promise her I will. As soon as I've put the phone down, I bathe, drown myself in Shalimar and jump into my favourite little black dress, which happens to be moss green: a silk, strappy nightie sort of an affair, knee-length, miraculously cut to emphasize the good points (bosom) while minimizing the bad (stomach). I throw on a bubblegum-pink cashmere cardigan, slip into a pair of purple raffia mules I've had for years, stick some hoops in my ears and race back downstairs to ask Frank's opinion, stopping on the landing to ring for a taxi.

Frank and Honey are lying on my favourite pinky-red Turkish rug, building stocky creatures out of Duplo: a very charming sight, except it reminds me of playgroup again. God, we have to go again next week – can it humanly be borne? Best not to think about it now.

'Well?' I twirl. 'What do you reckon – will this do?'

'You smell delicious,' Frank says.

Honey's in her blue pyjamas with rabbits on them; Frank, rather touchingly, is wearing matching blue pyjama bottoms (no rabbits, obviously) and a white T-shirt. Both have freshly washed hair. They look adorable.

'Mama,' says Honey.

I take her on to my lap and sniff her hair, wondering when her vocabulary is going to evolve.

'Good, but it's not the smell I care about! How do I look?'

'Great. Lovely.'

'Oh, Frank, honestly. Give details.'

Honey hops off my lap and returns to her Duplo. She looks rather like a rabbit herself, with her fat nappied bottom.

'Sexy. Like a smart gypsy.'

'But is that a good look? I'm not sure I want to look like a smart gypsy. Like *The Diddakoi* in black tie, do you

47

mean? God, I loved that book. Don't look so blank, Frank.'

'Who's the diddykoo?'

'*Diddakoi*. I'll tell you tomorrow, ignoramus. What I need to know now is, do I look potentially sexy and potentially businesslike at the same time? I mean, you're an artist, you go for that boho stuff. Would you still think I looked nice if you were – I don't know – a merchant banker?'

'Rhyming slang?'

'No – you know Isabella. She always has a couple of City types at dinner, or at least she used to.'

'If I were a banker, I'd want to ravish you before returning to my little wifey in Wimbledon, yes.'

'I do wish you'd be serious, Francis. And anyway, there aren't any bankers in Wimbledon.'

'Oi Womble,' Honey says, looking pleased.

'Clever girl!' I scoop her into my arms and kiss her: my baby genius. Honey and I love all those old shows on cable – I never saw them as a child, only *Barbapapa* in French, so they're new to both of us.

'Stella?'

'Yes, Frank?'

'Don't do it with a banker. Here, I made you a gin. To help your nerves.'

'Chin-chin. I wasn't planning on it, but actually now I think of it, banker-sex might be rather nice. They work long hours, don't they? So they'd be very tired and rich and one could have the most peaceful, ordered, suburban life. With maids. God, I *long* for staff, don't you?'

Frank rolls his eyes. We sit in friendly silence, watching Honey busily making Duplo stacks. I love my house now, I realize: the lilies are still scenting the air, the lights are giving off a yellow glow, the squishy sofas look inviting and comfortable, and the French doors to the garden (complete with impeccably mown lawn) are letting in a damp, bosky smell. We'll be able to light the fires in a month or so.

The taxi arrives. 'Hair up or down?' I ask Frank, suddenly feeling panic-stricken.

'Down,' says Frank, unpinning it for me and fanning it out with his hands.

'Easy, Casanova,' I grin.

He grins back, and wriggles his hips suggestively. 'I'll see you out.'

'Don't wait up,' I call, as I climb into my taxi.

5

Isabella Howard's Islington house is one of those interior-
designed numbers of the kind where the glacial, soulless
owner pays the designer thousands of pounds to make the
house look warm and soulful. This usually involves a kind
of update of the rich casbah look, with low tables, an
overabundance of cushions, overpriced rugs from shops
in Notting Hill and lots of little ethnic trinkets to suggest
that whoever lives here a) is well travelled, a global citizen
rather than an unimaginative provincial, and b) has an 'eye'
for beauty. The glass lights are Moroccan lanterns; the
throws on the sofas are antique saris; there is a stone
Buddha on the left-hand side of the mantelpiece. I recognize her interior, having seen many like it in houses from
Clapham to Hampstead, and can even tell that the décor
in question is by an ageing queen with an indeterminate
accent rejoicing in the name Ricky Molinari, absurdly
known to his clients as Mr Ricky.

Mr Ricky has two looks: de luxe ethnic, as in Isabella's
house (he rather invented this look, cleverly deciding four
decades or so ago to put his holidays in Tangiers to
professional use), and 'maximal minimal', which is basically
your old minimalist look – loft-like spaces, rubber or
concrete floors, uncomfortable linear furniture in black,
grey or chocolate brown – except roughed up with cherry
wood, books (which do furnish a room), contemporary
art (from my ex, Dominic, usually), and either orchids (bit

passé) or cacti or Venus Flytraps, planted in amusing and unexpected containers, such as petrol cans. Mr Ricky buys books by the yard, basing his choice upon the height and colour of the spines, with occasionally startling results: the faintly dusty, pretty pale green spines of *The Story of the Eye* or *120 Days of Sodom* in a Cheyne Walk lavatory belonging to an elderly woman who lives for Botox and egg-white omelettes, for instance.

I don't share any of my thoughts with Isabella, obviously, pausing instead to congratulate her on the beauty of her house.

'Do you really like it?' Isabella says, touching my arm. 'It's taken me absolute ages to put together.' (Actually, Mr Ricky tells his clients to leg it to the South of France, or wherever, for a couple of weeks, during which he and his armies of helpers 'do' the house at breakneck speed.)

Isabella, who must be about forty-five, was married for twenty years to Mark, a publisher, who left her six or seven years ago for one of his authors, a troubled young woman with very pert breasts. Mark was richissime, combining a hefty salary with family money, and eased his conscience by donating a large proportion of his annual income to his former wife. Isabella reinvented herself as a thin, spry champion giver of parties, stealthily inserting herself into every imaginable London social circle over a period of months, and returning home with the phone numbers of its principal players; she is particularly keen on 'young people'. She brings all of these together every week for dinner and thrice a year for what she refers to as 'my big dos' (which always raises a snigger from me: I do love a poo joke). I slipped off her list some time ago, although, judging by tonight, I'm back on – which I'm pleased about, because, say what you like about Isabella, she has a kind of genius when it comes to party giving and these evenings are seldom dull.

The other guests are already gathered in the drawing room, which is softly lit by pink-glass lanterns and candle-light coming from outsize scarlet candles. Some indeterminate jazz is playing in the background. The low, carved coffee table – about eight feet in length – is scattered with rose petals, and little silver dishes containing delicacies are piled on to each surface. (Frank would say that it is very like me to notice the snacks on offer before noticing the people.) The overall effect is mildly poncy – why are we pretending to be in Fez crossed with Jaipur? – but not without charm.

'Now, Stella, darling, have a drink. The usual selection, or one of my cocktails?'

'Mm, a cocktail please.'

Isabella hands me a flute of champagne, sugar and fresh mint.

'Now, do you know everyone?'

I peer through the seductive gloom: no, actually, I don't think I know anyone at all.

'Hello,' I say, boldly advancing towards the couple by the mantelpiece. 'I'm Stella.'

'Stella was with Dominic Midhurst,' Isabella says helpfully. 'Weren't you, darling? How is Dom these days? Do you know?'

'Fine, I think. He spends a lot of time in Tokyo.' Do I really still have to be defined by a man I was briefly attached to? It seems extraordinary in this day and age.

'Hello there,' says the male half of the couple. 'George Bigsby. Can't say I thought much of your husband's stuff,

I'm afraid.' He laughs friendlily, his eyes crinkling up. 'All those installations. More of a Rubens man, myself.' His face is rather red and rather fat, and he has a big nose. Jolly, though, and he looks kind.

'Me too,' I smile back. 'I couldn't agree more.'

'This is my wife, Emma,' George says, pointing to a pale, elfin woman, wearing what appear to be fairy clothes – pastel-coloured wisps of fabric clinging to her thin, boyish frame: more Giacometti than Rubens. I fleetingly wonder whether she has an eating disorder – who doesn't, these days?

'Hello,' I smile.

'Hi,' says Emma, looking me rather rudely up and down, not what you'd call wildly enthusiastically.

'And over here,' says Isabella – a lesser hostess would have left me standing in silence by Emma – 'is William Cooper, whom I particularly wanted you to meet.' She gives me a significant look from behind his back: here is the Designated Single Man. 'William's a cosmetic surgeon, so if you make friends with him you can have free tummy tucks!'

'Gosh,' I say, breathing in sharply. Great: the single man is uniquely positioned to make me feel physically lacking.

'Not that you need a tummy tuck,' says William Cooper smoothly, having a good old look at my abdomen. 'Not yet, anyway. Very pleased to meet you.' He raises his eyes until they come to rest on my chest, at which point he looks up and gives me rather a sexy smile.

Hello, I think to myself. *Hel-lo*.

William Cooper has a velvety voice and is ridiculously handsome (does he do work on himself? I must ask him) if slightly overgroomed: his skin is tight, polished, absolutely porelessly clear in a way that you don't see much in men of his age, which is roughly late forties-ish, at a guess (flattering lighting in here, though). His very white teeth shine in the half-dark, as do his fingernails (manicured?). His hair is black, and, peering closer, I see he has blue eyes: I always love that combination. I never quite know what to make of his kind of look: it is, aesthetically speaking, quite overwhelming, but there is a plastic quality to it that somehow doesn't look human. Still, there's no denying he's foxy.

'And I'm Tree,' says a woman, coming up to join us. Ah, this I know: this is familiar, a species I immediately recognize. Tree has long, straggly hair, very expensively cut and streaked though you wouldn't know it, held off her hard, make-up-free, not especially youthful (or indeed intelligent) face with glittery little clips. She is thin to the point of looking simian, and is wearing the *dernier cri* in bohemian chic – to you and me, a nondescript rag, to Tree, £800 worth of fabulous clothing. She has toe rings and, I expect, a couple of tattoos. I know she must live just off the Portobello Road in a five-storey house, must have a trust fund and a very rich husband, must do something 'creative' and – we'll see at dinner – must suffer from an unusually cruel number of allergies.

'I love your shoes,' Tree says sweetly. Her accent is perfect Estuary. 'Well wicked.'

'Thanks. I've had them ages.'

'Raffia,' she says. 'Beautiful. Natural, you know.' Tree stretches. 'I'm knackered, actually. Went for a swim before coming out and it's made me sleepy.'

'Porchester Baths?' I venture, wanting to test out my theory.

'Nah, at home,' Tree shrugs. Bingo! She has a swimming pool in her garden.

'What do you do, Tree?' I ask.

'I'm training to be a music therapist,' she says, looking more animated now.

'What's that?'

'You work with, like, really damaged people, and heal them through the beauty of music. I have a drum.'

'That's nice,' I say, hoping not to sound sarcastic. 'What kind of drum?'

'It's, like, a drum of wisdom and peace?' Tree explains. 'With beads. Abba Babu gave it to me.' Seeing me look blank, she adds, 'That's my guru. I go to an ashram for three months a year. India is such a spiritual place, don't you think?'

'I don't know. I've only been once. I really loved the shops.'

'It has feathers.'

'The guru or the ashram?'

'No, the drum.'

'Mmm,' I say, rather lost for words.

The low hum of conversation is interrupted by the late arrival of a woman so very masculine that you wouldn't be overly astonished to find that she did, in fact, have a penis. She is very tall, somehow broad in the beam without being in any way overweight, and her appearance is striking: she is wearing mannish black trousers and a mannish, but rather beautiful, black cashmere sweater over a pristine white shirt. Boots on her feet; six or seven thick, plain silver rings on her long, elegant fingers, and cropped grey hair that is slicked back to reveal flat, neat ears and a pair of cheekbones that would be the envy of women half her age: she herself must be somewhere in her mid-sixties. She has the palest blue eyes and an intelligent, take-no-prisoners face.

'Ah, Barbara, darling,' says Isabella, jumping up. 'So delighted you could join us.'

'Good evening, Isabella,' Barbara says in a sixty-a-day voice. 'Delighted to be here. Does me good to get out of the house every now and then,' she adds, turning to me and smiling. She smells of Guerlain Vetiver, one of the loveliest men's scents in the world. 'I sometimes feel my limbs are in danger of atrophying.'

'What nonsense, Barbara – you're hardly ever in,' Isabella says, affectionately patting her arm. 'You're a social whirl. Have a drink,' she adds, racing off to find one of her pitchers of cocktails.

'I'm Stella,' I tell Barbara.

'No surname? Then I'm Barbara.' She gives me a bold, frank look – right in the eyes, bang bang. 'Come and sit by me. I don't like standing when I don't have my stick.'

We walk over to the sofa and sit side by side. 'Who are these people?' Barbara asks.

'I don't really know any of them. He's a plastic surgeon.' I point at Cooper.

'Oh, yes, I know him – William Cooper. Raised my sister's jowls last year; she rather fell in love with him. Do you know, I think he may have had a fling with Isabella.'

'Really? How fascinating. When? I wonder whether she had anything done.' Good of Isabella to pass him on, I suppose. Is that what women *do* now? Probably: we're always hearing about how there aren't enough men to go round.

'Anything done? I should hope not. Ghastly business,

plastic surgery. So many women of my generation had their faces ruined. Lumps, you know, suddenly appearing *years* afterwards.'

'Eeeoo.' I make a face. 'Anyway, next to him is a woman called Tree who is training to be a music therapist.' Barbara looks over and smiles so knowingly at me that I grin back. 'And then the couple by the mantelpiece,' I continue. 'I don't know what they do, but he seems very jolly.'

'And she less so?'

'Yes.'

'And then dear Isabella. My god-daughter, you know.'

'I didn't actually. How nice. Do you have children of your own?'

'No, my dear,' smiles Barbara. 'What about you?'

'One, a little girl. Eighteen months. Her name's Honey.'

'What a sweet name.'

'Isn't it? She's a sweet little girl.'

'And what do you and Honey do all day?'

'Not much, actually. Well, I do the odd bit of translating now and again, but mainly we're at home in Primrose Hill. Her father and I are separated.' Blissfully, Barbara spares me the platitudes – the so sorrys, how sads, oh dear what happeneds that I never have any replies to.

'*I* live in Hampstead,' Barbara says instead. 'We could get together sometimes. Do you walk?'

'Yes – unless it's absolutely pouring, I try to take Honey to the playground once a day, and then for a trot around the park.'

'We could walk together, if you liked. I'm rather slow, I'm afraid.'

'I'd love that,' I say, meaning it.

I'm pretty sure Barbara is a lesbian, which is really

neither here nor there except for the fact that I think I must give off gay vibes myself, because lesbians absolutely always make a beeline for me. This occasionally leads me to wonder whether I am, in fact, batting for the wrong team: if every single lesbian I've ever met has looked at me in the manner of like recognizing like, *perhaps they know something I don't*. On the other hand, Barbara is a very old lesbian, and if I were to start exploring the notion of sexual fluidity, I'd rather do it with someone my own age. More to the point, I can't imagine what sex would be like without a flesh-and-blood penis being involved. Slurpy, I suppose, like glutting on oysters. I groan quietly to myself: try as I might, I really can't fancy the idea of hot lezzo action much at all. But surely it must have something to recommend it if so many people practise it? Very confusing. Perhaps the slurping is optional. And people's breasts *are* interesting, I remember from the showers at school: some girls had that thing where the combination of two nipples and one tummy-button made a perfect sort of face – huge, rather boggly eyes (the nipples), small nose (the TB), furry triangular mouth (the pubis) – which used to fascinate me. But the fact remains: fascination or not, I didn't yearn to get close to the faces, or to grope them.

Tree comes over to speak to Barbara, and I fall into a sort of reverie. William Cooper: what's the story there? Why is he still single? Is he a professional escorter of women – an older, sadder, more humourless Frank? Or perhaps, also like Frank, he is a master of his craft, a shagging supremo, and generously spreads himself around to aid womankind. I am feeling quite sexually desperate, actually, and although I wouldn't normally go for the smoothie plastic surgeon option, I am not quite myself at the moment. Besides, he *is* incredibly handsome, even if he doesn't look entirely human. And at least he has a penis. I imagine. It must be terribly pale in comparison to his face, unless he rubs bottles of St Tropez tan into it.

Why am I thinking these things? What is the *matter* with me? Sexual frustration is a terrible thing.

William Cooper does not rub fake tan into his proud member, it turns out. I know, because I saw it.

I was seated next to him at dinner. Cooper, it quickly became clear, was very much on for it: what started off as mildly flirtatious banter, of the kind you might have with your husband's half-gaga great-uncle, turned into something rather fuller on as the evening progressed and the claret flowed. I went along with it: everyone enjoys being flirted with, and I haven't had anyone flirt with me for ages. Not exactly subtle, though, Mr Cooper's flirting, consisting as it did of *double entendres*, compliments addressed to my bosoms and much flashing of his weirdly white teeth. Funnily, the harder he flirted, the more I found myself flirting back (the wine helped, as did his face). His technique may have been unspeakably naff, but in the half-light, he really looked pretty sexy.

And then it was pudding: a cheese plate, passion fruit crème brulée and imported figs. I'd turned to my left to speak to George Bigsby (I was right about Tree: absolutely *riddled* with allergies to wheat, dairy, fish and alcohol, poor thing) when I felt my calf being stroked by somebody's foot – somebody's cashmere-sock-clad foot, by the feel of things. I stared at George, who stared back somewhat blankly, and then turned my head to my right. William Cooper winked, and carried on stroking. The stroking was oddly vigorous – like having a good rubdown – rather than sensual, but none the worse for it. Looking around the table, I noticed that everyone was deep in conversation. I turned back to William to say something – I wasn't quite sure what – but one look at his face left me (and this is quite a rare occurrence) absolutely speechless. Cooper was performing cunnilingus on a fig.

He held the hapless fruit, which he had split open, with two tanned, square hands, its flesh glowing pinkly in the candlelight. Then, turning his body to enable him to maintain eye contact with me at all times, he proceeded to – well, to *eat it out*, with his pink tongue, which he'd made rigid and pointy: slow, languorous licks up and down and then, horribly, faster, more insistent, probing licks aimed at the centre of the vagina-fig: pressure applied to, as it were, the fig-clitoris. At this point, he half-closed his eyes and (I swear) murmured a throaty 'Aaah', his tongue moving faster and faster until, presumably, he felt the fig had come. The whole performance took about a minute and a half, and when I looked around the table again, no one seemed to have noticed, amazingly.

I was *astonished*. A-s-t-o-n-i-s-h-e-d. As you would be. I mean, good grief. And then I was astonished further when Cooper wiped his mouth, licked his lips and whispered in my ear, 'Are you wet?', using, I thought, rather a complacent tone of voice. It took me a few seconds to compose myself, and then I managed to say, 'Bone dry, actually. Dry as a bone, which is coincidentally the name of an Australian type of coat.' This was pretty much true, although I have to confess, shamefully (and yes, I was – I am – ashamed), to having felt a slight, a *tiny* twinge during his ludicrous figgery. Not that I'd admit it to him in a million years, hence my – I hoped – off-putting reply. But instead of looking down shamefacedly and muttering, 'I don't know what came over me' (to which the correct answer would have been 'A fig, mate'), Cooper smiled in rather a pleased way, winked again, and put his hand on my thigh under the table.

Now obviously there comes a time when a girl has to make decisions, and clearly this was one of those times. What to do? I'd seldom found anything as profoundly ridiculous as the fig display – thank God we didn't have oysters, or mussels, or clams, or he'd have probably tongued those as well, making some ghastly remark about them 'tasting of the sea' – but, on the other hand, beggars etc. Not that I think of myself as a beggar, quite, but this definitely constituted an offer, and offers have been thin on the ground in my neck of the woods. (Still, what a thing to do: I couldn't – can't – conceive of a situation where I'd be out at dinner and get it into my head that it would be a really terrific idea to impress the man next to me by cheerfully fellating a sausage. Imagine if you got it all the way in and choked a bit and had to be rescued by your hosts, the head, as it were, of the sausage peering helplessly out of your parted lips.)

So, *que faire*? I was given a few minutes' respite by Emma, on Cooper's left, asking him whether it was really true that liposuction was bad for you, and during these minutes I am sorry to say that I decided, Yes. I decided that since I was practically rusty from lack of sexual use, I'd give Cooper a go. Why not? He was remarkably good-looking, he clearly had the horn, he had quite a long tongue and I never needed to see him again, so who cared if his seduction techniques involved violating fruits? The more

61

I thought about it – fortifying myself with another couple of glasses of wine – the more it seemed to me that Cooper coitus was really rather a good idea: the perfect way of easing myself back in the saddle, as it were – a neat, no-nononsense solution to my problem. I'd go somewhere with him after dinner, have a quickie, prove to myself that I was still capable of having sex, perhaps an orgasm, and go home. Perfect. It was about time I slept with someone who wasn't Dom, and got on with my life. Once the decision was made, I began rather looking forward to it.

Barbara and I exchanged phone numbers over coffee in the drawing room, and then I looked at my watch and started making noises about baby-sitters. 'Could you call me a cab?' I asked Isabella.

'Which way are you going?' William Cooper asked, on cue.

'Primrose Hill.'

'I'll drop you off,' he said.

'Yes, do,' said Isabella with tremendous unsubtlety.

'I'll do that.'

'It's not much of a detour. We can't have Mrs Midhurst going home on her own.'

'Quite,' said Cooper.

I thanked Isabella – pausing briefly to wonder whether it was the done thing to say, 'Thanks so much for organizing a rogering for me' – said goodbye to the assembled crowd – Tree pressed her phone number on me too – and got my coat ('Get your coat, you've pulled,' I giggled to myself, knowing by now that I'd had too much to drink). William's coat was a navy-blue number with a velvet collar, of the kind favoured by small nanny-accompanied children in Kensington Gardens.

His car was parked just outside the house: a black Jeep with leather seats. Once he'd opened the door, we sat in the particularly harsh, unforgiving light for half a minute, during which time I realized that his tanned face – what is it with me and men with orange issues? – came out of a bottle, and that his hair was most probably dyed. Both these observations were sobering. But only a little bit.

'Well,' said William, once the light had gone out, giving me a wolfish grin, his teeth glinting in the dark, quite sexily: there's something about oddly sharp incisors that gives me the horn.

'Hmm,' I said, thinking. Obviously, we couldn't go to my house: it'd be like soiling your own nest. Well, not *soiling*, quite, but it wouldn't necessarily enrich my home environment, either, to be reminded of William lying there, all bare, every time I looked at my cosy bed.

'Would you like a nightcap?' William asked, turning the key in the ignition.

'Yes,' I replied.

'Your place or mine?' he asked smoothly, flashing his teeth again.

'Yours.' I smiled back.

'Good,' said William, squeezing my knee. 'Very good. It's not far.'

It suddenly occurred to me that Dr William here might, for all I knew, be a murderer, or a wild perv, or anything else at all. He might perfectly well take me back to his flat and tie me up and, I don't know, torture me with electrodes, and keep me in a box, and feed me cat food. Sure, I'd met him in respectable circumstances, and doctors aren't usually loony types – *but on the other hand, Dr Crippen.* I decided to quickly text Frank, so that at least one person would know where I was.

'What are you doing?' William asked.

'Just letting my house-mate know I may be back late.'

'You certainly will,' William leered. He licked his lips and squeezed my knee again, getting my upper thigh instead: either he thought I had freakishly short legs or he was revving up. 'Good. Why don't you just ring her?'

'Him, actually. This is faster.'

'What are you saying?'

'Oh. Er, just "Back later" really, so he doesn't worry.' Which was a lie: I'd typed *Hv plld dr fr sx bck 2 am ltst or rng 999* before pressing 'Send'. I've never quite got the gist of text messages. They all remind me of that ad there used to be on the Underground years ago: *If u cn rd ths msg, u cn bcm a scrtry & gt a gd jb.* Which made me think for years that secretaries were a bt hlf wttd.

'All done?' asked William.

'Yes. Now I'm ready to check out your bedside manner, Doctor. I have a terrible ache in my, you know, lower regions.'

William looked exceedingly pleased by this, and stroked my thigh.

'Mmm,' I added. 'Ow. I can't wait. Will you wear your stethoscope?'

'Would you like that?' William husked, pulling off the Euston Road into Marylebone High Street.

'I'd rather like a full exam,' I said, slightly revving up myself. I suddenly had a thought. 'But not including rectal, obviously. No bottom action at all, in fact.'

'What?' said William, swerving to avoid a Fiat Punto. 'What did you say?'

'I dislike anal sex,' I explained. 'I'm just letting you know early. Being helpful. To avoid disappointment. I do hope you're *not* disappointed?'

'Er, no. No,' he said. 'That's, er, quite all right. Here we are, then,' he added, pulling up outside a Victorian mansion block.

Cooper, predictably, lived in a shag-pad, though the shag-pad was so Seventies that I had to ask him how old he was (the reply, conclusively, was 'old enough to show you a good time'). There were black leather shag-sofas all over the living room, and recessed shag-lighting, and long, tufty shag-pile, and one entire wall was made up of smoky shag-mirrors.

'Got any Barry White?' I asked, which was supposed to be a joke.

'Of course,' William Cooper said smoothly and somewhat solemnly.

'Baby,' I growled, in my deepest voice, and then laughed to myself because my Bazza impersonation is so eerily exact.

Cooper, who had his back to me, fiddling about with the Bang (ha!) & Olufsen, seemed surprised by my sound.

'Here we are,' he said, turning around and giving me a strange look. '*The Greatest Hits.*'

It happened very quickly after that. On came Barry, down went the lights, off came his coat, and mine. And then – oh no, oh *no* – he started to dance. He danced a snaky, writhy little dance, and as if this weren't bad enough, he started untying his Turnbull & Asser tie, thrusting all the while, not quite in tune with the music. His clenched fists were down by his swivelling hips, pumping in and out like a choo-choo train. I constantly ask myself whether prowess on the dance floor is indicative of prowess in the sack; if so, then I was clearly in for a bit of a spasticated ride. I was just standing there, watching the display with mounting dismay and wondering whether I ought just to go home, when he spoke.

'Come here,' said Dr Cooper, his voice sounding all hoarse. 'You make me hot.'

'OK,' I said, unnecessarily, moving forward. 'Do you, um, want me to dance too?'

'Yeah,' said Cooper, pushing his face into my neck and – eeeuww – licking it. 'Dance with me, hot lady.'

You know when you really, really want to laugh, but you're not allowed to, and how the forbiddenness makes it so much worse? It was like that. I wanted to snort, to honk, to *bray* with laughter, to lie on the floor and clutch my stomach and *howl*, but I didn't. I also really, really wanted a shag – and I know how bad it looks, or at least how mysterious, but you've got to trust me: there was something inexplicably sexy about him. He had a nice body, even if it was writhing about all over the place malcoordinatedly. So I danced.

Eventually – quite quickly, really – I was dancing with his hand in my pants. This was when he turned me around and moved behind me, so that we were both facing the wall of mirrors. I've never had a great desire to watch myself bobbing about half-naked to Barry White, so I shut my eyes, which of course William interpreted as a sign of deepest ecstasy.

'Do I make you come?' his voice whispered wetly into

my ear, followed by an odd sort of whinnying noise: he sounded like Austin Powers crossed with a pony, and like the kind of man who spells 'come' c-u-m.

'Mmm,' I said, because, really, what can you say without sounding rude? 'Not yet, actually.' Which *did* sound rude, so I added, sounding to myself strangely like a dowager duchess, 'But I'm, er, I'm sure you will. Soon, you know. Later.'

'I'm gonna make you come so hard,' Cooper stated, very categorical. 'Harder than you've ever come before.' He made the strange whinnying noise again: 'Neeiiiigh.'

'Jolly good,' I said uncharacteristically. All that whinnying reminded me of Thelwell ponies, and I'd adapted my language accordingly, obviously. 'Shall we, er?' I asked, gesturing to what I imagined to be the bedroom.

'You can't wait, can you? You *can't wait*,' Cooper said, looking pleased. He stared at himself in the mirror, one hand quickly reaching up to push his hair back. 'You dirty girl.'

'Quite. Shall we go?' I said, because really we had to, before I lost my nerve or started laughing dementedly.

'Dirty, dirty girl,' he repeated. And then he led me by the hand to the bedroom, doing his weird dancing all the while.

6

I'm not going to go into too much detail here. On the plus side: the sheets may have been satin, but the ceiling was not mirrored, which was a bonus. Dr Cooper had rather a large penis, ditto. He was very athletic, though still in his oddly plastic way: I was reminded of contorting an Action Man into unlikely positions. He knew a couple of neat tricks. He left my bot alone, as decreed. I had one small orgasm. Mustn't grumble, really, since that was pretty much what I came for.

On the other hand, I'm not really the mustn't grumble type. So, on the minus side: when we were in the bedroom and I was getting undressed, he crawled all over the bed and roared like a tiger. Yes, really: raaah. And then he talked *non-stop*. I don't mind a bit of commentary, but this gave me ear-ache – not helped by the fact that the vocabulary used was, as I've already mentioned, on the Austin Powers side. Also, I think that if you're going to go down the dirty-talking route, it helps to have an almost unintelligibly rough accent – council-house Glaswegian, say, just to pick an entirely random example. Dr Cooper's upper-middle-class cadences didn't really sit comfortably with the language he was using, and after a little while I became tired of the way he said 'pooseh' and 'cork'. I think Dr Cooper dyes his chest hair, too, because when we'd finished there was a strange, dark grey sheen to my breast. He must immerse himself completely in a bath of dye. And his penis was stubbornly untanned; ghostly, glimmering palely in the darkness, looking somehow both blind and albino.

Once the deed was done, I waited ten minutes or so and then started getting ready to leave. All sorts of thoughts were whizzing round my head: 1) how I don't think being on top is really *at all* an option after the age of thirty-five, as everything sags forwards horribly; 2) how it was surprisingly unsurprising to have sex again; 3) how perhaps I should have saved myself for someone I found less ridiculous; 4) how I did exactly the right thing – he may have been slightly ridiculous, but it was a perfectly decent shag; 5) how I really hate it when men lie there not taking the condom off afterwards, so that their penis looks all small and wrinkly and like it's wearing a poor-quality, cheaply transparent anorak.

'How was that, baby?' Cooper said as I struggled into my pants.

'Great,' I said, looking for my tights in the dark. 'Very nice. Thank you.'

'Where are you going?' he asked. 'Don't you want – ' he licked his lips, which shone like mucus in the darkness – 'don't you want . . . more? Huh? Huh? More, you dirty girl.'

'Not really, William. I have to get home. I have to get my daughter up in a few hours.' Mentioning Honey made me feel grubby, somehow, unmaternal, slappery. I continued to gather my things, which were scattered all over the floor.

'Nurse,' said Cooper. 'Nurse?'

'What?' Why was he speaking without verbs? 'No, actually, I mainly bottle-fed. Anyway – thank you for, you know, *having me*, ha ha, and, er, see you.'

'Nurse, Mrs Midhurst is ready for her exam now,' Cooper leered, addressing his imaginary colleague. 'The full physical, I think.' He whinnied again, his hand fumbling horribly under the sheet.

Oh, stupid, stupid *moron* me. Why did I mention playing doctors? Suddenly, the idea filled me with something not a million miles away from disgust.

'I'll just get my instruments,' Cooper continued, getting out of bed now, still addressing the invisible attendant.

'I really have to go,' I said, standing up and following him out of the bedroom. 'But it was very nice to meet you. No, really,' I had to add, as he started rustling about in his doctor's case and re-emerged triumphantly clutching a stethoscope and a pair of latex gloves. 'I *really*, really have to go. So, um, goodbye.'

'Come by next week for your examination,' Cooper said, standing by the door naked except for the pair of rubber gloves, which he'd snapped on. 'I'll ring to confirm,' he winked.

'Bye,' I said, and ran all the way down the stairs.

'Raaaa,' he called at my back. 'Raaaaaaah!'

Standing in Marylebone High Street looking for a black cab, I didn't know whether to laugh or cry, so I did both.

'Well?' says Frank, the following morning. 'I thought I'd let you lie in. Mary's here and she's taken Honey to the zoo, by the way. Some special owl thing, apparently. What happened?'

'You got her up? That's incredibly kind of you.' I haven't

had a hangover for months, and also – though this may be psychosomatic – my pelvis hurts slightly: I feel like I should be walking with my legs in the shape of a Y.

'No problem. Anyway, so?'

'Hang on, I'm just making myself some tea. Was everything OK last night?'

'Absolutely fine. She went to bed at seven thirty and she didn't budge. I read her two *Angelina Ballerina* stories. She really loves them, doesn't she?'

'Yes, more than life itself. I looked in on her when I came in, about two-ish.'

'I didn't hear you. Come on, Stella, for God's sake: *so?* What happened? Who's the doctor? Some sexy locum?'

'Oh, Frank.'

'You look knackered, actually.'

'Shagged out,' we both say at the same time.

'Not quite sexy locum,' I explain. 'A sexy-ish plastic surgeon. Name of Cooper. Was at Isabella's. Dyes his hair and has very white teeth. Also, orange skin.'

'Stella!' Frank says, half-horrified, half-thinking I'm making it up. 'You went to bed with an orange plastic surgeon? Tell me you're joking, love.'

'Alas, Frank. No. I'm not.' I take a sip of tea. All my head feels hot. 'He roared like this: raaah,' I tell Frank.

'What?'

'Naked. On the bed. He roared. Raah. Also satin sheets, natch. Chocolate brown.'

'Christ,' Frank says, sitting down next to me. 'Why did he roar?'

'Because he thought it was animal and passionate, I expect, Frankie. Why, is the roar not in your seduction repertoire?'

'Nah,' says Frank.

'Well, no,' I said, 'I suppose I'd have heard by now. One must be grateful for small mercies.'

'Whatever,' said Frank, giving me a long look.

'He also made this really funny horse noise,' I tell him.

'For God's sake, Stella. He sounds like Dr bloody Dolittle. Anything else?'

'Yes, actually. He called me hot lady.'

Frankie spits out his coffee. I am trying to butter my toast casually, but it's too much. Before I know it, tears of laughter (at least I think it's laughter; I very much hope so, at any rate) are pouring down my face; Frank appears close to hyperventilation.

'Raah,' says Frank, beside himself. 'Hey, hot lady.' He leaps up and starts parading about the kitchen absurdly, throwing imaginary paws about, thrusting wildly, growling like Eartha Kitt, winking at me 'hotly' and, of course, roaring.

'Don't,' I sob, practically choking with laughter. 'Don't make fun of my love.'

'Sorry.' Frank comes up to me, licks a finger and presses it against my face. 'Sssssss,' he says, making a sizzling noise. 'Wooh! Hot lady!' And then he collapses again.

I actually think I'm going to pee, I'm laughing so hard. 'Do men do this?' I ask him when I've calmed down. 'I mean, have hysterics the next morning?'

'Sometimes,' says Frank, who is still wheezing. 'Not this badly, though. Oh, Stella. Stella, Stella – what did you think you were *doing*?'

'The thing is, the actual shag was fine,' I tell him. 'The preliminaries . . .'

'Ssss,' says Frank.

'The preliminaries were on the comical side, I'll grant you . . .'

'Raah,' he adds unhelpfully.

'But the actual doing it was OK.'

'I should hope so,' Frank says. 'I should bloody well hope so, Stella.'

'And yet I feel the whole thing left something to be desired, really. Why's that, do you think? You told me – promised me – that doing it after a long while was easy and not at all stressful, remember?'

'Yes, but I didn't mean for you to go out and knob men with satin sheets who think they're tigers. Apart from anything else, it seems an awful lot of palaver to go through if you just wanted a shag. I mean, you could just go to a party and pick up someone, you know, normal. What's that mark on your chest, by the way?'

'He *is* normal. Where? Oh, that. Hair dye, I think. I think he dyes his chest.'

'Sexy,' says Frank. 'Bloody right horny, that.'

'Enough now,' I say. Because I don't want my new sex life to be hysterically funny; I momentarily feel rather annoyed, actually: it's true, Frankie did promise, and I should be sitting here looking sated and replete with sex and mysterious, not giggling like a loon with him. 'At least he's not covered in ginger fur. You might like to take a leaf out of his book, Frankie. Nothing wrong with hair dye, you know.'

'Well, back in the knife drawer, Miss Sharp,' Frank says, somewhat campily. 'Don't be cross. I was only teasing. Anyway, I have to get to the studio now. Are you about tonight?' I nod. 'I'll see you later, then. Have a good day. Don't overheat.'

'Just go,' I say, feeling a giggling fit coming on again. 'Just leave. Now. Go.'

I don't really know what I was expecting: not quite to strut about the house feeling pleased with myself, bellowing 'We are the Champions' for emphasis, but close. After all, it *is* quite a feat to have sex again after nearly a year, and not with one's husband. So I really should be feeling a little more delighted, and a little less sickened. Well, not sickened, quite, but somehow *grubby*, like a teenage girl who's let someone Go Too Far in an alley behind the school disco. Oh, arse. I wouldn't be feeling like this if I were a man: I'd be down the pub boasting about my giant member, and about how women cried hot tears of gratitude every time they were allowed to glimpse it.

Still, at least that's that over and done with. I am back in the saddle. Yee-hah and giddy-up and good for me.

Today, of all days, is the day Rupert, my first – and, on paper, only – husband decides to phone me. As I think I've mentioned, Rupe gave up the west London playboy life to go and live on a remote Scottish island and hang out with birds 'of the feathered variety', as that strange man next door would probably put it. Because we were so young when we married, I sort of feel like Rupert is one of those boys you knew at school who's really more like a girlfriend: I don't speak to him very often (although he does regularly send sweet postcards with pictures of seals or puffins), but when we do speak it's easy, and giggly, and you can more or less say anything that comes into your head without worrying about the consequences.

So really, who better to share my happy news with?

After asking him the usual questions about wildlife, I drop my hot gossip.

'I had sex with a man last night, Rupe,' I tell him.

'Oh, well done,' he drawls in his funny posh voice – half Harrow, half Ladbroke Grove.

'Thank you. I'm quite pleased with myself.'

'I rather assumed you weren't living the life of a nun.'

'I was, actually, Rupe. I was nunnish. Getting none. But no longer.'

'Very good. Who was he?'

'Doctor called William Cooper.'

'Plastic surgeon? My mother goes to him.'

'Does she? What for?' Why does everyone go to the plastic surgeon except me?

'Don't know. Stells, he's, er, quite old, isn't he?'

'I don't think so, darling. He's about our age – maybe a bit older.'

'Actually Mummy went to his sixtieth, if I remember rightly, and that must have been a couple of years ago, at least. Er, rather fiercely *tanned* chap. Rooms near Harley Street. Huge teeth.'

'Nooooo!' I wail. 'Nooooo! Noooo! Rupert, that can't be right. I can't have wasted my first shag in ages on someone old enough to be my *dad*. Oh, *God*. Oh, *no*. No fucking wonder it was so dark at his flat.'

'Old Cooper. He'd have been twenty-four when he sired you, by my reckoning,' Rupert says, like an irritating bloody mathmo. 'Terribly well preserved, though – by his own hand, I gather. Although a bit on the smooth side for you, one would have thought. Still, there must be benefits. Was he awfully *experienced*?' He's laughing to himself, I can tell. No, he's about to keel over laughing.

'I suppose so. Tricks, you know.'

'How ghastly.'

'Not really. There's a lot to be said for a trick. English men don't know enough. They think it's OK to just sort of *prod* you for two and a half minutes and pant in your face.'

'Do they?' says Rupert, sounding interested. 'Where does one acquire knowledge of these marvellous tricks, then? I must learn some.'

'I don't know. Books, maybe. Or prostitutes. Ideally, very wide sexual experience, or an innate talent for raw sex. Speaking of which, Rupert, how's your love life?'

'Don't be sarky and horrible and defensive. You're the one who slept with the grandad.'

'As I was saying, your love life, stud?'

'It's looking up, actually – that's sort of why I'm ringing.'

'Yes?'

'I was wondering whether you could put me up for a night or two next week. I've sort of got a date.'

'Of course. Seems an awfully long way to come for a date, though. Couldn't you meet somewhere in Scotland? And who is she?'

'Well, she lives in London. She's called Cressida, works in nannying. Met her at a cousin's wedding – Harry, remember him? Anyway, seems a bit much to ask her to schlep across Britain for dinner with me.'

'Oh, but Rupert – I've just remembered. My dad's coming to stay from Friday night. Is that OK? There's plenty of room for you both, but you don't mind him being here, do you?'

Rupert has always viewed my father with extreme suspicion; he is convinced that Papa fancies him. As far as I know, there is no evidence of this whatsoever.

'No, that's fine. Could probably teach me a trick or two, old Jean Mary.'

'He's not called Jean Mary, you arse. He *is* my dad, Rupe, so, you know, a little respect. You might at least get his name right.'

'Sorry. Old habits, etc. Really kind of you, Stells. I'll make my way there, probably tea time-ish on Friday. Just don't leave me alone with him.'

'I'm out Friday night, actually, so you will be. Which serves you right. See you then. Don't forget to wash.' (English men of his class – he's quite posh – are always a bit flannel-shy in my experience. I was always telling Rupert to wash when we were married, and he never did; he smelt of dog and wet wool, which isn't as romantic or easy on the nose as it sounds.)

'Oh, God. Will I really be alone with him? Well, needs must, I suppose. I'll keep my back to the wall. Bye, darling – don't be cross. And well done on pulling Cooper.'

I could swear there's the faintest snort of laughter just before the line goes dead.

Three days later, Meals on Wheels telephone, thanking me for my application and telling me that there are indeed people in Camden who need my help; would I like to come in for a chat with my Area Supervisor? I am non-plussed, until, when the post arrives, I find a card from Rupert: 'Thought of a really nifty way for you to combine your two favourite things, darling – eating and old men. See you on Friday, much love, R.'

I am very stressed. Back to the drawing board, I think, sex-wise. Because while it's all very well being sexually active, I have no desire to become ridiculous.

7

Tuesday already, which means only one thing.

'Oi bunny,' says Honey.

Yup, it's playgroup. But it's not all grim: we're going round to Louisa's afterwards, for lunch – a silver lining, but one surrounding an exceptionally large cloud. Since all the women at playgroup seem to dress in a manner that is deliberately hideous, I aim to do the same, in the hope that perhaps we'll warm to each other more if we're all wearing equally disgusting clothes. I feel a bit mean Louisa-wise, since she, brave thing, was wearing rather a pretty pale pink cashmere twinset last time, but needs must: I can't spend two or three mornings a week hating every single second of my time. I must try and blend in.

And so here I am. The outfit I am wearing actually hurts my eyes (sharp stabbing pains just behind the corneas). I am wearing a tie-dye T-shirt, which some grubby friend of Dominic's left behind years ago and which, laundered, has been lining the bottom of my tights drawer for ages. The T-shirt is brown. Brown like poo, rather than brown like conkers or chocolate. Brown like diarrhoea, actually. In the centre of the T-shirt are concentric gingery-orange swirls with creamy-beige smears dotted about. These last look like guano. It is an amazingly ugly garment, as though created by blind Aborigines while a lot of pigeons were flying overhead.

But wait, we're not done quite yet: over my T-shirt, I

am wearing a pair of enormous Seventies-style dungarees. These used to belong to Frank – he wore them to paint in – but even he discarded them on grounds of taste. The dungas (there's a dung sort of theme to my clothing, come to think of it) are enormous, so I have to roll them up; they're also smeared with cow-coloured paint, so that it looks just like I've been rolling happily in russet-coloured pats. I finish off the look with a pair of battered Birkenstocks I keep by the garden door: gnarled, muddy, brown, of course. I scruff up my hair, smear some Vaseline into my lips, forgo scent and race downstairs.

'Ee,' says a wide-eyed Honey, which is her own peculiar brand of yokel-speak for 'oh look, a *really* horrible sight'.

'I know,' I whisper, smoothing down her little curls. 'I'm in disguise. Shall we go, then?'

'Oi go,' says Honey, so we do.

It's not better the second time, I am sorry to report. It's not better at all: it's *so* worse. By break time, I can't stop swearing to myself, deep in the throes of internal Tourette's, and I feel a sort of murderous rage boiling up inside me: I want to kill the Happy Bunnies mummies in a very slow and painful way – roasting on a spit, perhaps, followed by tearing limb from limb.

What's the matter with them? Freaks, all of them – fucking *freaks*. Is there anything worse than feeling like the odd one out when all the ones that are 'in' are the bloody geeks, the gimps, the abnormalities-on-legs? You know how you occasionally get that I-wish-they'd-pick-me-for-the-netball-team feeling in adulthood – that lonely, abandoned, I-can-do-it-really-I-can-just-give-me-a-chance feeling? Well, this was the same thing, but in reverse. I'm the cheerleader being ignored by the nerds. They should have been begging *me* to pick *them*: I'm the normal one here, the non-tonto one, the one who washes her bloody armpits every once in a while and has non-loopy opinions about child-rearing. But no: despite my cunning disguise, I could still feel the air thickening with disapproval every time I wiped a nose, told some little brat to be quiet at story time or wondered out loud whether four wasn't quite old to still be in nappies. It's not, apparently. Apparently, at Happy Bunnies, 'we' let the child decide when it's had enough of nappies, Marjorie tells me. Potty-training forces our principles of what constitutes acceptable behaviour upon children in a way that 'we' find reprehensible. It isn't fair on the child, apparently. (I'll tell you what isn't fair: expecting me to deal with strangers' children's shit, that's what. Actually. Since you ask. Not that any of them did.)

The morning went on and on. And on. I got told off every time I behaved like a normal human being: not only for wiping noses, but also for separating squabbling kiddies, or for cleaning sticky surfaces up with squirty Domestos (bleach, apparently, is dangerous, and dirt isn't), or for choosing *The Elves and the Shoe Maker* at story time rather than some *bien-pensant* volume about, say, handicapped children – sorry, differently abled – having two mummies. I thought this kind of thing had gone out in the Eighties, but no: if it's a slim little volume about siblings with no arms you're after, or a ploddily written account of life as a five-year-old in the Kalahari, you'll be overwhelmed by choice (both books, of course, written by white middleclass women who live around here).

Bloody Ichabod got slap-happy again at the Painting

Station (that's another thing: every crappy bit of dirty, broken second-hand equipment has a grand-sounding name: Book Corner is a pair of grubby beanbags, the Kitchen is a chipped table with grey Play-Doh on it, the Play Area is a splintery old climbing frame, the Treasure Chest is a box full of toys I'd feel embarrassed about giving to Oxfam. Mystery heaps upon mystery: the women in this room all live in houses or flats that cost upwards of £300,000. What's the problem? Why can't we buy some new fucking toys and a bit of decent equipment? Why do we have to *pretend we're poor*? I must ask Louisa. I've noticed this before, with the English middle class: they're the ones who buy second-hand clothes for their children and pride themselves on wheeling around rusty, disintegrating push-chairs. At the park, working-class children are the ones swathed in goose-down, being wheeled in Land Rover buggies; the middle-class children are the thin, pale ones – the ones who look abused. Why?).

Still, I learned a new word today. The word is: pee-pee tail. Nice, no? Has a ring about it, wouldn't you say? Pee-pee tail is what Marjorie – the breast-feeding obsessive with tits like udders – calls willies. 'Don't forget to shake your pee-pee tails,' she instructs the children – all two of them, practically teenagers – who have managed to work out how to use a lavatory by themselves.

'Pee-pee tails?' I ask, finding it hard to keep the note of appalled horror out of my voice. I mean, you're a four-year-old boy and suddenly you're told your penis is a tail – a back-to-front tail; worse, a tail that pee-pees. How disturbing is that? How *Freudian*?

'Yes,' said Marjorie, who never ever smiles at me. 'That's what we call them here.'

'What's wrong with "willy"?' I ask.

'Everything,' says Marjorie, who needs to do something about the hair on her upper lip. 'Not least the fact that it's a child's name. That kind of thing can often lead to bullying,' she sniffs disapprovingly. 'And we none of us condone bullying,' she adds, excluding me from the 'us' in a manner that is, well, somewhat bullying in itself. She shifts her massive bulk and looks me slowly up and down for the second time this morning: insolent is the word that springs to mind, fatly, lazily insolent. Annoyingly, William Cooper's willy pops into my head uninvited at this point, all larval and white. I repress a shiver and soldier on.

'Oh,' I say. 'Well, how about "penis"? That's not anybody's name.'

'No. We only recommend using the biologically correct terms from age six plus. For the under-fives, we like friendly names at Happy Bunnies.'

'Really? And how do "we" come to these decisions? Do any of us have any qualifications in childcare, for instance? You see, I'm going by instinct. What about you?'

'I am highly qualified,' says Marjorie. 'That's why I'm Play Leader.'

'In what way? Because, correct me if I'm wrong, this room – ' I gesture – 'looks pretty crappy to me. It isn't safe or clean. The equipment is broken and out of date. The lavatories are disgusting. I just wondered, you know, in what sense this playgroup actually qualifies as a playgroup. Or in what sense you actually qualify as a Play Leader. I mean, Marjorie, with respect, you don't actually *play*, do you? You breast-feed Euan in that corner there and get people to bring you cups of tea.'

'I'll have you know,' Marjorie hisses, 'that I've been

running playgroups all over north London for the past five years. I'm appointed by the parents.'

'I don't doubt it,' I say, bending down to wipe Perdita's nose. 'I just wondered what qualifications you had, that's all. But if you don't want to tell me, that's fine. What were we talking about? Oh, yes, pee-pee tails. You see, I think that's a kind of disturbing name, as I was saying. What about "thing"?' I suggest helpfully, just to be irritating – even I am aware of the fact that calling your penis your 'thing' would probably lead to many adult years on the psychiatrist's couch.

'Certainly not,' Marjorie says, po-faced yet radiating intense disapproval. 'As for your remarks, I don't care for them much. If you're really unhappy with Happy Bunnies, Stella, it seems to me that you should perhaps consider another playgroup.'

'Honey likes it,' I say. 'Which is why I'm here.'

'Precisely my point. You don't have to like it, but the children do. And in all my years of experience, I've never run a playgroup that children didn't like.'

'Everything all right?' says Felicity nervously, popping up behind me like a jack-in-the-box.

'We were just having a little chat,' says Marjorie, smiling tersely. 'I was putting Stella straight about a few things.'

'Golly,' says Felicity, fiddling with her pearl necklace. 'Oh dear. Stella *has* been working hard, you know, Marjorie.'

'With the tissues and the Domestos,' says Marjorie. 'Yes, I've noticed.'

'Quick,' I say. 'Hygiene alert! Call the child police!'

'She,' Marjorie says to Felicity, 'made a derogatory comment earlier about the book of the week.'

'I didn't know there *was* a book of the week,' I say. 'What is it?'

'*When Mommy Died*,' they both reply in unison.

'For fuck's sake,' I say.

'You see?' Marjorie asks Felicity. 'You *see*? That's what she said earlier, too.'

'It's a difficult subject,' Felicity winces. 'But we all thought it was handled beautifully in the book. Sensitively. Marjorie's friend sent it to us from America.'

'This is a playgroup for under-fives,' I say. 'I'm not reading them a story about dead mothers.'

'These are important issues,' Marjorie says. 'We all die. We are all dying now: you and I and all the kids. The kids are dying. It benefits children to learn about death early, in as natural a way as possible. Death *is* natural.'

'Does the mummy go to heaven?' I ask.

'No,' they say.

'Does she go anywhere comforting at all?'

'She is buried in the earth, and is once again at one with Mother Nature,' Marjorie says. 'To me, that's beautiful. It's the circle of life.'

I don't have the time for this, I really don't: I could stand here arguing with Marjorie until the cows come home. 'We'll agree to disagree,' I say, more conciliatorily than I feel.

'We're all growing, Stella,' says Marjorie. 'And perhaps you too will grow as a result of your time at Bunnies.'

'Perhaps. And do you know, Marjorie – perhaps you will.'

'I am always open to anything that aids personal growth,' she says. 'Always.'

Felicity leads Marjorie away, and I begin to butter the

bread with Economy strawberry jam. Trouble ahead, I expect, but never mind.

It starts pouring with rain just as we leave Happy Bunnies, and it's really bucketing by the time we get to Regent's Park Road. We ring Louisa's doorbell, but to no avail: she must still be at the dentist's. It's really sloshing down, so we huddle under the organic bakery's awning, waiting.

We've been there three or four minutes – Honey safe and dry under her plastic pushchair-cover, me brollyless, getting soaked by the wind pushing the rain sideways – when I notice a man walking towards us. He's doing the pimp roll – a sort of loll from the hips – and wearing Eighties-style track pants with two go-faster stripes down the side, a huge black hooded top with a logo I can't understand and one of those little hats favoured by black teenagers that looks like it's made out of tights. Ali G, basically, but for real, and wearing the requisite shades even though it's raining.

The apparition stops by the health food store and fishes about in his pockets for keys, which can only mean one thing: if Louisa's Flat B, he must be Flat A. Which means he can let us in – I'd rather sit on the dry stairs than hang out here drowning. So I leap out from under the awning.

'Excuse me,' I say.

'Yo,' says the man.

'Do you live here?'

'Yeah.'

'I'm supposed to be having lunch with your neighbour – Louisa?'

'Aye,' he says, oddly northernly, or perhaps, 'Ai.'

'Well, she's not back yet, and – ' I gesture at the sky – 'we're getting soaked.'

'Ai,' he says again, pushing the key into the lock. He is wearing extraordinary trainers.

'So I was wondering whether you could let us in – we could wait on the stairs.'

The man gives me a long, up-and-down look, much as Marjorie did earlier, but with a smidgeon more approval.

'Sweet,' he says. 'Come in.' His accent is purest south London.

I struggle to manoeuvre Honey's pushchair through the narrow entrance: I'd lift her out, but she's fallen asleep.

'Thank you,' I say to the man.

'Safe. Cup of cha?' he says. 'Was just about to brew up meself.'

'That's *so* kind, yes please, if you don't mind.'

'Wha' about the sprog?'

'I'll leave her here, I think – she's fast asleep and it seems safe enough.'

''S upstairs,' he says, leading the way.

'I'm Stella, by the way,' I tell him as I start to follow.

'Yang-Tza,' he says, which seems bizarre: surely I can't have heard properly.

'I'm sorry,' I say, as we get to his front door, which is cleverly painted to resemble camouflage. 'I didn't quite get your name.'

He has removed his sunglasses now and, although the hall is dark, I can't discern any sign of Orientalism about his features: I must have misheard.

'Yang-Tza,' he repeats.

'Oh, right,' I smile. 'OK.'

'Y-u-n-g-s-t-a,' he spells helpfully.

'Gosh,' I say, sounding like Felicity. 'That's unusual.'

'I's da DJ,' he says, as if this explained everything, which indeed it does. 'MC Yungsta. You know?'

'Sorry, no – I'm more of a Radio 4 girl,' I shrug apologetically. 'I last went to a rave in 1988, nearly fifteen years ago.'

'I'm the daddy,' Yungsta says simply, which confuses me temporarily. 'I is the daddy,' he adds, correcting himself.

'Cool,' I say. 'That must be fun.'

'Kickin',' he says, pushing the door open. 'Here we are.'

Yungsta's walls are plastered with flyers and posters, all of which advertise him. He's considered a great draw, it seems, from King's Cross to Ibiza to Aya Napa. I've never really thought about DJs much: this is a part of youth culture which I am way too old for, though I've caught glimpses of it on satellite TV. I like Abba and camp pop music, like Kylie Minogue, and I wasn't being entirely truthful when I said 'Radio 4' – I have my Radio 2 moments too, singing along to Dean Martin. (I used to get depressed about this, but I've come to terms: the ravey kind of music which Yungsta plays just hurts my ears and puts me in a bad mood.)

'PG, Earl Grey or camomile?' Yungsta asks from the kitchen, which surprises me somewhat.

'PG, please, milk, no sugar.'

I gaze around the room as he's fiddling about with the kettle. It's done out in beiges and taupes, like a very groovy take on William Cooper's apartment: it's the Seventies revivalist look, with suede sofas, a cowhide on the black-painted floor and lots of sculptural plants dotted about. The far wall is full of LPs and bits of what looks like recording equipment. There are joint roaches in the ashtray and socks on the floor. The room is sparse and very masculine, but clearly belongs to someone with a sense of style.

'Here you go,' Yungsta says, reappearing with two steaming mugs.

'Thanks. Sorry about this. I'm sure Louisa won't be long, but if you have things to do, you know, do kick me out.'

'Nah,' he says, kicking off his trainers, removing his shades and stretching himself out on his mushroom-coloured sofa. 'Just got up. Not much to do until tonight.'

He yawns, while I note that he is capable of normal speech. I also observe that Yungsta is a bit of a dish. I mean, he is ridiculously dressed (mutton dressed as lamb isn't in it: he's an ancient ram, the grandaddy of rams, Da Ram, dressed as the littlest, babiest lamb in the land). And he talks like he wishes he were black, and yes, he appears to be wearing a hairnet, but if he were mute and bareheaded, you certainly wouldn't kick him out of bed. He has very piercing greenish eyes, for example. Can't tell about the hair, as it's all hidden under his hat, but he appears to have a Number 2 crop. Still, he seems to be about my age, which I'd have thought was quite old for a DJ. Seems a bit churlish to bring this up now, though, as I'm sitting in his armchair drinking his tea. So I sit quietly, admiring the view, while Yungsta offers me a cigarette and smiles for the first time. I smile back, wondering whether to have a little flirt while my daughter sleeps downstairs, until I remember my clothes: I'm still in the dunga outfit, for heaven's sake. It did me absolutely no good at all at playgroup, and now it's impeding my flirting.

But then, miraculously: 'I like your T-shirt,' Yungsta

says of the Abo-guano number that is gracing my chest.

'Good God,' I say. 'You can't be serious.'

'It's well safe,' Yungsta says. 'Retro – I like that. Old skool.'

I wiggle my Birkenstocked toes with pleased disbelief. Yungsta looks down at my feet as if they were shod in Manolos.

'So,' Yunsta says.

He is interrupted by a trilled 'Yoo-hoo' wafting up the stairs. Louisa's home, and thirty seconds later she appears by the front door, which has been left open.

'Stella,' she says, out of breath. 'So sorry. Dentist took ages. I bought us these to compensate,' she adds, brandishing two bottles of white wine. 'Hello, Adrian. Thanks for looking after her.'

'Adrian?' I say, nonplussed, gazing from Yungsta to Louisa.

'No trouble at all, Loz, mate,' Yungsta says, looking frankly embarrassed.

'Well, um, thanks for the tea,' I say, rising, 'and, er, it was nice to meet you.'

'Sweet,' Yungsta says again. 'See you,' which, the way he says it, really ought to be spelled 'C Ya'.

A couple of hours later, after lunch – a bottle of white wine, some organic olives and a plate of cheese – Louisa shows me her hats, a picture of her ex-husband, her wedding album and a photograph in *Vogue* of some shoes she covets. Thanks to the wine, we've bypassed any awkwardness or shyness and got straight down to the nitty-gritty, exchanging life stories. Honey and Alexander are playing on the floor with Brio, with brio.

'Does she have an afternoon nap?' Louisa asks.

'Normally, yes, at about this time, but she fell asleep in the buggy, so I don't know. She's rubbing her eyes, though.'

'Alexander usually has a nap about now too. Won't go to bed, though. I normally put a video on and we snuggle down on the sofa until he falls asleep. Which doesn't take long. Shall we try it?'

'Absolutely.' I nod. 'I'm going to the loo. After which, I don't suppose you fancy that second bottle?'

'My thoughts exactly,' she giggles. 'So pleased you're a responsible parent too.'

'Well, they're sleepy and it's raining, so I can't think of anything I'd rather do. But if you're busy . . .'

'I have no life, Stella,' Louisa says sadly. 'This is the most fun I've had in months. I'll get the corkscrew.'

The video is already playing by the time I get back from my pee. Alexander is sucking his thumb and Honey is twirling her hair: they'll both be asleep in minutes.

'I don't know if I've seen this one before,' I whisper.

'Lucky you,' Louisa whispers back.

'They're an odd-looking bunch, aren't they?'

'You can say that again. Oh, look, Honey's gone.' My daughter's eyes are closed and she is already snoring softly. Louisa puts a fleece blanket on her. Within ten minutes (half a bottle of wine: we're making good headway) Alexander has nodded off too.

'Stella?' Louisa asks.

'Mmm? I love Orvieto, don't you?'

'Delish. Anyway. Stella?'

'Yes,' I reply, except it comes out as 'yus', which makes

us both giggle. 'That wasn't a very substantial lunch,' I chide. 'And now we're drunk, and it's your fault.'

'Oh, but I'm having such fun,' Louisa smiles, stretching. 'Top-up?'

'Please. What were you about to ask?'

'Oh, yes. Now, which one gives you the horn?'

'Sorry?'

Lou gestures at the video.

'This lot. Which one would you snog?'

'None of them, for God's sake.'

'No, really.' Louisa has another sip of her wine. 'If you absolutely had to. If you were desperate.'

'It's an unappetizing selection we have on offer here, Lou. Honestly – none of them really do it for me.'

'Oh, come on,' Louisa says, her contagious giggle starting up again. 'There must be *one* you slightly fancy.'

I lean forward, feeling more sober now, and take a good look at the faces flickering on the television screen.

'With tongues?' I ask.

'The works. I quite fancy Toby,' Louisa says thoughtfully. 'Have done for some time, actually. That's him now. What about you? Come on now. Apply yourself.'

'I don't like his nose,' I say, squinting at the screen and gesturing. 'It's got that Lloyd Webber piggy thing going on. That Fred West thing.'

'How could you compare sweet Toby to Fred West?' says Louisa, aghast.

'Well, I don't know much about his character – he does seem very sweet,' I concede. I stare at the screen again. 'And anyway, why does he talk like that? I suspect he has learning difficulties.'

'Bless,' says Lou, making a concerned and loving face.

'Ah, but now you're talking,' I say, pointing at the screen again. 'Who's he? I quite like *him*. There's something quite forceful about him, I think. What's his name?'

'James.'

'That's right. I've seen this before somewhere, but I can't remember where.'

'You'd do it with him?'

'No!' I scream in mock horror. 'I said he looked quite forceful. Doesn't mean I'd want to have rumpo with him, though. I'd do it with Tony Soprano, though, wouldn't you?'

'They're the same type,' Lou points out, 'James and Tony. James definitely has a naughty streak, which is quite appealing. But I know his type,' she adds darkly. 'Couple of dates, fantastic shag, no phone calls.'

'Yes, but at least you'd have a good time. Your Toby's a ridiculous shape, as well as piggy-nosed. Sort of boxy – look.'

'Size isn't everything, Stella. And I don't think it's an indicator of pant-content, either. Toby's hung, if you ask me.' Our second bottle of wine is finished. Louisa cranes her head and examines Toby from all angles.

'What are you doing, Lou? Checking out his bulge?'

'Yes,' she answers solemnly. 'But I can't see anything.'

'Well, that would be because . . .'

'I'm really glad – so glad – that we met,' Louisa says. 'I'm really happy you're my friend. But I think you're sizeist. I mean, Tom's – that's him now – may not be the biggest of them, but I'd give him one any time. I suppose it's because I know him best.' She sighs thoughtfully. 'Well, not in real life, obviously – but I feel that I do. That's the

93

thing with this programme – it really gets into your head, like *EastEnders*.'

'Louisa! He's Thomas, not "Tom". He's the most appalling square. *And* he's wet. And I hate his big round eyes – I'll bet he has some kind of overactive thyroid disorder. He looks like he'll run to fat, too, within a couple of years. At least James would show you a good time. James is quite rakish, quite 007. And lean with it. He's a lean machine.'

'We'd do it from behind,' Louisa says matter-of-factly, 'me and Thomas – so his round eyes wouldn't come into it. I suppose,' she adds, draining the last of her glass, 'I suppose you'd pick Gordon, wouldn't you, because of his size?'

'Who's Gordon?'

'There, in green.'

'No way! I would not!'

'Would.'

'Would NOT.'

'Well, at least he's big. Not to mention hard. Not to mention throbbing.'

'Stop making me laugh, you'll wake the kids.'

'I can't believe you'd do it with Gordon,' Louisa persists. 'That's just dirty.'

'I would not do it with Gordon. I can't believe you'd do it with Thomas, frankly, with his great big round thyroidy eyes staring down at you creepily. You disappoint me, Louisa.'

We sit in companionable silence, sipping the last dregs of our wine.

After a while, Louisa says, 'We are in our thirties. We are in our prime. And we are sitting here discussing possible sexual intercourse with Thomas the Tank Engine and his mates. Do you think, Stella, that possibly, possibly, we ought to get out more?'

8

From having no social life at all, I suddenly notice, with delighted amazement, that my diary now has a little string of dates scribbled across its once pristine, virgin pages. Nothing wildly thrilling, mind you, but, as the Americans say, hey – it's a start. I could even have dinner with William Cooper if I wanted – he's left a couple of messages with Frank – but I think I'll pass on old glow-peeny (funny, that. Well, I *say* funny, but actually, not so very funny at all because I still get armpit-shame – you know, that really sharp prickling – whenever I think of my PARTS rubbing along in conjunction with Cooper's). Besides, Frank says he found it hard to speak to the glowster without the kind of intense smirkage that is audible even down a phone line ('I'm sorry, Stell – I just couldn't help it'), so with any luck old sex-tiger will have been put off, and that will be the end of the good doctor. Rah. Yeurch – it hurts my *underpants* to think about him.

So I rush to the phone with a song in my heart and a skip in my step when it rings at about eleven that morning. This singing and skipping are based a) on the thrilling and aforementioned semblance of a social life and b) on the news that Louisa passed on to me yesterday – namely that Yungsta, a. k. a. Adrian, had asked her for my phone number after we met. Oh good, I'd said, to which she replied '*Quite* good' and asked me, matter-of-factly, whether I wanted to know his age or his surname. I declined, on the basis that any woman who lies in bed at night dreaming about doing it doggy-style with Thomas the Tank Engine is frankly in no position (boom boom) to offer dating advice.

And anyway, I don't care how old he is, or what he's called: he's quite nice-looking, or would be if he got rid of his facial hair, and he sounds like he'd be a laugh, or at least interesting, what with his deep understanding of youth culture. It's important to keep up with these things, I'm always telling Frankie (whose reply, inevitably, is a rather disparaging 'You wish', usually after I've tried to get him to explain why a crusted pair of pants lying on a floor, say, is as culturally and aesthetically important – to say nothing of accomplished – as a Vermeer. I used to have this argument with Dominic, too).

Still, I may not understand about Young (is forty young?) British Artists, but I'm willing to give Yungsta's kind of music a go – although I must confess that I didn't understand much when I listened to his radio show yesterday: he seems to talk in patois, like people in St Bart's (a favourite holiday destination of my father's), though it's entirely possible that I misheard, as I was playing with Honey at the time and not wholly concentrating. Also, I'm at a distinct disadvantage musically, in that I was brought up listening to Johnny Halliday, Claude François and Sylvie Vartan (my beloved Claude, or CloClo, as he was known, electrocuted himself to death in the bath with a plug-in dildo. I think they gave him a state funeral. The other two, now grandparents, are still going strong. *Vive le rock!*). But he – Yungsta, I mean, not the poor frazzled out-with-a-bang ghost of Claude – could always explain the complexities of contemporary music over lunch at Le Caprice, for instance: there *are* advantages to being called Adrian. Brring brring, goes the phone: that must be him now.

'Weeeeelll,' says a voice I don't recognize. 'Mrs Midhurst.'

'Is that you, Dominic?' I doubt it: my non-husband is in Tokyo, as far as I know, but no one else calls me that, except for what Mummy likes to call 'the men'.

'Nooo,' says the voice – rich, oily, drawly. 'Guess again.'

'I don't know who you are,' I say genuinely. Must be one of 'the men', though unusually well spoken. 'British Gas? The electricity? The phone people? Salesman, in which case, sorry but no thanks?'

'Wrong,' says the voice, sounding very slightly less confident.

'Give me a clue,' I sigh. I hate these phone games, and besides, for all I know, my interlocutor could perfectly well be an obscene caller.

'Mmm,' the man says, sounding hoarse. 'Grrrr.'

Oh, no. *No.* It's Cooper. I can't stand it. Shall I just hang up? No. I can't. The poor man gave me what I wanted, after all: he can't help being slightly revolting or having a penis that is so palely loitering. How did he get my number? Isabella, I expect. Oh, God.

'Oh,' I say, forcing the rictus of horror off my face and a smile into my voice. 'Well, hello there.'

'You had me going there, with the who-are-you business,' Cooper says, all confidence again, as if he might suffix the sentence with a fruity 'you little tease'. He lowers his voice a little, and makes it croakier. 'Come to think of it, you had me going the other night too. Hot filly.'

I expect Cooper must have thought he was actually on

the phone to a real live pig at this point, because I let out the most massive, hideous, unmistakable snort – an obscene-sounding noise that was exactly like the oral version of a really ripe fart. 'Snorrrrt,' I went, and then – just for added sex appeal – started choking on my own laughter.

Silence. Then: 'I say, are you all right?'

'Haaaaaah,' I whimpered, not quite able to breathe.

'Good Lord,' said Cooper.

I really *was* choking, so I put the phone down on to the coffee table and my head between my legs. I stayed there for about half a minute, breathing heavily through my mouth in the manner of a badly handicapped person who's just discovered they're rubbish at swimming, or an emphysemic, until I was able to draw more or less regular breaths.

'Sorry,' I said, sounding very raw about the throat, when I picked up the phone again. 'Don't know what happened there.'

'I do,' said Cooper.

Oh dear, how extraordinarily embarrassing. I may have no intention of ever seeing Cooper again, but I don't necessarily want him to think I spend my mornings being sow-like, either.

'Don't let's talk about it,' I tell him, clearing my throat, which still feels all funny. 'What have you been up to?'

'Thinking about the other night,' he replies smoothly.

'Hmm,' I say noncommittally.

'I know what happened just then,' Cooper says, a knowing, randy note creeping back into his voice.

'Hmm?' I say again, because I can't trust myself to actually speak.

'That noise you made . . .'

'I'm sorry about that,' I quickly interrupt. 'I'm ill. Very ill. Throat bug. Sometimes I can't breathe.'

'Nonsense,' he laughs wetly. 'I've heard that noise before. Can you guess where?'

'No,' I say, nearly whispering with dread: whatever he's got to say is likely to set me off again.

'When you came,' Cooper growls.

I nearly drop the phone with shock.

'*Excuse me?*' I hiss, doing a passable impression of Miss Jean Brodie in her prime. '*What* did you say?'

Cooper laughs his comfortable, complacent laugh.

'When you came the other night,' he repeats. 'When you had an orgasm.'

'I bloody did not!' I shout. My God, is the man mad?

'You did, I assure you.'

'I may have come, William, but I most certainly *did not* snort as I did so. Good grief! The *idea*! Like in *Jabberwocky*! Burble burble! No! No! God!'

'And you came again just now, didn't you?' he continues, completely ignoring my outburst.

'NO!' I yell, as exasperated as I am indignant. 'No, no and NO again. Fucking bloody hell. I did not come. I just, er, snorted by mistake. And I can assure you that I have never, ever snorted at the point of orgasm. What a grotesque suggestion! How dare you, actually, hatefully ring me up and tell me I squeal like a sow when I come? How *dare* you, William? I mean, *Jesus*.'

'Steady on,' Cooper replies. 'I was simply pointing out the truth as I found it to be.'

I've been pacing up and down the room in an absolutely frenzied state of agitation. Now I sit down, dazed with horror.

'William.'

'Mrs Midhurst.'

'Do call me Stella – we did fuck, after all.'

'Mmm,' says Cooper. 'I remember.'

'Are you being serious? I mean, is there a gram, an ounce, a speck of truth in what you've just said?' I quite want to cry, actually.

'That you snorted uncontrollably at the point of, shall we say, no return?'

'Yes,' I whisper. Uncontrollably? *Uncontrollably?*

''Fraid so,' Cooper says cheerily.

The phone actually falls from my hands, like in a film.

'Stella?' Cooper's voice says from the floor. 'Hello?'

I pick up again.

'Swear on your life. Swear on your *dick*.'

'I swear,' he says. 'But I wouldn't worry about it, my dear. Some women pee slightly, and a mutual friend of ours brays, rather like an donkey. I've known more than one girl – they're often from Clapham – who called out "Daddy".'

'I think,' I say, as a last-ditch attempt to claw back some dignity, 'that I'd know. I mean, it's my body, and my, you know, *sound*.'

'Quite. I was actually ringing to ask you to dinner.'

'What do you mean by "uncontrollably"? That I snorted and snorted again?'

'Just the once, as I recall. There's rather a marvellous local Italian . . .'

'I'll have to call you back. I have to go now,' I say. My stomach is swirling with shock and bells are ringing in my head.

Oh, my God. I snort when I come. *There is no hope.*

*

I don't think I have actually ever been so ashamed. I once peed in my pants in kindergarten – a horribly vivid recollection, actually, thirty-five years later: I can still recall the exact, dazzlingly golden shade of yellow, trickling weirdly sonorously on to the lino tiles – and *that* was shameful enough. And sometimes I haven't been as kind, or as tactful, towards my fellow human beings as I might have been, granted – but I've had the grace to feel bad afterwards. I have, um, mixed feelings towards both my parents, but good heavens, who doesn't? Nothing that I have ever done could merit this *grotesque* punishment. Has the Lord taken leave of his senses?

I take to my bed, because that's all I can think of to do, and pop a Xanax to calm me down. At first, I decide I am going to ring every man I have ever slept with and ask them outright, while I am mildly sedated and the shock might be cushioned. But I don't have current numbers for any of them, only Dominic and Rupert, and Dominic's sleeping in Tokyo and Rupert's coming here tomorrow. I could always ask him then.

It can't be true. Someone, surely, would have mentioned it.

They just have.

Oh, *God*.

I have to emerge from my lair to give Honey her lunch when Mary brings her back from playgroup (I couldn't face Marjorie today). She is at the kitchen table, trying to make coils ('Oi snail') out of Plasticine while I stand at the cooker, warming up some of the delicious chicken curry Frank made a batch of yesterday. There's still a weird throbbing feeling in my stomach and talk about prickly armpits: mine feel like they're on fire. I could weep. No, really. Because as if the shame weren't bad enough, I clearly can't have sex with anybody ever again.

Actually, that's not true. There are options. I could learn to sign and find myself some deaf people. Or some mutes (with no hands: can't have them writing anything down). Where are the amputee mutes around here when you need them? As I say, I could weep.

'Hey,' says Frank, coming in through the garden. 'What's up? Why the long face? Hello, love,' he tells Honey, nipping her fat little cheek.

'Lo,' she says.

'No long face,' I tell him, grinning fixedly to show that I am as happy as the lark, chirrup chirrup. 'Nice morning at work, darling?'

'Fotherington in Accounts is rather a bother,' he says (see? Frank always gets the joke).

'Is there enough for me, or shall I have a butty?' he asks, peering into the fridge. 'Juice?'

'Please, for Honey. There's tons. And anyway, it's yours – you made it.'

'Cool,' says Frank, getting the plates and clicking Honey's plastic bib around her neck. 'Looking forward to tomorrow night?'

'What's tomorrow night?'

'Friday night, Stella. We're going out.'

'Oh, yes,' I say, remembering how excited I was when Frank offered to take me out and teach me how to pull. That seems like aeons ago now, a lifetime ago, before my entire sex life was ruined.

'There's a do in Shoreditch, then a party in Soho, and then, if you still fancy it, another party just off Old Street.'

'There's also Papa arriving, and Rupert. I feel rather bad leaving them.'

'Stella!' Frank says sternly. 'You *told* them you were going out – I heard you.'

'Mmm,' I shrug. 'This is exquisite. Is there cardamom in it?'

'Yes, and cinnamon.'

'You're such a good cook,' I say, reaching for more rice. 'Why don't you feed any of your dates?'

'Because they're not interested in dinner. Don't change the subject.'

'OK. About tomorrow: I don't know if I can come, Frankie.'

'Why? And why are you all red?'

'In homage to you.'

Frank rolls his eyes.

'No. Because, literally. I don't know if I can come.'

'You've lost me, love.'

'I can only date the deaf,' I whisper, hanging my head. 'Or the armless mute. And I know that's OK – do you know any deaf people, Frankie? Please, it's important – but, you know, it leaves out quite a lot of people.'

'Are you on drugs?' asks Frank. 'You're not making sense.'

I glance at Honey, who is trying to get the rice in with one hand and stroking her 'snail' with the other.

'I . . .'

'What, Stella? Are you ill? What are you talking about, woman?'

'I make . . .' I can't tell him, actually. I am burning with embarrassment: I can feel the tips of my ears and they're *roasting*.

'What do you make, Stella? Love? War? Bubbles? Come on, for God's sake.'

'I don't think I can tell you. Well, I could, but as the joke goes, I'd have to kill you afterwards.'

'What do you make?' Frank demands, sounding annoyed now, and coming over all forceful.

'I make horrible, horrible sounds when I come,' I blurt out, half-sobbing.

Frank puts his apple juice down and stares at me, his mouth half-open.

'Don't laugh, Frankie, I beg you,' I whimper melodramatically.

'I'm not laughing,' he says, but a smile is curling around his lips, causing me to throw a clod of rice at him.

'What sounds?'

'I . . . I . . . I *snort*.'

'Oh, my Christ,' Frank says. 'Oh, my fucking Christ.' He is trying to look solemn and sympathetic, but it isn't working: I know he wants to laugh.

'My life may as well be over,' I tell Frank sadly. 'Do at least *try* to be sympathetic.'

'Snort, like what? Like this?' Frank oinks richly.

'Yes, I expect so.'

'What, you go . . .' He oinks three times, each snort louder than the last, and then gawps at me in disbelief.

'Piggy,' says Honey, through a mouthful of chicken. She snorts too, which causes her to splutter all over the table and to collapse into giggles.

'You said it, Honey,' says Frank, by now openly sniggering. Oink, he goes, oink oink OINK, with Honey gleefully joining in, until the kitchen sounds like a sty, its walls echoing with pig-noise. 'Well,' says Frank, when he's calmed down, which takes a few minutes. 'Wow. Sophisticated lady. Miss Parisian charm.'

'Just leave it, Frank,' I tell him, trying to be cool and stern while still hot and floppy with shame. I wish I hadn't told him. I feel like I've got a family of wriggly hedgehogs under my armpits, flexing their spikes.

'Stella?'

'Don't start. Please. I shouldn't have said anything. And anyway,' I retort, gathering strength, 'you can talk. You may not make inhuman noises . . .'

'Snorrrrrt,' interrupts Frank rudely. 'Snoort.'

'But you've come on a woman's face at least once in the last three months. So I think we're quits.'

'I bloody have not,' Frank starts saying, but I don't let him, since as a matter of fact he has.

'I have the incontrovertible evidence of my own ears,' I say. 'So let's just *know* these unattractive things about each other and place them at the backs of our minds, like adults.'

Frank has been peeling an apple for Honey. He now, rather absent-mindedly, starts feeding her small pieces of it. His mind, understandably, is elsewhere.

'But Stell,' he says. 'How do you *know*? Did you hear yourself?'

'No, of course not. There's a sort of mini passing-out, isn't there, at the point of orgasm? One is hardly listening out for unusual sounds.'

'Well, then, how can you be sure?'

'Someone told me.'

'Who? They might have been joking.'

'They have no sense of humour. Besides, it's not funny. And anyway, I *said*, let's leave it. Let's talk about something else. What shall I wear tomorrow night, for instance?'

'The grandpa,' Frank murmurs, as if this were a particularly devastating insight. 'The doctor gramps from the other night.'

'Well, hey, Sherlock. Bravo. *Now* can we leave it?'

'Quite a menagerie that night chez Gramps, it must have been, with the tiger lying down with the lamb's little piggy pal,' irritating Frank persists biblically.

'Frank!' I yell, echoed by Honey: 'Fwank!'

Frank stops talking, but carries on feeding my daughter bits of apple with a strange expression of barely repressed hysteria on his face. This makes his eyes bulge.

I stomp over to the counter and clear away our plates. I can feel Frank's eyes burning into the back of my neck. He just can't help himself – he just can't leave it alone.

He says, 'Has anyone else ever mentioned it, like Dom?'

'No.'

'Never?'

'No. No one's ever said, Stella, you snort like a fucking pig when you come, darling. Odd, that.'

'Don't get cross, babe. It was probably a one-off.'

'I doubt it. And don't call me "babe" – you sound like Frank Butcher.' I unclip Honey's bib and lift her, and half a ton of squishy apple, out of the high chair, just as Frank bursts out laughing.

'I didn't mean it in the Frank Butcher sense,' he honks. 'I meant it . . .'

'As in the film,' I suddenly twig. 'Babe. Very fucking hilarious, Frankie. Honey and I are going to make up the guest beds now,' I tell him with as much dignity as I can muster. 'And that, by the way, was a really mean joke.'

As we make our way up, I can hear Frank at first shouting

and then screaming with laughter. I hear his big hands slap against his thighs. He drops something, at one point. He is practically delirious.

'Oink,' Honey snorts quietly against my neck as we head for the second landing. 'Oi piggy.'

'No, darling. *Oi* piggy,' I tell her sadly. 'Oi Piggy of Shame.'

9

Friday morning, and chaos. There's no food in the house except rusks, bananas and a scraping of cold curry, so I'm just about to rush off to Waitrose to stock up when the phone rings. It's Rupert, who informs me that he's decided to drive down from Scotland rather than train or plane it, which means he doesn't quite know when he'll be arriving. 'So,' he tells me, 'I've asked Cressida – that's my date, Cressida Lennox – to come straight to yours at half past six. I'll either be there myself by then, or I'll be just around the corner. Is that OK?'

I suppose it is; he's booked dinner at a restaurant called Odette's, ten minutes' walk from my house. 'That's fine,' I tell Rupert, 'but do please try and be here on time – my dad's arriving, plus I'm going out myself and I need to get ready, so if you're not here, I'm not going to stand in the living room for hours making small talk to your fancy woman when I should be in the bath and generally beautifying.'

'You'll love Cressida,' Rupert says breezily. 'You can talk about babies and things.'

'Why? Because we both have wombs?'

Rupert chortles fruitily; one of the sweet things about him is that he never takes offence at my snappier jokes. 'That too. But she works in childcare so, you know, you'll have lots in common. I expect. Anyway, I'll be there. Don't worry about it. Cheerio.'

So then I'm trying to rush out to Waitrose for the second time, and just scribbling a note for Mary asking her if she wouldn't mind giving the living room a quick once-over while Honey has her nap, when the doorbell goes.

'*Bon-jewer*,' says Tim, my next-door neighbour. He is standing with his hands in the pockets of his trousers – they're more slacks, really – stretching them out.

'Hi,' I say. 'I'm actually just on my way out – house guests. No food. Need to get to Waitrose and back before the child-minder finishes her shift.'

Tim just stands there, fiddling with his pockets, staring. He mowed my lawn this time last week, come to think of it: obviously doesn't go to work on Fridays.

'Hello?' I say, keys in hand. 'I'm sorry, Tim, but I'm late as it is – I really need to get going.'

'I'll drive you,' Tim finally says, selecting a weird, burbly voice, as if speaking from the bottom of a bog, from his panoply.

'No, really, it's OK,' I tell him, stepping out and slamming the front door shut behind me. He doesn't move back, so for a second or two we are both perched awkwardly on the top step. Why is he so peculiar and off-putting?

'I'll drive myself,' I say.

'I'd like to drive you,' he replies.

'Sweet of you, but . . .'

'I'm at a bit of a loose end, what with Janice and the kids away,' he explains, now sounding perfectly normal and looking entirely plausible, in a beslacked, suburban husband twenty-years-married kind of way. 'I need a few things from Waitrose too. Go on,' he adds, seeing my confused expression. 'It'll be fun.' He points his key ring at the street and the lights on a black MPV (natch) flash as the door catches – click – are released.

'Come on,' he calls out, striding ahead purposefully now. I don't quite see how I can't get into his car without seeming unnecessarily rude. He *is* odd, and he is marsupial, but if he wants to drive me to Waitrose because he's bored, or lonely, and if supermarkets are his idea of 'fun', then really I don't see why not.

'Belt up,' Tim says as I park my behind in the front seat. His seat belt is already fastened, and as I glance over it seems unusually taut and neat, sitting across his proud chest like a sash. Tim was probably the kind of boy whose school uniform trousers were slightly too short, and too tight over the copious expanse of his buttocks (because he was a fat-arsed child, I can just tell). He probably tucked his regulation V-neck in tightly too, and had horrible sandwiches that stank of unrefrigerated egg, and ignored his contemporaries' mean comments by applying himself to elaborate fantasies about trolls or Tolkien. I suddenly feel sorry for him.

'So,' I say cheerily. 'You don't work on Fridays, then?'

'Not at the moment, no,' he says, not elaborating.

'That must be nice. Longer sort of weekend, I suppose.'

'Yes.'

'More time with the kids.'

'Uh-huh,' Tim says.

'They look nice boys.'

'That they are, mam'zelle, that they are.'

We drive in silence for a while, up to Swiss Cottage. The Swiss cottage itself, an Alpine wooden chalet in the middle of a busy junction, has always struck me as especially incongruous, but the minute we catch sight of it Tim grabs my knee and says, 'Yodel-ei-hee-ho,' very, very loudly, causing me to jump.

'Gosh,' I say.

Tim is holding the steering wheel with one hand and rotating the other encouragingly at me.

'Come on,' he says. 'Come on, then.'

I smile at him blankly. What is it he wants me to do?

Tim sighs deeply. 'Yodel-ei-hee-ho,' he repeats. And then, helpfully, he whispers, 'You reply, "Yodel-ei-hee-*hee*."' He raises his eyebrows expectantly.

'Oh, haha, yes,' I stammer. 'The *Swiss* cottage. I get it. Yodelling. Yes. Ha ha.'

'Yodel-ei-HEE-HO,' Tim bellows, po-faced. 'Join in, for God's sake. Join in, woman.'

'I don't want to.'

'Yodel-ei-hee, yodel-ei-hee,' he sings furiously, his voice rising all the while. 'Yodel-ei-heehee, yodel-ei-hee-ho, yodel-edle-yodle-edle-yodel-EI.'

Bloody hell. I don't know what to do, so I stare out of the window.

Tim doesn't speak again until we're halfway down the Finchley Road.

'Look,' he then says. 'I'll be straight with you.'

'Right,' I say. 'Straight about what?'

'My needs,' Tim says simply. 'I have needs.'

'Oh,' I say, flummoxed. 'What kinds of needs?'

'Very real needs,' he says. 'And you strike me as a woman of the world.'

'Oh,' I repeat. I wish I could remember the bit in the Worst Case Scenario handbook about jumping out of moving cars.

'Being foreign and all that,' he continues.

'Quite. Though possibly you attribute too much exoticism to me, Tim. I'm half English, you know.'

'Weren't raised here though, were you? I can tell.'

I concede that no, I was in the main raised Abroad. Tim nods knowingly and parks the car. We jump out and head for the trolley rank.

'What's your point, Tim?'

'My point is this,' Tim says. He takes me by the hand and leads me to a little concrete bench, usually frequented by drunks. 'Sit yourself down,' he says magnificently. 'My point,' he repeats – he is standing, and doing the thing with his pockets again – 'is this. I know about you single women.'

'Right,' I say, glancing at my watch. 'I don't really have that much time, Tim, so . . .'

'Precisely. You're, what, thirty-five?'

'Thirty-eight, actually.'

'And time is running out,' Tim says, looking very pleased at the idea.

'What for? Time is running out for what?'

'For the likes of you. I mean, look at you. You're divorced, single, not getting any younger . . .'

'That's right,' I say pleasantly. He is annoying me now. The 'Allo 'Allo French stuff is bad enough, but this really takes the biscuit.

'And you're gagging for a man. You all are.'

'There's only one of me. Actually.'

'I mean all of you . . . you women. You types.'

'Gagging for a man?'

'Of course,' says Tim. 'Let's go in, shall we? They always run out of rhubarb yoghurt.'

Tim's idea, in a nutshell (because it takes him three aisles

– pasta, crisps and snacks, dairy – to articulate it), is as follows: he and I have an affair. Nothing heavy. Janice, it seems, is going through some kind of early menopause thing which is affecting her sex drive. Only temporary, probably. But meanwhile Tim has very real needs and I – well, I am old and single and gagging for it. True, there isn't much in it for me in the long run, but in the short run I get all the sex I want. With Tim. In the afternoons. I'll love this, because a) I am French and thus gagging for it even more than my English sisters and b) it would give me a chance to air my mother tongue, which Tim says he would find very erotic when used 'in a bedroom situation'.

'So,' he says, standing by the cheese counter and actually rubbing his hands together. 'What do you say?'

I say nothing. I stare at a Stilton with blueberries and wonder why the English, with so many fabulous and underrated native cheeses at their disposal, insist on buggering about with them. Blueberries in Stilton. Imagine. What next? Sultanas in Brie? Jelly Tots in Chèvre?

'That's a disgrace,' I tell Tim, gesturing in the direction of the counter. 'A disgrace to cheesehood.'

'I like a bit of Jarlsberg myself,' he says.

'I can't have an affair with you, Tim,' I snap. 'But thanks for asking.'

'Why ever not?' he asks, looking genuinely astonished. 'Why not, woman?' He isn't in the least sorry for himself at being turned down: he is indignant, just as he was when I wouldn't yodel.

'Your taste in cheese offends me,' I tell him truthfully.

'I suppose you like those stinky French numbers that taste like old socks,' he sniffs, not remotely conciliatory.

'I do, as a matter of fact. Though I am also devoted to Laughing Cow.'

'Very unattractive in a woman,' Tim continues, flinching away from me as though I were about to lick his face with Chaumes-scented breath.

'Well, then,' I say.

'Well, then, what?'

'Well, then, we couldn't possibly have an affair, because I eat stinky cheese all day long. For breakfast. For elevenses. Lunch and dinner. Snacks in the night.'

'Do you really?'

'Yes. That's how French I am. Cheese all day, walking around in basques all night.'

'Basques, eh? Basques. Braun do an excellent electric toothbrush. The Plaque 3-D. Most efficient. Janice has got one.'

'No doubt.'

'You could use that, before coming over. And Listerine.'

I've had enough of this by now. Oddly, though, I can't get quite as cross with Tim, or feel as amply insulted, as the occasion warrants. There's something about him that makes me feel protective: he's so pitiful and weird and throwbackishly *English*. He is beyond gauche. He is a social cripple. He thinks you ask your next-door neighbour for sex because she's foreign and so, in some weird way, it doesn't count. He yodels. He wears slacks and puts on funny voices; he probably goes to pubs, 'takes a pew' and addresses the landlord as 'mine host'. He also hates women, I suspect, and has overly macho, robust relationships with his male friends, give or take a little bare-bottomed towel-flicking after the weekly game of squash.

'I won't be coming over,' I tell him, stuffing basmati rice

and two jars of chutney into my already bulging trolley, 'because we won't be having an affair.'

'I don't mind about the cheese. Not with modern mouthwash.'

'I don't fancy you,' I tell him bluntly, loading up on claret.

'House guests alcoholics, are they?'

'No.'

'Well, I fancy you, even though you're quite old.'

'That's nice.'

'Oh dear,' says Tim, now standing in line at the till, stretching out his pockets again. 'Oh, Lord. What will I do instead?'

'You could always just *wait* until Janice gets HRT. Or masturbate,' I tell him loudly as I unload my trolley on to the conveyor belt. The latter suggestion seems to thrill him, because he squirms slightly and goes red and smiley before throwing me a disgusted look.

We drive home in silence, avoiding Swiss Cottage. So you see, the thing about single women over the age of twenty-five never getting any offers is a complete crock, and so's the thing about desperation. Some of us may be desperate, but there's desperation and there's Weedy Neighbour Sex, and never the twain shall meet.

Tim helps me unload my shopping bags and then goes home, throwing a cross-sounding, '*When* you change your mind . . .' in my direction. I spend the next couple of hours cooking and cleaning – we do actually have a cleaning lady, but I can never tell whether she's been or not, a state of affairs I must remedy at some point – and generally making things attractive.

My father arrives just before four, while Honey, clearly exhausted from a morning spent at her weekly Music and Movement session, is still napping.

'Estelle!' he bellows from the front doorstep, not bothering to use the knocker. 'I have arrived. Help me.' I am fiddling about with the fire in the living room and can hear him through two sets of walls.

'Hello,' I say, opening the door and embracing him. 'It's so nice to see you. Did you have a good journey?'

'Passable,' Papa says, thrusting luggage at me. 'Although one feels most *oppressed* by the ocean when actually under its mighty weight.'

'Yes, it's an odd idea, isn't it? Come in, come in. Coffee? Something to eat?'

Oddly, counter-intuitively, this conversation is not conducted in French: my father loves speaking English.

'A glass of wine, I think. And perhaps one of your exquisite British sandwiches. Aaah,' he says, looking happily around the living room. 'It's much prettier than when I was last here. More aesthetic. Less hideous.'

'I redid it after Dom. White or red?' I call from the kitchen.

'Red, darling. Red like the corpuscle.'

I walk back through. 'Here you go,' I say. 'And here are some cucumber sandwiches I made especially for you. Chin-chin.'

My father taught me to say 'chin-chin' when I was a child, believing this to be charmingly and authentically English. I've never met another person under sixty who actually says it, unless they're French.

'*Santé!*' he smiles, taking a huge gulp. '*Oh for a beaker full of the warm South,*' he continues, waving his arms about like

117

a third-rate actor – I'm sparing you the phonetic spelling: suffice it to say that his accent is cartoonishly, comically French and that he speaks very fast. '*Full of the true, the blushful Hippocrene.*' That's another thing he taught me. Until I was about sixteen, I believed the done thing was to quote this particular bit of Keats whenever presented with a glass of wine: according to my father, it was what *le tout Londres* always did. My mother just smiled vaguely (smiling vaguely is my mother's forte), and never disabused either of us.

My father, who is seventy, is enormously tall and occupies a space like no one else. Already, he seems to have taken over the whole room. He doesn't just sit down, he *inhabits* the sofa, and his crossed ankles commandeer the carpet. He is somewhat corpulent – he has the stomach of a *bon viveur* or professional ball-swallower – but leggy with it, like a tree with a knot in its middle. His once-black hair is now salt and pepper; his small, crinkly blue eyes – they're almost turquoise – bore into one like lasers and fizz like sparklers.

Today my father is wearing a pink shirt – he has about a hundred, though he also favours violet and primrose yellow – and a loose, but beautifully cut, toffee-coloured corduroy suit. He smells of Mouchoir de Monsieur and his socks are pea green. There's something camp about his hands: long thin fingers, too expressive, and frequently bejewelled. I love him very dearly.

'Where is Honey?' he demands, devouring each sandwich in one bite.

'Asleep. She'll wake up in a minute, I should think. So, Papa, how long are you here for, and what will you do?'

'The weekend only, I think. I shall roam,' he says. 'I shall revisit some haunts. Scenes of the crimes. Above all,

I shall revisit my tailor. Only the English still know how to dress. In Paris, men dress like Arab pimps.'

'All of them?'

'Evidently.'

'Let me know if you want company.'

'You could maybe meet me in the Ritz bar at six tomorrow.'

'Yes, maybe.'

'Where is this Frank?'

'On his way back, I expect.'

'Do you sleep with him?'

'No.'

'Hmm,' my father says, throwing me a beady look. 'It is very unhealthy to deprive oneself of sexual intercourse. On top of that, it is very *ageing*.'

'Mm. Frank's lovely, but I don't think sleeping with him would be a good idea.'

'Very bad for the nerves, that deprivation,' my father persists. 'Are you seeing anybody?'

'My nerves are fine, Papa. No, not really, but there are . . . offers. There was one only this morning, in fact.'

'Excellent. As it should be. May I have another wine?'

'Of course.' I go into the kitchen and come back with the rest of the bottle, pouring myself a glass too.

We gossip companionably for a while and then I go and get Honey, worried that her extended nap means she won't sleep a wink tonight. Papa makes squeaking noises at her, pronounces her 'a beauty' and immediately starts playing peek-a-boo with a cushion, much to Honey's delight, even though he gets bored after a couple of minutes. Honey, nevertheless, gazes lovingly up at him and amuses herself by his feet with her toy puppy.

'I've left you a tomato tart and salad,' I tell Papa. 'And a pavlova for pudding. By the way – ' I glance at my watch – 'Rupert will be arriving later. With a girl called Cressida.'

'The husband?'

'Yes, the husband.'

'Very good,' says my father, smiling. He loves frightening Rupert: that sort of blethery, chinless (as Papa sees it) Englishness amuses him no end.

'And I'm going out, remember? With Frank.'

'Whom you do not sleep with.'

'That's right.'

Frank's key jiggles in the lock on cue; two seconds later, he strides into the living room.

'Enchanted,' my father says, jumping up and giving Frank an appreciative up-and-down look. '*Thrilled*.'

'Likewise,' smiles Frank easily. 'Hello, love,' he tells Honey, ruffling her hair. 'Hi, Stell.'

'That Titian hair!' my father says, to no one in particular. '*Comme un renard*. Like a wolverine.'

'Fox,' I correct.

'Fox. Ravishing. You look a most capable young man.'

'I try my best,' Frank shrugs. He is clearly more my father's type than Rupert or Dominic. Despite what Rupert chooses to think, his former pa-in-law regards him as a risibly poor physical specimen. Of Dominic as husband material, all Papa had to say was, 'Charming, I agree, but he looks like a feminine lesbian.' Frank, though, is obviously much more to his taste.

I suppose the thing about Frank is that he is very butch. He couldn't be anything other than male. Rupert's on the pretty side (if you squint), and Dominic's effete, but no one could ever accuse Frank of effeminacy. He is *bien fait*, nicely put together – tall and sinewy, with long limbs. And he has that square-jawed, manly facial thing going. It's true, he does look capable. But the colours! He is *so* ginger. If he weren't, I suppose – if his hair were brown or black or blond – he would be a catch. Which he already is, given his improbable number of sexual partners, so it's hardly as though he needed my pity. Very, very fleetingly, I ask myself whether I'd sleep with Frank if he dyed his hair. And recognized his family, of course.

'Stell?' Frank says. 'Oo-ee, Stella, wake up.'

'Hmmm?'

'I was saying, do you want to go and get ready now? I'll be the host.' He smiles at my father. 'And keep an eye on Honey. Has she had tea?'

'No.'

'Omelette all right?'

'Oh, Frank – you're not the nanny. I'll do it.'

'You've been with her most of the day. Go and have a bath,' he says, scooping Honey up with one manly, ginger-haired arm. 'Papa and I will do it.'

'Papa?' I ask.

'Yeah. That's what your father asked me to call him. I'm very flattered.'

'This man is a phenomenon,' Papa says happily. 'No, Stella? A *phenomenon*.'

I'm lying in the bath, wallowing in Shalimar (the scent of which actually reminds me of my mother in a way that is not entirely welcome; I'm convinced the reason my father is so, shall we say, ambisexual is that he's had to be both a father and a mother to me). I am thinking about Frank. He is extraordinarily good with Honey, is what I'm thinking: he really seems to love her. He volunteers to give her her tea, or tuck her in, or take her for the odd stroll. I know he actively enjoys playing with her, because a genuine enthusiasm for playing with small children can't be faked for more than fifteen minutes. I also know she loves him: he inspires love in her.

And sometimes I get very uncomfortable with all of this. Not on my behalf, or Honey's, but because *he has his own child*. The silent, invisible, never mentioned child that Dom alerted me to. Is that why Frank's so kind to Honey? Is she a substitute for the child he so horribly never, ever sees? Let's be blunt: for the child he abandoned. A little girl too, Dom said. I know life is complicated, and that there are usually compelling enough reasons to explain random acts of emotional brutality, but I just can't get to grips with this one. Frank is a slag, but he is a nice man. Why does he pretend his own daughter doesn't exist?

It feels odd to me never to bring her up in conversation. Frank and I talk about everything, bluntly, crudely sometimes. But whenever I've alluded to Newcastle, or home, or Frank's life before he came down south, he tells me about pubs, bars, his mum, his brothers and sisters, the footy, the shipyards – anything, really, and everything, except what I really want to know about. It makes it almost impossible to bring the subject up, really. I suppose I could just ask him outright – just drag it out into the open – if I didn't feel so strongly about the issue of men abandoning their children. But since I find the very idea of it so utterly offensive, I know that I would lecture, and hector, and argue, and end up not liking him. And I don't want not to like him. So we don't go there. He doesn't let me, and I don't trust myself to ask dispassionately. Doesn't stop me wondering, though. God, how I wonder. I suppose I could always ask Mary – she's known his mother for years. She must have heard something about it.

My somewhat depressing train of thought is interrupted by the doorbell. I hear Papa answering, and a female voice: Cressida, presumably (an amusingly English name, Cressida, like being called Tomata. The one that always stumps me, though, is Candida, as in *albicans*, as in thrush, as in vaginal infection. This is little Candida, and this is her brother Non-Specific Urethritis, and *this* – proud flourish – is Genital Warts, our eldest).

Where the hell's Rupert, who'd promised to be here in time? I hop out of the bath and into the bedroom, wondering – again – what on earth one wears when one is a woman of thirty-eight out on the pull. Because that, I remind myself, is the purpose of the evening after all: Frank kindly offered to share his pulling tips with me. I'm not wildly in the mood for a repeat of the other night, I must say, but then, I sternly remind myself, the best policy when one has suffered a trauma, e.g. falling off a horse or shagging a man with a penis that is somehow *larval*, is to immediately get back in the saddle again.

Ten minutes later, I emerge into the living room wearing a little black dress (with red and pink flower embroidery – very pretty, though I say so myself), low slingbacks and a string of pearls, which is perhaps a little formal. But I have a horror of being underdressed, and since I know nothing about any of the parties we're going to, I'd rather be overdressed than skulk about in a corner trying to look 'street' in a pair of torn jeans when everybody else is in black tie. (I hate people who do this: it's supposed to say 'I don't care', but in fact screams 'Look at me', and rather adolescently at that.) I'm grateful to Cressida for turning up: if I hadn't felt I needed to come downstairs, I'd still be in front of the mirror trying to figure out what to wear. You sometimes read about rich women who put on a sort of uniform every day, and while in the past this has struck me as a poor, denying-the-joys-of-fashion approach, I am beginning to see its charms. Open the closet and pick one of ten black jumpers, to team with one of fifteen pairs of black trousers and one of twenty pairs of black shoes: I have to admit, it has appeal.

Cressida is a nice pink-and-blonde Sloane in, I would say, her late twenties: on the chunky side, good legs, nice breasts, wearing an LBD of her own for her date, with flat shoes and a matching handbag. Her hair is shiny and hangs in a neat bob; she is wearing clear lip gloss and a smidgeon of brown mascara. She sits chatting to Honey, who is on the floor constructing squat little Duplo towers.

'Hello,' I say, hand outstretched. 'I'm Stella. Rupert shouldn't be long. Would you like a drink? Frank, why haven't you offered Cressida a drink?'

'Air, hell-air,' says Cressida. 'I'd love a glass of white wine, if you have one. Vair dry. Sweet little girl,' she adds, pointing at Honey. 'She almost knows her colours, clever thing.'

'Yes, we've been learning them.'

'I was just about to,' Frank says, sounding hurt that I should so denigrate his hostly skills. 'Offer drinks, I mean. But Papa was in the kitchen with me, wanting me to explain about my pictures . . .'

'And wouldn't let you get away,' I finish. 'I quite under-stand. He does it all the time. Where is he now?'

'Gone to "refresh himself" and get something from

upstairs. I'll do the drinks now,' he says, smiling at Cressida. 'White wine, wasn't it? What about you, Stell?'

'Papa will probably stick to red, but yes, I'll have white too.'

'Gosh,' Cressida murmurs at Frank's retreating back. 'He's rather a dish, isn't he?'

'If you like that kind of thing,' I smile back at her. 'Which I must admit, I don't. He's *lovely* though,' I add helpfully. 'He's the nicest man I know. But . . .' I wave my hands around my head. 'You know . . . very red. And, er . . . well, let's leave it at that.'

'Goodness,' says Cressida. 'That's an awfully modern way of speaking about your husband.'

'Oh, no! No, you've got the wrong end of the stick. Frank isn't my husband.'

'Isn't he?'

'No, not at all. He's my friend. He's my house-mate.'

'Oh,' says Cressida, looking perplexed.

'Easy mistake to make,' I say reassuringly.

'So the baby?'

'Honey? She's Dominic's. We split up a couple of years ago.'

'I'm sorry.'

'Don't be.'

Cressida looks expectantly at me, her steady blue gaze demanding more of an explanation.

'It was a very friendly split,' I shrug. 'He lives in Tokyo now, most of the time. He's an art dealer – he's Frank's art dealer, in fact.'

'Oh, is he an artist? How romantic. Still, being divorced can't be easy.'

'We weren't actually married. That was Rupert.'

'Was it? Where?' Cressida springs to her feet and smoothes down her dress. 'He's awfully nice, isn't he? I do like him, I must say. Met him at Harry Redstone's wedding, do you know him? Gosh, your hearing's good. But some people's car engines are like that, aren't they? My flat-mate had a Fiat Cinquecento that made a particular sound – I could tell she was home from half a street away.'

'No,' I start to explain. But by some weird coincidence, the door goes half a second later and it is indeed Rupert, looking his usual dishevelled self and proffering a news-paper-wrapped parcel.

'Hello, Rupe.'

'Hello, darling. Brought you a salmon. Wild.'

'How delicious. Come in. How was the drive? Do you want to have a wash or anything? Cressida's here already.'

'Do you adore her? I do.'

'She seems very nice.'

'Hmm.' Rupert is hovering about the hall, blinking and doing a passable imitation of a grubbier, less groomed Hugh Grant. 'Tell you what – if you can hold the fort for a couple more secs, I'll just go and brush my teeth, wash my hands, that kind of thing, and be with you in five minutes. Think I should – I've got car-breath.'

'OK. You also smell slightly of dog.'

'Yes, but that's a nice smell. Women love it.' He smiles and makes his way up the stairs as I go back into the living room. Cressida is standing, a pink blush about her cheeks.

'Just gone to freshen up,' I tell her. 'Long drive.'

Sweetly, Cressida looks as though she is about to explode with excitement.

'Here,' I say, 'have a refill.'

'One hardly *ever* meets any nice men,' she blurts, taking

a couple of great gulps. 'They're all married, or divorced, or gay, or strange . . .'

'Well, Rupert *is* . . .' I begin, only to be interrupted by my dear papa, who has changed into a dark red velvet smoking-jacket all the better to tend to his baby-sitting duties.

'Good evening,' he says to Cressida. 'Jean-Marie de la Croix.'

'My father,' I explain. 'Papa, Cressida is here because she has a date with Rupert. He's just upstairs.'

'Rupert?' says Papa, giving Cressida a long, unsettlingly knowing look. 'Ah, yes. How charming.'

'How do you do,' says Cressida, a touch nervously. 'Are you French? I love Provence.'

'Of course,' says Papa, with a courtly bow. 'What English person doesn't? *Ils ont si peu d'imagination, les pauvres.* Where is Frank, Stella? I would like to offer him a cigar. Romeo y Juliettas,' he says, waving a box at me. 'And this, *ma chérie*, is for you.' He dumps a large, extravagantly beribboned square parcel on to my free arm.

'Thank you, Papa. How kind. He's in the kitchen, I think – I'll get him. I'll just go and put this fish in the fridge.'

'And then you must open my gift.'

'I can't wait. What is it?'

'A surprise, of course.'

I totter into the kitchen, where Frank is filling an ice bucket.

'I made some crostini,' he says.

'What?'

'When you were out this morning. I had to pop back for something, and while I was here I made some crostini.'

'Are you being serious?'

'Yes, Stella,' Frank says patiently. 'They're on those two green plates, under the tea towels.'

'But how?'

'How what? Your dad's great, by the way.'

'How did you know how?'

Frank gives me a look and shakes the ice down.

'I went to a Swiss finishing school,' he says drily. 'I can also get in and out of cars without showing my crack. You look nice, Stell. I thought we'd leave here at about eight-ish, and maybe go and get a drink first?'

'You really are a paragon,' I tell Frank, kissing him on the cheek. 'That is just *so* kind. I am *incredibly* impressed.'

'They're only bits of bread with stuff on top,' Frank says northernly, 'so don't get too excited. Bring the plates through, will you, and come and introduce me to your ex-husband.'

We soon have rather a jolly little drinks party on our hands. My father refuses to be detached from Frank, for whom he has clearly conceived something of a passion, although he does occasionally throw Rupert one of those long, knowing looks of his, followed by a wink.

'Look,' says Rupert, who is standing next to me and speaking through a mouthful of mushroom crostino. 'He's doing it again. I've told you a million times, Stella; I know he fancies me.'

'Don't be *absurd*,' I reply. 'He only does it to annoy. If you didn't react so dramatically, he wouldn't do it in the first place.'

'No,' says Rupert. 'He can't help doing it. He's always

done it to me. I used to get looks like that off boys at school.'

'Er,' says Cressida. 'Surely you aren't suggesting that Stella's father wants to . . .'

'He does,' Rupert states. 'I know it. It's *terribly* nice to see you again, Cressida.'

Cressida, who's been looking both puzzled and not a million miles from appalled, beams. 'And you.'

We sip our white wine in silence for a moment. Honey is roaming about the room, gnawing on crostini and climbing on to random laps before returning to her Duplo stacks.

'And your Frank,' says Rupert, turning to me, 'is a really top bloke. Nice chap. Like him tremendously. Are you and he . . .'

'No.' Does everyone I meet have to ask me this?

'Well, you could do worse. He's absolutely sweet with my god-daughter. She's absolutely sweet with him, too.'

'Yes, they get on very well.'

'And he's really nice to be around. You know, easy.'

I burst out laughing. 'Easy? Yes, you could say that.'

'Well, I like him,' says Rupert. 'I like him a lot more than that horrible Dom. Now there's the opposite of a top bloke. Sneaky. Manipulative, if you ask me. Don't like the cut of his jib one jot.'

'Jib one jot? You sound like Edward Lear. I know you didn't like him, Rupe – you've told me a million times. Never mind. Don't lose too much sleep over it.'

Cressida, whose attention has been elsewhere, touches Rupert's sleeve.

'How do you know him?' Cressida eventually asks Rupert. 'Stella's father, I mean?'

I'm about to answer this when, to my astonishment, Rupert very carefully places his foot, which is shod in a seen-better-days brogue, right on top of mine (which is shod in nothing, at this point – my shoes are in the hall), and pushes down, hard. He does this very quickly, rather as one might stamp on an ant, but in such a smooth, gliding sort of motion that Cressida appears not to notice.

'I'm an old friend of Stella's – we met at university. So I know her father from way back.'

'Oh, yes, that's right – you've told me before. Where did you go?' asks Cressida breathlessly.

'Cambridge,' Rupert says, pretending it's irrelevant.

'Goodness!' says his date. 'You must be awfully clever.'

'Oh, you know,' Rupert and his Third in Geography shrug modestly.

'We need some more wine,' I announce. 'Rupe, come and help me with the ice, will you?'

'I'd rather not,' Rupert says, much to Cressida's pleasure. 'I love it where I am.'

'I need you to. Now.'

Rupert rolls his eyes theatrically at Cressida, who giggles.

'Don't go away now,' he husks.

Bloody hell. Love's young dream.

'Don't tell me,' I say to Rupert the second we're in the kitchen, 'don't tell me, Rupe, that you haven't told her.'

'Haven't told her what?' Rupert asks innocently. 'Lovely kitchen you've got here.'

'Haven't you told Cressida we used to be married?'

Rupert puffs his cheeks out.

'I don't think she'd like it.'

'She doesn't have an enormous amount of choice, Rupe – I mean, it happened. It's not particularly significant . . .'

'Thanks.'

'You know what I mean. It's not particularly significant, but you're going to have a problem trying to keep it from her with my dad here, not to mention Frank. Anyway, I think it's rather insulting. To me, I mean.'

'What I really adore about her is that she's so old-fashioned. Rather sweet, you know. Unspoiled. Probably believes in the Tooth Fairy.'

'Well, I must say, she makes a nice change from all those girls you used to hang around Westbourne Grove with – the Taras with the trust funds and the coke habits.'

'Don't remind me. But that's exactly my point. She's not *urban* in that way. She wouldn't know what E & O or Soho House was. She's probably never taken drugs in her life. She's just really, really sweet, like a puppy. Do you know, she still rides?'

'Don't tell Frank that, or he'll start laughing.'

'Why?'

'It's a northern thing. He gets hysterical whenever he sees a Dial-a-Ride bus.'

'How odd. Anyway, Stells, do you see? I didn't think I'd get married again . . .'

'Steady on! You've known her two minutes.'

'I know, I know. But I really like her, and I think she's just the right sort of woman for me. We could still live on the island and I can just sort of *see* her there, Stells, baking bread and so on. Shining light of the WI, that kind of thing.'

'And you're trying to keep your terrible past from her in case it puts her off? There's nothing so awful about having been married for two seconds over ten years ago, you know.'

'I'll tell her eventually, Stella. But I'd rather not tell her now. Do you mind?'

'Not really,' I shrug. 'But in that case we'd better go back through before someone says something they shouldn't and this evening turns into . . .'

'A French farce.'

'Exactly.'

'You're an angel. Thanks, Stells, I owe you one.'

The parcel from my father, which I am urged to open in public, contains, as suspected, a costume masquerading as a dress. This time, Papa has seen fit to buy me a Native American outfit consisting of a fringed suede dress, matching boots, a little feather-holder to wear around the forehead and a useful container for keeping my arrows in. Despite his cries of regret, I don't try it on there and then, or indeed wear it out with Frank.

Honey goes to bed at seven thirty and falls fast asleep, compounding Papa's disappointment. 'I hope she wakes up later,' he moans, 'or I shall be very bored.'

Cressida and Rupert slope off to their restaurant at ten to eight, and Frank and I go half an hour or so later, leaving my father comfortably ensconced with claret, cigar and cable television.

'Amuse yourselves, my children,' he says, seeing us out. 'Come back late.'

I pull on my coat and force Frank to wear his (he usually does that absurd macho northern coatless thing, even – especially – when it's freezing). And Frank and I step out into the night.

We start off somewhere in the East End of London. Frank orders lychee martinis, which are new to me and delicious in the extreme.

'So,' says Frank, once we're settled in. 'Nice bloke, but doesn't seem your type.'

'Who, Rupert? He's not, but he was then, because he was so un-French – it was *years* ago, Frank. We used to have such a laugh. It was like being married to one's brother.'

'Did one have sex?' Frank is wearing a suit, amazingly, with a black shirt and a black tie, which ought to look ludicrously, Guy Ritchie-ishly wannabe bad boy but works, somehow, on him: he looks naughty but nice, like an Eighties cream cake. More naughty than nice, actually – almost surly, until he smiles.

'One did, actually,' I tell him sternly. 'Giggly, stupid sex. You know – the way you do when you're really at ease with somebody. Falling about laughing and giving our genitals excruciating names.'

'Yeah,' says Frank, with a very small sigh. 'I do. I love that. Haven't had that for years.'

Aha! This would suggest a relationship that was longer than a one-night stand. It must, in fact, be a reference to the mother of Frank's child. He must remember her, surely, sometimes? Or does he really never spare her a thought at all?

'Do you ever think you're actually oversexed? I mean, I've been through periods of, you know, in the past, but I can't believe the number of people *you* go through. It can't be good for you.'

'Why not?'

'It must be exhausting, for a start.'

'I manage,' says Frank. ''Nother martini? You shouldn't gulp them down like that, you'll be ill.'

'Yes, please. Utterly delicious, aren't they? And don't worry about me. I could drink you under the table, I think you'll find. *Actually.*'

Frank raises one eyebrow and grins, then gets the waiter.

'I suppose perhaps you're on a sort of quest,' I continue.

'Yes, possibly.'

'What for, though, is the question? The ideal wife?'

'A dirty ride,' Frank smiles, raising his glass. 'Cheers.'

'Cheers.'

'Actually, the *ideal* dirty ride,' Frank elaborates.

'How do you define a dirty ride? I mean, what does it actually *mean*? I've always wanted to know – me and the entire female population.'

'I can't really explain it,' Frank says unhelpfully. 'Some people are dirty rides, and some people aren't.'

'In what way? Try and be specific, Frankie.'

'See,' says Frank, lighting a fag, 'the thing about dirty rides is they don't just turn it on.'

'How do you mean?'

'Well, the dirty ride just *is* a dirty ride. She's not *trying* to be dirty, because she already is. Being normally ladylike and then turning it on isn't actually being a dirty ride. It's *pretending* to be a dirty ride.'

'Oh.' Our second martinis arrive. 'But how do you

define dirty? You mean those women who always look like they've just done it and are leaking into their pants? That look?'

'Sometimes. Not always. Not by any means.'

'Who, then? Pamela Anderson?'

'Yeah. Have you seen the video?'

'No.'

'She's a dirty ride. But it isn't to do with the way she looks – it's to do with her, um, enthusiasm. I mean, you could have a trick pelvis and still not be a dirty ride. It's all in the delivery.'

'So if you fellate someone with the most tremendous gusto, you're a dirty ride?'

'You can be.'

'You're not being at all clear,' I sigh.

'Sorry,' he shrugs, smiling curiously. 'It's not that important.'

'That's a complete lie,' I cry. 'It is *hugely* important, other-wise it wouldn't be your life's quest and I wouldn't be so extremely interested. I can't overemphasize my interest, Frank. So come on. Give me examples. Who's a dirty ride? What about blue knickers a couple of weeks ago? Was she?'

'What, that short bird? Not especially.'

'The blonde who came in while I was having a shower, then – the one before the screamer. Remember? What about her?'

'Oh, her,' smiles Frank. 'Yeah. Yeah, she was.'

'Who else?'

'I don't think you've met any of them.'

'So can you tell in advance? Point out the dirty rides in here.'

'Really?'

'Really.'

'Oh, all right. Come and sit next to me then, otherwise you'll crick your neck.' I get up and swap my chair for the leather banquette. 'You can't ever be absolutely 100 per cent certain,' Frank says, 'hence Red Knickers. But you can guess.'

'Blue Knickers.'

'What?'

'She was wearing blue knickers, not red.'

'Whatever.'

'You're really revolting,' I tell him pleasantly. 'Anyway. OK. Where are they? Show me.'

The bar we're in is heaving with the usual assortment of identikit young trendies, as well as older people dressed, like Frank and I, in black. In the far right corner, huddled round a circular table, is an incongruous group of fresh-faced young women who look slightly out of place, though they've tried hard to blend in: despite the fashionable clothes, mussed hair and lashings of make-up, they all look like they should be frolicking with ponies in some sunny glade.

'Well, none of them, obviously. Even I can tell that,' I say.

'Where?'

'The big table on the right, over there. The out-of-towners. Hen party from Hampshire or something.'

'The one in the middle, in the pale pink,' says Frank. There's a head in my way, so it takes me a few seconds to see properly.

'The blonde? You can't be serious.'

The woman Frank has pointed out rather reminds me

of Cressida: same well-fed, milky complexion, same Sloane breasts, same benign expression. She looks like a milk-maid.

'She looks like a milkmaid,' I tell Frank dismissively.

'She's a dirty ride,' Frank says. 'I'm telling you.'

'But she looks really wholesome! Oh, I don't understand it at all. You said it was women who looked leaky that were guaranteed dirty rides.'

'No, Stell – that's what you said. And you were right, in a way. Some look leaky, as you put it, some don't. Sometimes it's the really clean ones who are really dirty. And sometimes not – see that woman over there, in the black?' He points to an emaciated stick with smeary, smudgy make-up around her eyes. Her dress is too short for her age and she is clearly in the throes of an appalling Mutton Moment. 'Her too.'

'I don't understand it,' I repeat. Rather chilling, no, this ability to point out such intimate things about women who are complete strangers? Bang bang bang: her and her and her. Wouldn't bother with her. Rather smooth. Rather horribly male. Compelling, though.

'They all look like they really love sex,' Frank explains.

'How can you tell? I mean, no one walks around looking like they *hate* sex. Although they sometimes do in the remoter Scottish islands, I've noticed. But apart from there . . .'

'They both look like they'd suck you off without you having to ask. And really enjoy it,' Frank says.

'You wouldn't need to push their heads down, you mean.' I start sniggering.

'Exactly.'

'Nice expression, "suck you off". You're a gent, Frankie.'

'Oi speak as Oi find,' Frank says, in an absurd accent, which makes us both laugh again.

'Your definition of a dirty ride is straight out of a porno magazine,' I tell him after a while. 'Basically, it's women who are gagging for it and practically cry with come-y gratitude if you let them touch your dick. You're like those sad men who write porn on the Internet – "Take me," she begged, "oh, take me, I'm dripping all over the carpet with desire for your huge, proud, bee-yoo-diful cock." That's what you're like, Frankie.'

'I don't think I've explained it properly,' he says, refusing (annoyingly) to deny my accusations. 'It's not as simple as that, although you're right – there *is* an element of pure male fantasy.'

'Well, what about me?'

Frank raises an eyebrow and takes a sip of martini. I wish he'd stop raising his eyebrows at me.

'No, seriously, Frank. If you were here with someone else and you saw me walking past, what would you say about me?'

'I'm getting you a coffee. They're very strong, those martinis, and it's only nine o'clock.'

'What are you now, my father?'

'Yes.' He grabs a waitress – literally, by the skirt of her apron – and orders me an espresso, and – ha! – another martini for himself.

'God,' I roll my eyes. 'You're so bloody northern. Mr Macho. I'll have a triple whisky, and a fruit juice for the little lady. Honestly, Frank.'

'I don't want you to be sick on my shoes,' says Frank bluntly.

I sigh loudly, to convey my irritation. 'As I was saying, what would you think if you saw me?'

'I'd think you were a ride, but I don't know about dirty,' Frank says, still looking around the room.

'One must be grateful for small mercies, I suppose.' I lean back and look around the room too, but not for long: Frank's little lesson in masculine prejudgement has left me feeling rather shaken.

'Do all men do that, Frank, or is it just you?'

'Everyone does it. Both sexes.'

'I don't. Not like that. And I don't think Rupert does, for instance, or Dom. Not that crudely. Do you not ever just think "She has pretty eyes" or "I like her face"?'

'Once or twice.'

'When, once or twice?'

'Not for a while.'

We're back to the wife, the girlfriend, whatever she was, I'm sure of it. But even though my stomach is slowly filling with alcohol, and even though I am burning to know, I can't ask. I just can't ask.

'I'm losing faith in men,' I say instead. 'You make it all sound extremely bleak.'

'Oh, Stell, I didn't mean to. It's just I'm supposed to be giving you a pulling lesson, and you asked. Come on, let's go. We're off to Shoreditch – we can walk.'

The party we're at is to honour a tralala new art gallery. Predictably enough, this consists of a huge white 'space' dotted about with funny little installations of giant latex insects encased in glass. It's incredibly noisy as we walk in: chatter, but also the kind of ultra-loud pounding, lyric-less music that gives me an instant headache. The canapés are all black: tiny parcels of squid ink pasta sprinkled with faux-caviare, pumpernickel with some kind of black butter and shavings of black truffle, black cherry tartlets in chocolate pastry. These latter are rather delicious. To drink, there are coffee-liqueur-based cocktails.

'Well, this is a blast from the past,' I tell Frank, who is steering me through the crowds with his hand on the small of my back. 'All we're missing is Dominic.'

'We won't stay long,' Frank says as a statuesque blonde shriekingly descends upon him. I take a few steps back, pretending to be interested in a massive pair of latex earwigs by my feet (titled, clunkingly and incorrectly, *Insexicide*). When I look up again, much to my dismay, Frank is talking to a brunette with such an effective push-up bra that her breasts rest crazily plumply just beneath her collar bones. I try and catch Frank's eye and fail, so I wander off on my own for a while. Inevitably, given the nature of the party, I bump into six of Dominic's friends in quick succession, including one of the married artists who lunged at me over lunch some months ago. He's here with his wife, who doesn't look entirely delighted to see me. Look, I want to say, your husband is physically repulsive. Just because you're grateful to have him doesn't mean every single woman in London is desperate to bed him. He's bald. He has a paunch. He also, I happen to know, has advanced halitosis. So, you know, drop the daggers and look at me normally. You can keep him.

Instead, I say, 'Hello, Sarah. How nice to see you.'

'You remember Stella,' the husband says. 'Used to be with Dominic.'

'Yeah,' Sarah says unenthusiastically, draping an ostentatious arm around her husband's sprawling waist.

'We spent the weekend with them once, do you remember?' the husband says. 'In Prague.'

'Not really,' says Sarah, now stroking the husband's jowls while maintaining eye contact with me.

'Never mind,' I say. What's up with these women? Why do they all seem to believe that given half a chance I'd fuck their horrible husbands' brains out on the spot? 'Nice to see you again. I must find my friend,' I mutter, peeling off.

'That should have given her the message,' I hear Sarah saying to her husband. 'I can't believe she tried it on with you.'

'She's just lonely,' he says, loudly and with considerable effrontery, considering *he* asked me out for lunch and *he* lunged. Men are so pathetic, I tell myself as I stomp around the room crossly, and so are women, always willing to apportion blame to others of their sex. *God.* Still, I'm clearly evolving as a person now I have a social life: three months ago, I'd have turned back and given Sarah a piece of my mind.

Instead, I head for the back of the room, where there's less of a crush, and am surprised to find myself face to face with the person responsible for the terrible din: Yungsta himself, resplendent in yellow track suit and bling-bling jewellery.

'Oh,' I say. 'How extraordinary. Hello! I'm Stella – we met the other day . . .'

'Yeah, yeah, I remember,' says Yungsta.

'You're doing the music?'

'Thass righ.' He gestures to some turntables, currently being manned by a mini-me version of Yungsta, also wearing a track suit. 'I was gonna ring you.' He mimes this, extending his thumb and little finger into an imaginary earpiece.

'Do,' I say, smiling my best smile. 'That would be nice.'

'Get together, yeah? Dinner or summink, yeah?'

'Sure.'

'I need to get back to me decks,' he says apologetically. 'But whatchou doin' later?'

'I'm with a friend, actually – I think we're going on somewhere.'

'I'm DJin' in King's Cross from about midnigh,' he says, handing me a couple of comps. 'If you fancy it. Come an say ello.'

'OK. And if not, we'll speak.'

'Deffo,' says Yungsta, nodding like a dog – what is he now? From Liverpool? 'For sure. Dope.'

I make my way back towards the centre of the room again, past all the you-remember-Stella-she-was-with-Dominics, looking for Frank. When I find him, he is, surreally, speaking with the father of my child: there's Dominic himself, looking slightly rumpled, holding court. I am briefly extremely depressed at the smallness of my world. And then I am lengthily quite seriously pissed off. Why didn't he say he was coming? One tiny phone call wouldn't have gone amiss. What about Honey? She sees her father rarely enough as it is – what if we'd been away?

'Good grief! Why aren't you in Tokyo?' I say, as soon as I've managed to wade and elbow my way through the mini-crowd surrounding him.

'Stella!' He detaches himself from the group. 'I only got in a couple of hours ago. Guy's an old friend – this is his space. How's Honey?'

'She's fine. She's lovely.'

'I'm over for a few days – business. Can I come and see her over the weekend, when I've had some sleep?'

'You might have warned me. You might have rung, Dom. We could have been away somewhere. But yes, come. She'll be so pleased. You don't see her nearly often enough.'

'I'll see her tomorrow. So what's up, Stella? You look fabulous. Frank said you were here – speaking of absentee fathers,' he adds, lowering his voice. 'Everything OK?'

'Fine,' I say. 'Fine. You?' There is *one* thing troubling me, but this doesn't seem like the ideal moment to ask my ex whether I snort when I come.

'Oh, you know, the usual. Tokyo is wonderful – inspirational. Did you meet Keiko, by the way, the last time I was here?'

'Yes, very briefly.'

'She's sleeping it off at the hotel, but I might bring her along at the weekend.'

'Sure.'

'Well, I'm out of here. Can I give you a lift anywhere? I've got a driver.'

'No, actually – me and Frank are on a night out.'

'Are you two . . .?'

Oh, not again. 'No, Dom.'

'Good. He's not right for you, Stella. And I know him very well, remember – too well.' He laughs. Dominic has a really unpleasant streak, I must say. 'He's doing brilliantly, of course. But I don't have you down as a Newcastle Brown Ale drinker.'

I give Dominic a dirty look, which he ignores.

'Plus,' he continues, 'he puts it about a bit. To put it

mildly. And he's not what you call reliable. As I told you, he has a . . .'

'Yes,' I say. 'I know. I remember.'

'Good,' repeats Dominic. 'Bear it in mind.'

Frank makes his way back towards us. 'Don't tell him I told you, will you?' whispers Dominic. 'Client confidentiality and all that. And anyway, better not to raise the subject with him, I'd have thought.'

'Thank you for your kind advice.'

'You're very welcome,' says impervious Dominic. 'Anyway, look, I'll ring in the morning. Maybe we could all have lunch or something. Great seeing you.'

'And you. Speak to you tomorrow.'

Dominic leaves.

'Enough?' whispers Frank in my ear.

I notice the woman with the push-up bra noticing this, and I also notice that she doesn't like it.

'Yes. Let's go. Where are we off to next, and will there be food? I'm starving.'

'Didn't you eat anything?'

'Only a couple of those cherry tarts. Out of vanity rather than reluctance – the other stuff would have given me black teeth. Stupid sort of food to serve at a party.'

'I'm quite hungry too, come to think of it. Do you fancy a curry? We're just round the corner from Brick Lane.'

'Oh, Frank, what a genius idea. Yes, *please.*'

He looks at his watch. 'It's half past ten. We could get something to eat and then on to the party.'

'Perfect.'

Half an hour later and we're sitting cosily in the fuggy,

flocked haze of the Star of India, a magnificent pile of poppadums rising between us.

'Do you enjoy those dos?' I ask Frank. 'Don't you ever get bored of them? God knows I used to.'

'Yeah, they begin to grind after a while. But then,' he shrugs, dipping a corner of poppadum into some coriander and yoghurt chutney, 'that's true of all parties. There comes a point where you'd rather be at home.'

'With your pipe and slippers and your Airfix kit. I believe you. Could you slow down with those poppadums please, pig? I want at least three.'

'We'll get some more. And you're in no position to call anyone "pig".'

I actually feel myself blushing at this.

He gives a wry smile and pushes the last poppadum my way. 'Sorry, babe.' He emits a tiny, barely audible snort, so I kick his shins under the table.

'Do you ever miss Dominic?' he asks, fiddling in his pockets for a lighter.

'No. Why, should I?'

'I don't know. People do, don't they?'

'Well, I don't. Do you ever miss your shags? Come to think of it, have you ever had a relationship that lasted more than an hour?'

'It's been known. What are you eating?'

'It hasn't been known while you've been living with me. What's that about? Traumatic early relationship that broke up? Teenage sweetheart? Are you trying to fuck someone out of your system?'

'No,' Frank says, laughing. 'Sorry. I'm thirty-five, not twenty.'

'Have you had your teeth capped? They're very neat.

I'm having the chicken tikka masala, one paratha, one plain yoghurt, pilau rice, one sag bhaji, and perhaps you'd like to share some spicy potatoes? Will you remember my order? I'm dying for a pee.'

'Off you go, Dr Freud,' says Frank. 'What do you want to drink? Another beer?'

'Please.'

When I come back from the loo, and from ringing Papa to check on Honey, who is up and watching *Bear in the Big Blue House*, Frank is leaning back in his chair, chatting to a couple of women at the table behind ours. They're doing that giggly, eyelash-batting thing that women do when they fancy a man.

I sit down again.

'See you,' Frank tells the women, before turning his back on them. 'I've ordered. Where were we?' he says to me.

'I was asking you about normal relationships. You know, anything more than ships in the night.'

'And I was telling you I've had them.'

'Who with?'

'Girlfriends, Stella. There were a few long-term ones. Went out with someone for three years, actually.'

'Who was she?' My heart is banging in my chest: here we go.

'Local girl, up north.'

I say nothing. Neither does he.

'Come on, Frank. And?'

'And we went out for three years,' he says in a patient-but-bored voice, 'and it wasn't really going anywhere, so we split up.'

'And how did she take it?'

146

'Not especially well. You don't, though, as a rule, when you're dumped.'

'No. So . . .' I brace myself by taking a sip of beer. 'Are you still in touch?'

'With Karen? No.'

'Why not?'

'What's this?' Frank laughs easily. 'The Spanish Inquisition? Do you keep in touch with your old boyfriends?'

'Yes, pretty much.'

'What, all of them?'

'No,' I am forced to admit. 'But *most* of them.'

'I guess we just sorta drifted apart,' he says in a corny American voice. 'Next subject.'

Why can I never get him to talk about this?

'What will happen, do you think?'

'Happen where?'

'To you. What's your plan? Do you want to, you know, settle down?'

'With my pipe and slippers and my Airfix kit?'

'Yes.'

'Eventually. But there's plenty of time.'

'Can I ask you something really old-fashioned, Frankie?'

'Ask away.'

'Do you ever feel that your life – your sex life, I mean – is sort of *empty*? You know, kind of unlovely.'

'Unlovely?'

'Yes.'

'No. I don't like living with people.'

'But you live with me.'

'But I don't sleep with you. Cheers,' he says to the waiter as our food arrives. 'I hate,' he continues, 'all that moaning and whingeing and bickering you get after a while.'

So he *has* lived with people.

'Perhaps you hate women,' I point out through a mouthful of spinach. 'Perhaps you're gay.'

'I've slept with a couple of blokes in the past, when I was at art college, but it wasn't really my bag,' Frank shrugs modernly. 'I prefer women.'

'But not to talk to or live a normal life with.'

'I'm talking to you, aren't I? Live with you, don't I?'

'Not the same thing.' We munch in silence for a while. I know it's immature, but I have to ask.

'Up the bum?' I say, trying to sound delicate.

'What?'

'With the men, did you do it up the bum?'

Frank is grinning at me quite wolfishly over the Bombay aloo.

'Do you really *need* to know that, Stella?'

'Yes.'

'Have you done it?'

'Up the bum?'

'Mmm.'

'No. I have a phobia. Hygiene-based. Have you?'

Frank sighs. 'You don't feel this conversation is in any way too much information?'

'No. I'm gripped.'

'You're exactly like a bloke,' Frank muses. 'You're like a pretty bloke.'

'But would you bum me if I were?'

'I haven't "bummed" a bloke, Stella, no.'

I nod, and then gasp. 'Do you mean you were the bummee?'

Frank pushes his hands back through his hair.

'You're unbelievable, you know that?'

'Tell me, Frankie. Tell your auntie Stella. Get it off your chest.'

'No bums, OK? No bums. Christ.'

I generously reward him with a dollop of my spinach, before continuing.

'What about with women?'

'Back to bums?'

'Yes.'

'Yes.'

'Gosh.' I look up at Frank, who is spearing his rogan josh, unperturbed.

'Don't you think it's sort of rude?'

'Stella, you are many things but I didn't have you down as a prude. What do you mean, rude?'

'I mean, a woman has a perfectly good vagina, which you completely ignore, and that seems to me to be very bad manners. Also, it's sort of rapey, don't you think? Overly forceful.'

'Makes a change,' Frank says blandly. 'From the other. That's all. And anyway, some women ask for it.'

'What, "Please do bum me"?' I say incredulously.

'Yeah. You know, treat me rough.'

'Does anal sex make one a dirty ride?'

'It can do. There's no set of things you *do* to be a dirty ride. It's possible to have dirty missionary position, if the girl's dirty enough. But yeah, anal sex's quite dirty.'

I go quiet for a bit, trying to take in all of this perfectly absorbing information.

'Who was that bloke in the yellow you were talking to?' Frank asks.

'That,' I tell him proudly, 'was my next date.'

'The DJ?'

'Yes. Why, do you know him? He's called MC Yungsta, or DJ Yungsta.'

'He's quite well known. Givin' it large,' Frank says in Yungsta's exact accent, throwing ridiculous shapes with both his hands. 'Make some noooooise.'

'He's called Adrian in real life.'

'They all are. There used to be one called Mista Killa, who turned out to be a bloody vicar's son from Penge. Called Nigel. Kickin'.'

We chuckle happily over this for a while.

'And you're going to go out with him? Christ, I'm stuffed.'

'Well, he's sort of asked, and I don't see why not, do you?'

'Nope. Well . . . No.'

'So. I mean, it can't be worse than Dr Cooper.'

'I don't suppose it can.'

'Oof, I'm stuffed too,' I say, pushing my plate away. 'Though I could possibly squeeze in one tiny kulfi, if they have almond.'

'Cheap date,' observes Frank.

'Oh, be quiet. Do you know,' I suddenly tell him, 'I've got a whole list of films about anal sex. It's a game I used to play with myself.'

'How do you mean?'

'Well, a film called *Deep Impact* came out, and I thought to myself that it sounded exactly like a film about anal sex.'

'You're a very silly girl,' Frank says, but he is grinning.

'And then I noticed there were loads of them . . . *Unlawful Entry*.'

Frank shakes his head and sighs, but his grin broadens. 'And *Backdraft*.'

'Oh, God,' says Frank, beginning to snigger out loud. 'Is this how you spend your time?'

'It was a few years ago, when I was very bored. But it's become a sort of ongoing thing. A hobby, if you like. I collect the titles now. There was an older one, with Lauren Bacall and Humphrey Bogart, which I caught on Channel 4 the other day. *Unlawful Passage.*'

Frank is really laughing now, choking on a corner of my paratha, gesturing me to stop. But I don't. I am very much enjoying sharing my carefully garnered information.

'There are the subtler ones, like *Lethal Weapon*, with Mel Gibson, do you remember? And *The Deep*. And *First Blood*. And *Blood and Thunder*, though that sounds more windy.'

'*The Wind Jammers*,' Frank chokes. 'It was a classic when I was a kid.'

'Oh, if you're talking classic, there's *Gone with the Wind* and *A Passage to India*.'

Frank motions at me to pass him my water. He takes a huge gulp.

'I see,' he says, sounding hoarse. 'They divide into two genres really, don't they – the actually anal and the more windy.'

'Exactly,' I beam back at him, pleased that he's noticed.

'Can I play too?'

'Of course you can.' I raise my beer glass to him. 'Bottoms up. Welcome to the game. You need to come up with at least one a week.'

'Done,' he says, clinking glasses. 'Do you know – ' he wipes his eyes – 'I haven't had such a laugh for ages.'

'That's because you should try *talking* to girls,' I explain patiently. 'Instead of immediately sticking your hand down their pants.'

'I don't immediately stick my hand down their pants.'

'Hmm,' I sniff. 'You could have fooled me. Here, taste my ice cream.'

Frank opens his mouth dutifully.

'Perhaps you're a sex addict, like Michael Douglas or your fellow ginge, what's his name, the really plain one?'

'Hucknall,' Frank says, not laughing any more. 'Mick Hucknall. Thanks.'

'Anyway,' I say chirpily, 'less of the pant-hand and more of the chat next time, I reckon, and you'd be pleasantly surprised.'

'Most women don't have your conversational skills,' Frank says with heavy sarcasm. 'Or your great charm.'

'Frankie, don't be so babyish. I didn't say you were *like* Mick Hucknall . . .'

'Could you stop saying "Mick Hucknall" please?'

'I didn't say you were *like* him, or that you *looked* like him, even. He's hideous and you're, well, you're very handsome, in a way. I mean, he's a *gargoyle*, a child-frightener. You'd have to be blind. You're much easier on the eye. Much.'

'Cheers,' he says, cracking a wan smile. 'It's just I can't *stand* Mick Hucknall, and people are always mentioning him around me.' He points upwards. 'It's a hair thing.'

Outside on the pavement, the wind is icy and it's been raining. I am clinging to Frank's arm, because standing up makes me realize how drunk I actually am. Frank's drunk more than me but seems entirely sober.

'Oh,' I moan, as we stand, frozen, waiting for a cab. 'I wish I had a lovely hot cup of tea.'

'Here,' says Frank, unbuttoning his coat. 'Get in.' He

holds both halves of the coat open. I step inside, and he closes them again. My bottom, I notice after a small while, is pressing right against his cock.

'Don't get aroused,' I tell him sharply, 'and try and impale me bummily.'

'I'm trying very hard to control myself, Stell,' Frank drawls. 'Shall we walk down to the minicab office?'

'Perhaps they could sweetly make us a cup of tea.'

'Doubt it. But they could take us home.'

'Home?'

'It's just a thought. If you fancy that party, I'm game. But I know what you mean about the cup of tea.'

'And we could make a fire.'

'And maybe watch a vid . . .'

'But you haven't shown me how to pull, Frankie. You haven't demonstrated.' We are walking down Brick Lane like a four-legged, two-headed monster, still huddled inside his coat.

'I'll show you later,' he says.

'Why, are you feeling lucky, big boy?'

'No, stupid.' He thwacks the top of my head from above. 'I mean, let's do this again later. Here's the cab office.' And then he says something that sounds like, 'Meynd thee divvent stomp in thon kakky.'

'Excuse me?'

'Mind the dog shit,' Frank grins. 'In normal language: Meynd thee divvent stomp in thon kakky.'

This renders me helpless, but *helpless*, for about ten minutes. I howl, I wriggle with laughter from inside Frank's coat, losing my balance twice and having to be caught.

'Did your accent really used to be that broad?'

'Aye. Spent too long in London,' Frank says. 'But I like to air it occasionally.'

'Air it with me,' I tell him. 'When we do this again.'

'Next week,' says Frank. 'We'll do it again next week. Let's go home.'

11

I go and check on Papa and Honey as soon as we come in: both are fast asleep and both are snoring, one more attractively than the other. Frank is making a fire as I totter back down the stairs and into the kitchen to put the kettle on. It's started to rain again. There really is nothing more blissful on earth than being inside, with tea, by a fire, when it's really bucketing down outside.

I've just got back into the living room, clutching two mugs of extra-sweet tea – Earl Grey for me, PG for him – when this rather charming and domestic scene is interrupted by Rupert's spare keys turning in the lock.

'Bugger,' says Frank, sounding intensely irritated. 'Who the fuck's that? It's one in the morning.'

'Just us,' Rupert slurs from the hallway. 'I've brought Cress back for a nightcap.'

'Oh,' I say. 'That's nice.'

Actually, I'm with Frank on this one: I was looking forward to our cosy, homely time *à deux*. I quite wanted to watch *The Godfather* on video. I wanted to get to the bottom of the dirty ride thing, and I wanted Frank to speak Geordie to me more. And, of course, give me some sex tips (though actually Rupert is the one who'd really benefit from these, given his technique, or the lack of it. Perhaps we could hold a quick seminar, *en famille*).

'Hello,' says Cressida, more pink-cheeked than before. 'We had a *wonderful* time.'

'Yes,' I say, 'it's a nice restaurant. Very romantic. All those mirrors.'

'Excellent wine list,' says Rupert, butchly addressing himself to Frank, who looks up grumpily.

'I'm not much of a wine expert,' he says. 'I prefer beer, or spirits.'

'I do wish you'd stop always making yourself sound like an oik with a lone O-level in welding,' I tell Frank, who is poking fire-things unnecessarily hard, with a cross look on his face. 'Rupert doesn't know anything about wine either – he's only saying that to impress Cressida.'

'Impress Cress,' Rupert says, which he and his date both seem to find almost unbearably funny. Har-har-har, they bray, like a pair of donkeys. They're standing immobile in the middle of the room, making eyes at each other, taking up space.

'What would you like?' I ask them, trying to conceal my irritation. 'The kettle's just boiled, or there are drinks in the kitchen. There's a delicious bottle of Calvados, actually, just on top of the fridge.'

'I'll have *oon petite Calva*,' Rupert says in his excruciating French. 'Cress?'

'I didn't know you spoke French,' Cressida beams.

'There's no end to his talents,' I mutter.

'I'd love another glass of white wine,' Cressida says, throwing me a mildly annoyed look.

'Rupert?' I say to the man, who is standing there rubbing his hands together and gazing idly at Cressida's well-turned ankles. 'The kitchen's through there. Surely you don't expect me to waitress for you?'

'Keep your hair on,' mutters Rupert, sloping off unsteadily. 'I'm just going. Got any crostini left?'

'Did you have a nice time too?' says polite Cressida.

'Great,' says Frank, coming over to perch on the side of my armchair. He bends down absent-mindedly and quickly sniffs my hair, as though I were Honey, whom he is always sniffing surreptitiously, I've noticed. Can't say I blame him: she smells delicious.

'What did you do?'

'We went for drinks, and then to a boring party where we bumped into Honey's father,' I say. 'And then we had dinner and lovely chats. Very interesting chats. About sex.'

'You're obsessed with sex,' Rupert says, coming back through with two glasses. 'Always were.'

'Really?' says Frank, looking amused. 'What a surprise.'

'Really?' says Cressida. 'And how,' she smiles plumply and fondly at Rupert, 'would *you* know, mister?'

'From giving her one,' Frank answers. God, the man's blunt. A little grace wouldn't go amiss every now and then, it really wouldn't.

'Charmingly put,' I tell him with a sigh. 'Nice one, Frankie.'

'Excuse me?' says Cressida.

'I said,' says Frank, 'from shagging her. Slipping her a length. Her. Here.'

'Don't call me "her",' I tell him. 'God, Frank, you know – *manners.*'

'From shagging Stella,' says Frank, correcting himself.

Cressida looks nonplussed, and not what you'd call overjoyed.

'A long time ago,' I say comfortingly. 'Once or twice.'

'Well, more than that, as I recall,' says Rupert with a chortle. 'Oh,' he suddenly remembers. 'Oh, yes. Oh, bugger and blast. Oh, damnation. Curses. Um, Cress?'

'Yes?' says Cressida glacially.

'Thing is, Cress . . . Thing is, darling . . . What I mean is . . .'

'Thing is, we were married,' I interrupt. Sometimes that blithering, stammery English thing gets right on my nerves. 'Ages ago. Aeons. For a tiny while. After Cambridge.'

'Didn't you know?' asks Frank.

'No,' says Cressida, in a small voice.

'Oh, fuck. Sorry, love,' says Frank.

'We were extremely young and it was a mistake,' I tell her. 'A disaster. Lasted thirty seconds.'

Frank laughs, and then looks penitent.

'I mean, the *union*,' I continue, tutting at him.

'And now you're just, um, *friends*?' asks Cressida, sounding a bit snuffly.

'Yes,' Rupert and I say in perfect unison.

'And you forgot to mention it when you told me your life story over supper,' Cressida says, looking at Rupert.

'Apparently so,' says Rupert, going pink.

'And you sleep at her house.'

'Darling, I live in Scotland. Where else am I going to sleep?'

'In a hotel,' says Cressida.

'But I have two spare rooms,' I tell her. 'Going to waste. This huge house. And besides, he only comes about once a year.'

Frank makes a funny sort of noise again. I don't think he likes Rupert much. In Paris, when he and I first met, Frank told me that he thought all middle-class people were 'knob-ends'.

'Really?' says Cressida, not remotely convinced.

'Really,' I tell her. 'I promise. And just in case you're wondering, we don't fuck.'

'I wasn't,' Cressida says, glacial again. 'Wondering.'

'Well, then,' I say cheerfully, graciously not pointing out that her last remark is in fact a lie. 'There's no problem, is there?'

'Course not,' says Rupert, putting his arm around Cressida's shoulder and kissing her cheek.

'It's, um, it's just a bit unusual, isn't it?' Cressida asks, ignoring the kiss and taking a sip of white wine. 'But I suppose that's modern life for you.'

'It is *entirely* usual, to me. Would you prefer it if two people who once liked each other enough to get married now had absolutely nothing to do with each other, like freaks?' I ask her.

I hate this. It's so *English* and puritanical that it drives me spare. I mean, here's Rupert. He was once an important part of my life, and I still like him enormously – love him, in a way. What am I supposed to do – cull him because we once shared a bed? He didn't beat me, or abuse me, or behave meanly to me in any way: we just got married by mistake, and divorced on purpose. And now Cressida – and there are plenty more like her – looks at me sniffily because we're still friends and he stays with me occasionally. Why? Why is this considered odd, when it is in fact the very opposite – when it is the acme of normalcy? My uncle Henri so liked his ex-wife that they slept together two or three times a year, for old times' sake. So what? What's it got to do with anyone else, sanctimonious prigs that they are? Still, not necessarily a good idea to hold Oncle Henri up as an example, in these particular circs.

'No,' says Cressida slowly. 'I wouldn't prefer that.'

'Well, then, for heaven's sake, *grow up*.' I say this slightly too ferociously, eliciting a 'Steady on' from Rupert.

'Do you not,' Cressida asks me timidly, 'worry about your daughter?'

'Honey? What about her?' I am inches away from losing my temper: I know what's coming next. I know it by heart.

'In my profession . . .' begins Cressida.

'Cressida's a nanny,' explains Rupert. 'What's it called again? Oh, yes: a career nanny. It means you only nanny for people in Belgravia.'

'It's just that in my profession,' she continues, 'I see what divorce can do to little people first-hand.'

'Really,' I say. 'Well, happily Rupert and I didn't have any little people together.' (I used to think that 'little people' was a euphemism for 'dwarves'. Everything in English is a euphemism, for people like Cressida.)

'But with your *second* husband . . .'

'We weren't married.'

Cressida sighs. 'Your "partner", then. In terms of social and personal development,' she parrots, 'the child really thrives most when it lives with both its parents.'

'Really,' I say again, taking a deep breath. 'Well, isn't that nice.'

'Your daughter,' Cressida continues, 'has an absentee father, you see.'

'And a mother who's obsessed with sex,' Frank adds with a grin, in a failed attempt at lightening things up. He's unbelievable, he really is: not a squirm of discomfort, not a blush, not a quiver at the words 'absentee father'.

'Lots of children have absent fathers,' I say, looking at Frank. 'It can't really be helped, Cressida. No one wakes up in the morning and thinks, I know, I'll get pregnant and then separate from my husband, just to make sure my child has an absent father, because that's what I really want for her most of all in life – an absent father.'

'I wasn't saying you'd done it on purpose,' she says, putting a hand on my arm.

'I should hope not. So what is your point, exactly? Because it's getting late and I'd quite like to go to bed.'

'Well, nothing, really. I was just, you know, *saying*.'

'Well, thank you for your insights. For your information, as far as I'm concerned, divorce doesn't mean the end of friendship, and separation doesn't mean your child automatically becomes a sociopath or a bed-wetter. OK?'

'OK. I'm sorry if I spoke inappropriately,' Cressida says. 'But I do so believe in the family, you see, and . . .'

'We all believe in the family,' I snap. 'Some of us have more extended families than others, that's all.'

'Mmm,' says Cressida, still not looking wholly convinced, but conciliatory now, unlike me.

'As for sex, frankly, I don't see why having a child should turn me into a nun, do you? I don't actually have sex in front of her, you know. I don't come home and say, Hey, Honey, Mummy's pulled, want to watch?'

'Um, no,' says Cressida.

'Glad we've got that straight. I'm going to bed.' To my horror, my eyes are prickling.

'Don't,' says Frank, putting his hands on the back of my neck and rubbing my shoulders gently. 'Stay.' But he makes me irate too, with his oblivion. This is why I can't ever have it out with him: I like him so much, we spend a really great evening together, and then he goes and makes a really crass joke a nanosecond after hearing the words 'absentee father'. I really feel there is something the matter with him morally. Yes, morally. Sorry to throw about the big scary words, but really: *this is a man who walked out on his own daughter.* And he has the temerity to make jokes about me being sex-crazed!

'Do stay,' says Rupert. 'Have a drink. Here, have mine.' He offers his glass of Calvados.

'Please,' says Cressida.

'OK,' I say, turning to Cressida. 'And I'm sorry. I tend to overreact a bit with that kind of subject.'

'It's all right,' she says. 'It was ghastly of me to bring it up. I've had a little too much to drink.'

'No, it wasn't. I just get very defensive over the idea that I'm bringing Honey up oddly, or that we're somehow *bohemian.*'

Frank silently hands me his rather revolting handkerchief and I blow my nose.

'Well, technically you *are*, quite,' Rupert pipes up helpfully, earning himself an expertly lobbed cushion at the head.

'She has a man in her life,' I say, pointing at Frank, 'so she won't grow up weird or scared of men. She has Rupe as a godfather. She has me, and I love her more than anything. She has a lovely child-minder. She has friends. Her father adores her and sends her presents and faxes, and rings her up. He sees her whenever he can – unfortunately, he happens to be based halfway around the world. But I'm not worried about her at all. And now let's talk about something else.'

We sit in awkward silence for a few minutes.

'Fancy that video?' Frank whispers.

'What's the time?'

'Just coming up to two.'

'Let's watch it another night. I might feel like a lie-in tomorrow, but Honey won't, and it's the weekend and I haven't asked Mary to come in.'

'OK. You're probably right.'

'I'm going to go up and have a bath,' I tell him, getting up. I'm not very steady on my feet at all: shouldn't have gulped Rupert's Calvados down in one like that.

'And I'm going to bed,' says Frank.

'So,' I say, turning to Rupert, 'what about you? Aren't you tired? It's two in the morning.'

'Not too bad,' says Rupert, looking at Cressida, who looks at the floor.

'You're very welcome to stay, Cressida,' I smile at her, heading for the door and leaving them to fathom it out for themselves – although she doesn't look much like a girl who puts out on the first date, I know nothing: she may be the dirtiest ride of all. 'Good night.'

I have a quick bath and fall asleep the minute my head hits the pillow. My last conscious, and unsober, thought is that I wonder what Frank would look like if he dyed his hair brown.

'I've got some juice for you,' Frank whispers, melding with my dream.

My eyes blear open. I have a terrible, throbbing head-ache, as though a giant fist had got hold of my head and was squeezing, squeeeeezing . . .

'Hoo!' I exclaim, scrabbling to remember what happened last night. This always takes me a while – I sleep very deeply; my sleeps are like comas – and the hangover is slowing me down further. 'What are you doing in my bed?'

'I'm not *in* your bed, Stell,' Frank grins. 'I'm in your bed*room*.'

'Oh,' I say, raising myself up on to the pillows.

'I can see your tits,' says Frank pleasantly. 'Are you cold?'

'Aaaaah! Stop looking.' I pull the duvet up around me. 'What's the time? Where's Honey? Why are you here ogling me? Stop looking, I said, Frank. Stop feasting your eyes like a, a, a *dog*.'

Frank laughs and rolls his eyes and then shades them, handing me the glass.

'Your dad left a note. Honey woke up at nine last night and they must have stayed up a while, because she's still asleep. He's gone out to the shops and he says, do we want to meet him in the Ritz bar at six. No sign of Rupert or Cressida, and his bedroom door's closed. It's half past nine. I really enjoyed last night. I'm sorry you got upset at the end. But you give as good as you get,' he smiles. 'At least. And,' he continues, 'if your head feels anything like mine, I thought you might like some juice. There's a pot of tea downstairs.'

It all comes flooding back, sort of. I think I was rude to Cressida, or was she rude to me? I rewind a bit further, back to Frank and lychee cocktails and curry . . .

'Oh, and there's a message on the machine from Dom,' Frank says. 'Says should he come to lunch. He's at the Sanderson.'

'Oh, God,' I croak. 'I don't feel well. Ring him back and say yes, would you? I'll be down in a second. Do we have any food in? Bless you for the juice. Do you think Honey's all right?'

'Probably had her first late night,' Frank says. 'Should I check on her?'

'No, no, leave her. Will you go now, so I can get up?'

He turns to go.

'Oh, and Frankie?'

'Mm?'

'I loved last night too. Now will you get out, please, so I can get dressed?'

Frank winks, and delicately shuts the door.

Lunch that day is like an advertisement for the extended families I was lecturing Cressida about last night. My father is absent, being otherwise engaged with his tailor, but Rupert's there, and a bashful, almost-silent Cress, and Dominic and his consort, Keiko (who is almost freakishly tall, especially considering she is Japanese), and me, and Frank, and Honey, who rose regally at ten and doesn't greet her father with as much crazed, hoppity excitement as he might have wished for, choosing instead to hurl herself strategically on to Frank's lap whenever he is sitting down. (I notice Dominic noticing this, and not liking it one bit.) She likes the Hello Kitty doll and accessories graciously offered by Keiko, though, and she *is* nice to Dominic; it's just she's nicer to Frank.

Despite our respective hangovers, Frank and I have been to the shops and roasted and stuffed two chickens and a truckload of pumpkin. He, heroically, did the peeling, and mashed some parsnips, while I topped and tailed a pile of green beans. We laid the table in the kitchen and collapsed at about eleven thirty, wondering whether a hair of the dog would be a bad idea. He eventually had a Bloody Mary. I decided against, until lunch time at least.

Rupert and Cressida appeared just before noon, she looking fresh-faced but somewhat sartorially dishevelled, he exuding contentment and thus, possibly, sexual satisfaction.

'Yummy smell,' said Cressida. 'Chicken?'

'Yup. Did you sleep well? Or are you a little bit shagged out?' I said blandly. 'It was a late night, after all.'

'Oh,' said Cress helplessly. 'Oh,' and she went red and stared at her feet.

'Beautiful morning,' Rupert boomed, rubbing his hands. 'Any chance of eggs?'

'No. It's nearly lunch. Have some coffee – it's in the kitchen. Dominic's coming to lunch.'

'Oh.'

'He's not that bad, Rupe. If you get stuck with him, you could always compare notes.'

'Goodness,' said Cressida.

*

After lunch, Keiko grabs my arm as I am loading up the dishwasher and says, 'You show arbum' three or four times in a row, smiling broadly all the while. 'What album?' I ask, to which Dominic, lying on the floor playing Mr Potato Head with a now only mildly recalcitrant Honey, replies, 'I think she'd like to see the wedding album.'

'I don't know where it is,' I wail. 'It could be absolutely anywhere.'

'It's on the third shelf in the little study upstairs,' says Dominic. 'Unless you've moved it.'

'Arbum,' says Keiko, smiling as though she might burst.

'Port, anyone?' This from Rupert, who, I suddenly recall, likes nothing better than spending urban weekend afternoons in an alcoholic haze.

'Yes, please,' says everyone, except me. I'm off upstairs to find my wedding pictures, which takes about ten minutes as I have, at some point, moved them out of the study. I eventually find them on top of my wardrobe, covered in dust.

I come back down clutching the leather-bound volume.

'Ooh,' says Cressida. 'Goody. I *love* weddings.'

'It wasn't actually a wedding,' I remind her for the *n*th time. 'We just had a party.'

'You wore a wedding dress, though, didn't you?'

'Of sorts. I did the big number with the meringue and the veil with Rupert.'

'Oh,' says Cressida, but she is kind-hearted and forces a smile this time.

'You marry Rupert?' says Keiko, whose accent I shall no longer attempt to convey phonetically.

'Yes, that's right. Long time ago.'

'Ho!' says Keiko, still grinning. 'Ho! Many, many husband!' She claps her hands together, like a child.

'Er, just the two. Just the one, really. Me and Dominic . . .'

'I know,' beams Keiko. 'Make fucking only.'

'Love,' booms Dominic from the ground, clapping his hands over Honey's ears. 'Say "make love", Keiko.'

'You say me, "make fucking now, Keiko". You say me. In bed,' she tells Dom reproachfully. 'Make fucking, Keiko,' she repeats, just so we're clear. 'Mr Dick.' This, understandably, brings the house down: even Cressida has a quick guffaw. Keiko nods, keeps smiling, and grinds her hips once or twice to show she understands.

'Yes, I think we get the picture,' says Dominic, who is, predictably, looking a little flushed around the gills, as well he might do. Mr Dick!

'Anyway,' I say to Keiko – who is, like the Eveready Bunny, still beaming her megawatt smile. I open the album. 'That was it there. The dress.'

Cressida and Keiko crowd in around me, kneeling on the floor.

'Aaah!' shrieks Keiko, right into my ear. 'Aaah! So cute!'

'It's pink,' says Cressida.

'So cute!' howls Keiko.

'Reddish. What can I tell you, Cress? It was a second marriage.'

'Lovely. Rather risqué, though. Gosh, look at your boobs.'

'Boobies,' says Keiko proudly, sticking hers out. Her nipples are rather prominent under her thin, candy-pink top. 'Titty-ride.' Good grief: Dominic's broadening his repertoire.

'As I say,' I continue, ignoring the pert bosoms thrust

into my face and the unwelcome images of Dom and Keiko hard at it which have popped, uninvited, into my head, 'I'd done the meringue the first time around.'

My explanation is interrupted by a veritable *roar* of laughter from the sofa. All three of us look up to find the men hysterical, quite beside themselves. Frank is lying on the floor and actually has tears coursing down his face. Rupert is coughing helplessly, eyes watering also, and Dominic is thwacking him (unnecessarily hard, I can't help but notice) on the back. Dominic is puce, his mouth a scream of laughter.

'Haaaa!' goes Frank. 'Haaaa! Oh, God, help me.' I've never seen anyone so amused in my life, though the other two are giving him a good run for his money.

'Hoooo,' howls Rupert.

'I'm going to *burst*,' shouts Dominic.

'Oi piggy,' says Honey, beaming at me.

Which rings alarm bells. Very serious alarm bells, actually. DING DONG, go the bells. DING DONG.

'Oi piggy,' says Honey delightedly, tottering across the room towards me. 'Snorrrrt. Oink.'

The men are nearly hyperventilating. Oddly – or not – not one of them seems willing to catch my eye.

'Excuse me,' I say, in my best schoolmarm voice. 'Hello?'

All three start to clear their throats and look busy. Frank, with one last wheezy giggle, gets up off the floor, mutters something about coffee in a strangulated voice and disappears swiftly into the kitchen. Rupert, who is as pink as his shirt, wipes his eyes and sits up straight on the sofa, fixing the middle distance. Dominic holds his head in his hands for a while, then pushes his hair back, wipes under his eyes and breathes out loudly. 'Pffft,' he says, before turning his attentions to Honey again.

'Golly,' says Cressida, addressing Rupert. 'What was so funny?' An eager smile is playing about on her lips: she too wants to be in on the joke.

'Oh,' says Rupert, very wide-eyed, sounding short of breath. 'Nothing, really.' He sniffs, and then blows his nose. 'Oh, God,' he mumbles to himself. 'I can't bear it. How *funny*.'

Dominic bursts out laughing again, catches my eye and turns the laugh into an unconvincing cough.

'Show more,' says Keiko, stabbing the photo album with an impeccably manicured fingernail.

I have to say something, since the alternative is spontaneously combusting with shame right on the spot, or running out of the room weeping with embarrassment.

'Do you still see all these people?' I ask Dom, gesturing at the album, not quite daring to meet his eye in case he laughs again.

'Onwards and upwards,' says Dominic. 'I've had to lose a few. Not the clients, unfortunately. I must say, one does sometimes pine for southerners with classical educations. Ordinary speech, that kind of thing.'

'You're a ghastly snob,' I tell him. 'You are really *ghastly*.'

'Oh, be quiet,' Dom replies. 'You didn't like them either.'

'I didn't like them because they were bores, not because they didn't go to Eton. And besides, the proles with the regional accents have made you extremely comfortable,' I point out. I hate Dom's snobby side, which he usually keeps under wraps.

'I've made them bloody comfortable too,' says Dominic.

'I've made them able to buy cars for their *mams*.' He nearly spits the word out.

'If Frank could hear you, he'd sack you.'

'What are you going to do, run and tell him?'

I sigh. Don't get me wrong: Dominic has always looked out for me, and he does have virtues. But sometimes they spread themselves a little thinly, and I really hate him. Still, this isn't the moment to have a row, and besides, he isn't my concern any more.

I know what is, though.

'Take Honey with you a second, would you, Cressida?' I say. 'And why don't you show Keiko the garden, while you're at it?'

'Oh. OK.' Cressida scoops Honey up with one hand and extends the other to Keiko. 'Come on, you two.'

I get up too, shut the living-room door and take a deep breath before marching up to the sofa.

'Right, you pair of bastards,' I tell Dominic and Rupert. 'You pair of treacherous, sniggering, babyish *turds*. Tell me why you were laughing.'

'I'd rather not,' says Rupert primly. 'If you don't mind.'

Dominic is shaking his head and grinning like a moron. 'Sorry, Stella. Private joke.'

'*Tell me.*'

'You wouldn't find it particularly amusing,' Dom says, hiding behind his floppy hair and biting the inside of his cheeks. 'Frank did, though.'

'Try me.'

'It was, um, it was a bloke joke,' says Rupert. 'About girls. That's all.'

'Share it with me.'

'No,' says Dominic. 'House looks nice. Not my taste,

171

but it's very cosy. Homely. And isn't Honey *sweet*? Little poppet. Speaks just like Frank, I notice.'

'Speaks like Pam Ayres, actually. Nothing to do with Frank, and don't change the subject.'

'They're taking a long time with the coffee,' Rupert says desperately, looking around him wildly.

'Shove up,' I tell him, plonking myself down on the sofa. 'Was it about, er . . .' I clear my throat. 'Was it about me?'

'Goodness me, no,' says Rupert, whose blush has spread to his neck.

'Absolutely not,' says Dom. His lips are quivering with suppressed mirth.

'Look,' I say, cutting to the chase. 'You *have* to tell me. I really need to know. Rupe?'

'There's nothing to tell,' insists Rupert.

'It has recently come to my attention,' I begin, but I can't go on.

Dominic and Rupert are staring at the floorboards by my feet.

I clear my throat and try again: I have to get to the bottom of this.

'It has recently come to my attention that . . . That perhaps I . . . I . . . I make an unattractive noise when . . . in bed.'

This conversation is painful on a number of levels, not least because it is forcing me to cast my mind back to a number of sexual encounters with both of them: pictures of Dom and Rupert, naked and eager, flow into my head.

'Really?' says Rupert, looking just over the top of my head. 'Fancy,' he squeaks. He makes to get up, but I push him down again.

'What kind of noise?' says Dominic, who's always had a sadistic streak.

'A . . . A sort of grunt.' It is my turn to blush.

Rupert and Dominic collapse.

'Snorrrrrrt,' yells Rupert, who's had too much to drink.

'Oink,' says Dominic, his eyes filling up again.

'No,' I say. 'No. It can't be true.' I can feel my shoulders literally sagging down under the weight of this information.

'Not always, Stells,' says Rupert kindly.

'More often than not,' says Dominic.

'Why haven't either of you ever mentioned it?'

'Didn't want to hurt your feelings,' says Rupert piously.

'Didn't seem appropriate,' says Dominic. They are deliberately not looking at each other in order to stave off another hysterical fit. 'And then Frank asked.'

'I'm sure we all do odd things at the, you know, moment of crisis,' says Rupert.

'You do, as a matter of fact,' I tell him, hungry – no, starving – for revenge. 'Shall I show you?'

'What on earth do you mean?' says Rupert.

'Shall I show you the face you make when you come?'

'Steady on, Stells.'

I push my chin right down into my neck, so that it is instantly tripled. I flare out my nostrils as far as they will go. I roll my eyes back. 'Eeeurgh,' I boom, in as deep a voice as I can muster. 'Waaaah.'

'That's what *you* do,' I inform Rupert pleasantly. 'You actually look facially deformed for a second or two.'

Dominic has collapsed into a helpless giggling heap.

'That isn't true,' shouts Rupert.

I raise my right eyebrow at him knowingly.

'As for *you*,' I turn to Dominic. 'As for *you*, Mr Dick: like this.'

Despite himself, Dom has to look. I make a grunting, pushing face, eyes screwed shut, mouth ground down, which I top off with an agonized pained-yet-relieved rumble.

'You,' I inform him, 'make this face. Exactly as if you were having a poo. And then you grunt like that, as if you'd finally got it out.'

'Stella!' he roars. 'You are the most *childish* and disgusting woman I have ever met. I do *not* make that face.'

'I'm afraid you do,' I say smugly.

'Do not.'

'Yes, you do, and I know it because I've *seen* it.'

'Bloody hell,' says Rupert slyly. 'I thought mine was bad, but at least I don't look like I'm taking a crap.'

'Fuck off, Rupert,' says Dominic.

'I don't think I would ever dare have sex again,' says Rupert, copying the face I've just shown him. 'I mean, one couldn't, could one, knowing that?'

So we're quits, then. Not much of a comfort in the long term, granted, but it feels like it helps right now. I can't believe Frank asked them, though. He shall be punished.

13

I'm trying with Happy Bunnies, I really am. But it's hard. First, before you've even managed to get your coat off, you're greeted by lumpen, tubby Ichabod and the words 'I've done a poo', the truth of the statement borne out by a bulgy wide-legged shuffle. You fleetingly realize that Ichabod doesn't really have any lips, only slits, like a fish, which creeps you out a bit. Then, before you have time to properly register your disgust, you have to go and change Icky, because everyone else is suddenly very, very busy looking at books, watching the kettle boil and arranging the pencils in a special way.

Today Kate, Icky's mummy, is absent: she's got an appointment in town, having extra hair transplanted to her upper lip or some such. It quickly becomes clear that I'm not the only one with, shall we say, in true Happy Bunnies speak, *issues* with Ichabod: Julia, mother of triplets Castor, Pollux and Hector, actually seems scared of him. And no wonder: he bites, along with the kicking, pinching and hand-stamping. He drools. I know all toddlers drool, but Icky has the full complement of teeth: why is he still dribbling like the Jabberwock?

'Do you think there's actually something the matter with him?' I ask Emma, mother of Rainbow, as we set out the Play-Doh and cutters. The Play-Doh today is pitch black, I notice, but it's past Hallowe'en. 'Seriously. And what's with the Gothic dough?'

'So the black children don't feel left out.'

'But there *aren't* any black children.' I laugh. It really is like being in a loony bin. 'And they'd probably be wildly offended if there were: I mean, no one's that colour, except crows.'

Emma shrugs, though I detect the hint of a smile playing about her mouth.

'Come on, Emma. Admit he's horrible.'

'He's just a bit of a handful,' she smiles nervously, not looking 100 per cent convinced.

'I'm getting rid of this dough. It's gruesome. I made some green last week – it must be in the cupboard some-where. To welcome the Martians among us. You know, the pretend Martians, playing in the corner with the pretend black kids and the little girl in the wheelchair, who is in fact invisible.'

'You're very naughty,' Emma says, actually smiling now.

'Look at him,' I whisper, emboldened and immediately forgetting all my good intentions, as Ichabod grabs hold of Susannah (mother of Mango)'s skirt and swings on it, as though it were a fence. Susannah keeps gently shooing him away, but he returns, hulking towards her, and has another go. Any second now, her skirt's going to tear: Ichabod isn't exactly a wisp of a child. 'He's a monster.'

'Stella!' Emma hisses reproachfully.

'Well, he *is*, though, isn't he? Come on, Emma.'

'He's difficult,' Emma concedes, keeping her voice low. 'But gifted children often are.'

'You think he's *gifted*?' I cry, raising my voice despite myself. 'Ichabod? On what possible grounds? I mean, I was wondering whether he was quite all there. Whether he was ill, even, in which case I take it all back. Ish.'

'Kate says he is a gifted child,' Emma says, bagging up the black dough and helping me divide up the green. 'She's having enormous trouble finding a school for him. They're always going to interviews, but no joy.'

'There's a surprise. In what way is he gifted, allegedly?'

'Kate says he's very musical and artistically talented. Also, she took him to a child psychologist who said that perhaps he didn't say much because he was so busy having really intelligent thoughts.'

'Really.'

'Really.' Emma stifles a smirk as we both turn to some of Icky's artwork, displayed on the wall behind us. His two paintings are a sort of homage to the dirty protest: even Honey, who is half his age, can draw a recognizable face.

'She's had him checked out by a doctor, then?'

'Oh, goodness me, yes – she's married to one.'

'And there's nothing wrong with him?'

'Nothing at all.'

'So he's just naturally horrible.'

'Yes,' says Emma, without thinking.

'See?' I say.

Emma smiles guiltily and looks over her shoulder. On cue, Marjorie galumphs towards us.

'Stella,' she says. 'A word, please.'

'Look,' I say, as we go into the kitchenette. 'I'm sorry about the other day. I shouldn't have spoken to you like that, or challenged your credentials. I had no right.'

Marjorie, in a pale blue T-shirt, clearly doesn't wear a bra, which I feel is a mistake when blessed with such an abundance of chest.

'We all have baggage,' she says, looking knowing.

'Excuse me?'

'Emotional baggage. We all carry it.'

'Um, yes. I suppose we do.'

Marjorie nods, spooning filthy barley-and-chicory coffee substitute into four waiting mugs.

'I threaten you in some way,' she says. 'You feel threatened by me.'

'I wouldn't quite say . . .' I start, but then stop myself. What's the point? I'd get more joy out of lying down in the mud of my garden and trying to have a conversation with an earthworm.

'Yes,' says Marjorie, in a forgiving, gracious 'I am a wise elder' tone. 'And you clearly have issues with your own parenting skills, which is why you're so disapproving of others.'

'I don't have any "parenting skills",' I point out. 'I just sort of get on with it. I don't understand why it is a parenting skill to make children play with black dough or read them books about death.'

'Quite,' says Marjorie, as though this proved her point, which perhaps it does. 'Anyway, let's hope we help you learn, shall we?' She stirs sugar into a couple of the mugs with a filthy spoon and squeezes past me. Louisa and Alexander have finally arrived: this time they're coming to mine for lunch. And I was right: Ichabod has torn Susannah's skirt.

We wheel our respective buggies back to the house through the sheeting rain – I can feel my mascara trickling down my face. Louisa quizzes me about my night out with Frank, about Rupert and Dominic (I keep the snort saga to myself), about Cressida, about whether it felt nice going to a glamorous party, and about what Honey says about her dad (not much). Alexander, she says, says very little about his.

'I don't understand,' she says, as we turn into my street. 'Frank sounds so lovely. That sounds like such a nice night.'

'I've explained it a million times, Lou. He *is* very lovely, in some ways.'

'Well, then?'

'I don't fancy him.'

'But why not?'

'He's a slapper.'

'Probably just needs the love of a good woman,' Lou says.

'Plus, he's really ginger.'

'So what? It can be very attractive – look at Nicole Kidman.'

'I don't fancy Nicole Kidman. So a lot, to me.'

We bump our buggies backwards up the steps, which always hurts my back. Being thirty-eight, sadly, means you notice things like this. I'm nearly forty, I think to myself. I'm *nearly forty*. It's a horrifying thought. Soon I will start smiling winsomely and telling people I feel twelve on the inside.

'And anyway,' I tell her, turning the key in the lock, 'there are other things.'

'Does he tear the wings off flies?' Lou laughs.

'No. But he's not necessarily as nice as he seems.'

'Who is?' sighs Louisa, trotting out all the platitudes.

'Never mind,' I say. I don't want to discuss it. 'We have a very cosy and nice set-up,' I add. 'It's like living with your really good friend, whom your daughter adores. It's bliss, really. I wouldn't want to go and fuck it up.'

'Fuck what up?' says Frank, who is standing in the hallway, flicking through the second post. 'All right? You look like a panda.'

'Nothing. Why are you here all the time these days? Aren't you working any more?' I rub under my eyes ineffectually, jabbing my eyeball by mistake.

'I live here. I come home for lunch most days,' says Frank. 'In case you hadn't noticed.'

'Hmm,' I harrumph. 'You didn't use to. Anyway, this is my friend Louisa. Louisa, Frank. Frank, Louisa.'

'Very pleased to meet you,' says Louisa, who actually licks her lips very quickly, which I thought only happened in movies.

'Likewise,' says Frank, fixing her with his flinty eyes. 'Stella's talked a lot about you.'

This isn't even true. I notice his eyes flick imperceptibly to her left hand, and clock the fact that her ring finger is bare. I can't believe Frank. It's like an illness, with him. He's probably gauging her ride-worthiness as we speak.

'And you.' Louisa giggles.

There's a charged sort of silence for a few seconds, until I bend down to unhook Honey from her buggy straps.

'Fwankie,' says Honey, stretching her arms out to him. 'Oi home.'

Frank scoops her up easily and perches her on his hip. 'And who's this?' he asks Louisa, glancing tenderly, *shamelessly*, towards Alexander.

'My son,' says Lou. 'Alex. He's a year older than Honey. They're great friends.'

'Hello, Alexander. Nice-looking little chap,' says Frank charmingly. 'Like his mother.'

'Eeurgh,' I say. 'Oh, vom, Frank. Polish up your technique a bit, would you?'

'What?' says Frank, laughing. 'It's true.'

'Heehee,' says Louisa, blushing now. Why do sassy, capable, *adult* women get reduced to quivering pools of jelly the second anyone says anything remotely nice to them? Louisa's really good-looking: people must say nice things to her all the time. Surely she's got used to it by now. Apparently not, though: quiver, quiver. God, it gets on my nerves.

I heave a great dramatic sigh and push past them to take off my coat, and then stride purposefully into the living room. Frank and Louisa fail to follow me: they're standing in the hall as though they've taken root.

'Hello!' I call out. 'Lunch, anyone? Louisa, I'm putting *Angelina Ballerina* on. Is that OK with Alex, or would he prefer *Bob the Builder*?'

'Bob,' yells Alexander in tones of crazed excitement, charging into the room. 'Bob, please.'

'Bob, please,' echoes Louisa, coming into the room as I hear Frank going up the stairs. 'It's his favourite.'

'Are you hot, Lou?' Louisa's cardigan, previously done up, is now held together by a mere two buttons, revealing a generous expanse of upper chest and, I notice with a twinge of annoyance, rather an impressive glimpse of flat-as-a-board stomach.

'Yes, I am, a bit, as a matter of fact,' Lou says defiantly. 'Must have been the walk.'

'Must have been,' I shrug, reaching for my bobbly old pashmina shawl off the back of the armchair. The truth is, it's freezing in here, as evidenced by Louisa's nipples.

'You,' I whisper, 'are a hussy.'

Louisa winks at me. 'He has enormous eyelashes,' she simpers wetly. 'And that chin – *so* masculine.'

'I hadn't noticed.'

'Stella, he's *gorgeous*. Do you, would you . . .'

'Mind? No. And you'll succeed, by the way, if that's your mission.'

'Did you get anything for lunch?' Frank asks from the doorway.

Bloody hell: how long's he been standing there? I look at him, as casually as possible. He looks back at me: Mr Inscrutable.

'I got some wine,' I say, 'and there's tons of stuff in the fridge.'

Frank wanders off to have a look. He is a man of many appetites.

I lower my voice and address Louisa again. 'But I wouldn't expect a wedding ring if I were you. I *have* warned you, Lou: he's a total one.'

'Ooh,' says Louisa, shuddering with pleasure (that's another thing: why do sassy, capable, adult women so like being told that someone is a bad boy? Some creepy mothering instinct, probably. Yuck). 'God, Stella, I can't believe you undersold him like that. You know, physically.'

'I could make pasta with goat's cheese and peas,' Frank shouts through.

'My God!' says Louisa. 'He *cooks*!'

'Whatever,' I shout back churlishly.

'That sounds delicious,' shouts Louisa. 'Thank you.'

'Will the children eat it?' asks Frank, coming back through.

'I don't see why not,' I say. 'Lou?'

'I expect so. Do you know, Rainbow came round for

tea the other day and it turns out she only eats oven chips. That's literally all she eats. And chocolate.'

'I can't stand that. It's so English.'

'Well, it can't really be helped,' Lou says. 'Picky eaters.'

'Yes, it can. I mean, obviously children like some things more than others, but the idea that they only eat bland, plastic food is just a crock. If they're hungry, they eat what they're given. And if you only give them crap, they turn into the kind of adults who haven't met an aubergine until they're twenty-five and don't like going abroad because the food's funny.'

'You're in a good mood today,' says Frank. 'That legendary charm pouring out of you.'

'I'm going to open some wine,' I say, ignoring him and making my way majestically to the kitchen.

He's right, though: I was in a perfectly good mood until we got into the house and Frank started his I'm-on-heat routine and Louisa fell for it. I pull the cork out of a bottle of white Burgundy and pour myself a glass. With what I thought was admirable prescience, I've asked Mary to come on Thursday afternoons from today, since we're at playgroup all morning. She's coming at two, which means I can have a drunken lunch and mooch about all afternoon without having to worry about poor Honey (quite an appealing thought, as poor Honey slept in my bed last night – well, I say 'slept', but 'chatted and giggled and wiggled her way through the night' would be more apt. I love those nights, and I love kissing her little damp head when she finally falls asleep, but I do really feel the lack of a good rest in the morning).

I take a cooling sip of wine and click the button on the answerphone. There's a message from Yungsta asking me to have dinner with him tomorrow; perhaps I'd also like to come and watch him in action afterwards somewhere in the East End. This cheers me, so that I feel much more kindly disposed when Frank returns to the kitchen, Louisa in tow.

'They're watching the video,' she says. 'Then lunch, then naps, I think. Frank says he might show me his pictures.'

'It's not far,' says Frank, reaching for a pan. 'I thought maybe you could keep an eye on Alexander for a little while, Stella.'

'Come up and see my etchings,' I say, which comes out quite tersely, by mistake. 'Of course,' I say, more pleasantly. 'No problem. And anyway, Mary's coming in an hour or so.'

Frank puts the water on to boil, and then pours Louisa and himself a drink.

'Cheers,' he says.

'Cheers,' says Louisa. Flutter flutter.

'Your neighbour just left a message,' I tell her, 'asking me out.'

'Are you going to go?'

'God, yes,' I say, with a degree of enthusiasm that, pleased as I am, I don't actually quite feel. 'You bet. Tomorrow.'

'Where's he taking you?' Frank asks. 'Penne or spaghetti? Penne's probably easier for the kids.'

'Some restaurant in Shoreditch. You'll know it, probably, seeing it's your stamping ground. Called Melon.'

'That's a bar,' says Frank. 'Very busy. Not quite your cup of tea, princess.'

'Well, the message said dinner, so maybe he'll take me

on somewhere,' I say, with my nose in the air. 'Somewhere fabulous, I expect.'

'Do you feel shy about it?' asks Louisa.

My nose comes down again. 'Actually, a tiny bit. I haven't had a date-date for years.'

'Would you like some company?' Louisa offers generously. 'I mean, it's not so bad if there are other people around.'

'Like who?'

'Like me,' she beams. 'I know Adrian pretty well. And maybe Frank would care to join us,' she adds flirtatiously, sliding him a look.

'Why not?' says Frank. 'Might be a laugh.'

'No! I'm not having the pair of you sitting there like, like an *audience*, watching my date.'

'I was thinking,' says Louisa, 'more of a double date kind of a thing.'

'Blimey,' says Frank. 'You don't waste much time.'

'I just meant . . .' says Lou, taking another glug of wine for courage. Her eyes are shining. She looks very pretty. 'Well, I just meant that it would be nice, I suppose. Fun. But if you don't fancy it . . .' She suddenly looks crestfallen. 'I mean, nothing serious. But you don't *have* to . . . Obviously. Er . . .'

'Nah,' says Frank casually, rustling around inside the freezer for peas. 'I'm game.'

'*Quelle surprise*,' I mutter, despite myself.

'What?' says Frank, turning around and giving me the benefit of an especially flinty stare, accompanied by an amused raised eyebrow.

'Nothing,' I say. 'You have needs, that's all.'

'Stella!' says Lou, like a hypocrite: for all her subtlety,

she might as well be advertising her own needs on a giant billboard strapped to her chest.

Frank shakes his head, smiles, and starts doing things to the goat's cheese. I can't believe it: people actually *beg* him for dates. What's the matter with Louisa?

'What's the matter with you?' I ask her, steering her back through into the living room under the pretext of checking on the children, who have fallen into one of those toddlers' video-comas. 'Have you gone mad? I mean, asking people out like that! It's so *pushy*.'

'No, it's not,' Louisa replies. 'It's what modern women do. And I am quoting *Vogue*, I'll have you know.'

'There's asking people out and there's throwing – *hurling* – yourself at them in a desperate kind of way,' I explain. 'Still, if that's what you want . . .'

'It is, actually,' she says, looking pleased now that she's finished looking shocked at herself. 'I reckon it'll be a laugh. And you *said* you didn't mind.'

'I don't. How long since you've had sex?'

'Oh, God,' she groans. 'About two years.' Her eyes are shining again.

'That makes you a born-again virgin, and as such susceptible to feelings of abandonment and disappointment if he doesn't follow through with a second date,' I tell her. 'And I'm quoting myself. Honestly, it's true – I've noticed it happening. So brace yourself.'

'Oh, I'm braced,' says Louisa with a grin. 'I am *so* braced.'

14

Try as I might, I can't seem to get excited enough about this double date. Frank and Louisa disappeared for an hour and a half yesterday, when he took her to look at his paintings. I sat and watched a sleeping Honey and Alexander, which was initially sweet but subsequently so dull that I joined them and had a quick nap myself. By the time my only two friends in the whole of London – the two people I am closest to – came back, I'd been awake for twenty minutes and was suffering agonies of annoyance. Bloody Frank, ruining my girly afternoon. I scanned their faces for signs of guilt (pointlessly, since, as I know, Frank doesn't do guilt), as well as for signs of snogging, but I didn't get much chance for scrutiny because Louisa only stayed another ten minutes and Frank went straight back to the studio. Mary was in the living room – I'd asked her to come because I thought – hoped – that Lou and I might get drunk again, and have another funny, silly afternoon – so I couldn't even ask the questions I wanted to ask, assuming that I would have done so. Which isn't a given. Ignorance is bliss, and, failing ignorance, doubt: there's always the possibility that you've got hold of the wrong end of the stick.

Louisa scooped Alexander up and wheeled him home, and I was left feeling lonelier and crosser than I've felt in quite some time. I sat and drank tea with Mary for a while, and then paid her off, thanked her for her wasted journey, told her I'd see her the next night – Double Date Night – and went to bed at the same time as Honey. I didn't hear Frank come home. I'm not sure he did.

So here I am twenty-four hours later, trying – again – to get ready; feeling – again – that my heart isn't quite in it. Why does one have to *go* on dates, anyway? What's so wrong with being single, and content, and just sort of pottery? Nothing, I sigh, pencilling in my left eyebrow, nothing at all if you *are* content. But I'm not. I don't want to live the rest of my life on my own, without sex, lonely again. And so needs must, as Tim the neighbour might say. (His wife came back from Majorca today, and I felt an odd sort of pang as I watched them all pile into their absurd people carrier, no doubt going out for a celebratory meal. Silly, weird Tim, his over-made-up wife, their two slouchy, trainered sons . . . so neat and dull and naffly 2.4-ish: for one fleeting moment, I'd have swapped places with any of them.)

My eyeshadow's gone wrong and I look like Joan Collins. I rub the worst of the excess away, and take a good look at myself in the bathroom mirror. Me, or a twenty-three-year-old with no conversation and fabulous tits? No contest. No, really. If I were a man, I'd go for the pert-breasted retard every time. No wonder women like me all end up either having affairs with married men or becoming lesbians. Frankly, there isn't a wild amount of choice. Speaking of lesbians, I should ring that nice old Barbara. Perhaps I could become that nice old Barbara's faithful companion.

I am beginning to depress myself, and I haven't even got dressed yet. Lou rang this afternoon, quizzing me about the kind of 'look' Frank liked best – how should I know? The female look, I told her. The look that has a vagina. Don't bother getting dressed, I said. She giggled stupidly and said she was off shopping. Meanwhile, I hate all my dresses and the kind of look Yungsta likes is not, I imagine, a look I am capable of mustering up: I'm twenty years too old. Why am I about to spend the evening with a man whose vocabulary flummoxes me and whose hand gestures make me want to laugh?

We're on to lipliner now, and I smile as I remember Frank's pitch-perfect imitation of Yungsta's patois cadences. I smile, and I don't know what comes over me, but suddenly I wake up. Get over it, I tell myself. Get over whatever's bugging you. You don't have to take a vow of chastity, or become a lesbian, or have an affair with a married man. You've been asked out on a date by someone nice-looking, and single, who is clearly interested in you. Now pay attention. Sort your face out, fish out your sexiest dress, and *be grateful*, you whining cow. Go get 'em. Be fabulous. Look like you're a dirty ride.

I can hear the front door slam and then Frank, not seen since lunch time yesterday, chatting easily to Mary and Honey downstairs. I hear him come up and call my name. 'I'm in the bathroom,' I shout back, 'getting ready.'

'Let's go together,' he says through the door. 'Louisa and, er, the DJ are making their own way from Regent's Park Road.'

'OK. I'll be out in ten minutes.'

'No hurry – I have to have a shower and shave and so on. Find some clothes. I'll see you downstairs. Call a cab, though, would you, if you finish first?'

'OK.' Why is he making such an effort? Usually, when

Frank goes on dates, he brushes his teeth and maybe – *maybe* – changes his T-shirt. He is going to unusual trouble for Louisa, I realize. So what? So bloody what? I am making an effort for Adrian. And, I realize in a flash of lucidity, I am going to pull out all the stops.

I'm really glad I know how to do make-up properly. I cleanse my face free of modest, wholesome, gild-the-lily Take 1, and spread all my brushes out in readiness for Take 2, the paint-myself-a-new-face option. I fish around in my make-up bag: here we go, I tell myself, my stomach contracting. *Here we go.* Concealer. Light-reflecting foundation, custom-mixed. Touche Eclat. Minutely subtle shading, around the nose and under the chin. (Oh, yes, I can be *very* professional: my Parisian adolescence didn't go to waste.) Cheeks: with my two blushers, I can give myself cheekbones like paperknives, and I do. New eyebrows, with the help of tweezers, some brown powder and a hard pencil: straight and demure, very vampy. Eyes like a cat's: three shadows, which change the shape of my eyes completely and turn them into long, wide almonds.

Eyelash curlers. Three coats of mascara, and an eyelash comb. And Vaseline, on my lips, because I don't actually want to look like a prostitute. I take a step back and admire my handiwork: fabulous. Five stars. Someone else's confident, pouty, sultry face stares back at me: I don't know her, but she's pretty lovely, and she winks at me. My work is done. I shove my brushes back into the make-up case and turn off the light.

'Blimey,' says Frank, looking me up and down rather solemnly. 'You scrub up well.'

'Thought I'd make an effort,' I reply breezily, as though

I didn't already have face-ache from my two tons of slap. 'You know, for my date. For Adrian. Sexy Adrian of sexiness. Sexy Adrian of total ride-worthiness. Just as you have, I see. How sweet. New shirt?'

'Yeah,' Frank shrugs. His duck-egg-blue shirt works very well with his grey eyes. 'But it's hardly the same thing. I've never seen you with proper make-up on. Your sexy make-up of sexiness.' He is grinning, but also sort of gawping, *boggling*, immediately making me feel that I've overdone it by a mile, which I expect I have. 'New dress?'

'This?' I shrug back. 'Pah! No, it's ancient.' I am wearing – and already feeling slightly uncomfortable in – a heavily corseted black number, purchased a couple of years ago in a moment of madness. (Mary had to come and lace me in earlier, making me feel like Scarlett O'Hara.) Still, as pulling dresses go, this one is fairly impressive: up go the bosoms, in goes the waist, out sticks the bottom. It's got arms, so I don't have to expose my thirty-eight-year-old's crêpiness, and it's got a longish, straight skirt, so ditto re thighs. It's pretty sexy, the dress, but it does make me feel slightly on display. I mean, all that flesh: too much information, really. Too much information, too soon.

'And you've grown, I see,' says Frank, still staring, looking down at my fuck-me footwear, a narrow, black suede pair of pointy boots with killer stiletto heels. These hurt like crazy, and will prove to be a fatal mistake if we have to walk anywhere, or – God forbid – dance. I really, really hope my DJ date doesn't take us dancing. It hadn't occurred to me that he might until now, stupidly.

Frank looks at my knees, then his watch. 'Nice pins. Did you call the cab?'

'Yes, he'll be ten minutes.'

Frank is pacing around the living room like a child.

'Calm down, Frank, we won't be late.'

Frank smiles briskly, and carries on pacing. I've never seen him so filled with anticipation for a date before, especially considering he saw Louisa only yesterday. Only this morning, perhaps, if he really didn't come home, the filthy, disgusting pig-stopout. With this elaborate whale-boned corsetry, it would be agony to sigh, so I don't. I put my pink velvet coat on instead – my favourite coat, this, with its wide belt and no buttons.

Twenty slightly awkward minutes in the taxi later – he preoccupied, me longing to ask him about Louisa but thinking the better of it just in case I didn't like his answers – we pull up outside Melon, which is heaving with young trendies with eccentric facial hair (boys) and facial piercings (girls) and stupid low-slung trousers (both).

'I feel like I've come to collect my daughter from the school disco,' I whine. This all suddenly strikes me as a very bad idea. What am I doing here, and dressed like this?

'I feel like you've wrapped me up, stuck a ribbon around me and handed me to your mate,' says Frank – his first complete sentence in twenty minutes – but I ignore him.

'Hello,' I say. 'I've come to collect Honey from Year 5. Honestly, Frank – I feel ancient.'

'If this were the school disco, you'd be the mum all the boys fancied,' Frank says kindly, 'so don't worry about it. Come on,' he says, giving me the nicest smile of the evening so far and taking me by the hand. 'Let's go and find them.'

We squeeze and weave our way through a packed crowd of people standing shoulder to shoulder and shouting through their goatees. The music is very loud; the décor industrial: concrete, lots of grey paint, exposed ducts. (Funny how this look never goes away: I remember being in places like it fifteen years ago. We thought it was *really modern* even then.) Beyond the hall-like bar area, though, the space opens out into a sitting area of sorts: an angular, spiky-looking row of concrete tables, hard-seeming chairs and functional, brown banquettes – not quite the comfortable den one would have wished for, but better than nothing. Adrian and Louisa are sitting down, facing a small rectangular table, drinking cocktails out of Duralex glasses. We see them first; Frank's warm, dry hand tightens imperceptibly around mine, and then he lets go.

'Wow,' Adrian whistles loudly, standing up. 'You look amazing.' He says the words in a perfectly ordinary Home Counties voice and then corrects himself, coughing. 'Fly,' he says, puzzlingly.

I kiss him hello demurely. I think I'll keep my coat on for a while. A pin from my chignon is digging into my head.

'Hello,' says Frank to Louisa in a low voice. She is looking extraordinarily pretty, like a flower, or an angel, all fresh-faced, blonde wholesomeness, but with a killer body. One look at her, and I immediately feel overegged. Her low-slung, embroidered Maharishi trousers show off that enviably flat and bronzed stomach; a slinky little vest top shows off her tight, pert chest and muscular upper arms. Her eye make-up is a perfect example of the 'I've spent three hours putting on make-up that looks like I'm wearing none' look so popular, I've noticed, with men, who claim such women are natural beauties until they accidentally catch them bare-faced and vomit with shock. But Louisa *is* a natural beauty. Even bare-faced, she looks like a prettier, softer, fresher version of Madonna. With the make-up, she looks sensational.

I feel extremely overdressed and not natural at all. Even my coat looks like it's about to go to the opera.

'You look *great*,' says Frank to Louisa.

We all sound like teenagers going on their first date.

'You don't look too bad yourself,' says Lou from beneath her eyelashes. 'Come and sit down.'

Adrian pats the banquette beside him, so I sit down too. Alas, I am not able to return his sartorial compliment: my date looks like an arse, as Frank might put it. He is certainly handsome under all the clobber, but seems intent on ruining his looks with a series of grotesque accessories. The first problem is facial hair: in honour of our date, Adrian has trimmed his goatee so that it is perfectly minuscule, a tiny tuft of black hair sprouting like a growth or squashed bug from his otherwise more than presentable chin. He is also wearing huge coloured plastic shades, à la Bono, in pale pink, which makes his green eyes look like rabbits'. Plus, if there's one person I physically can't abide, it's Bono (Bono! *Bono!* What's wrong with these people?), so the look doesn't do much for me – it dimly reminds me of insects with huge boogly eyes, in fact. Further down, we have gold jewellery around the neck and wrists, and *a beige track suit*, apparently two sizes too big, though curiously tight around the crotch, I notice, glancing down. Still, he looks comfy, at least, and the tracky's worn with nothing underneath so that I can see his well-developed, gym-friendly chest, which is mildly sexy. It is a sign of my advanced years, though, that instead of focusing on the perfect pecs, I imagine him, yearningly, in beaten-up jeans and a cashmere jumper. He'd look so much nicer. Why is he wearing so many rings on his fingers? Does he have bells on his toes, too? And has he never watched Ali G, for heaven's sake?

'Whatchou drinkin'?' Adrian asks, his thigh pressing against mine.

'Champagne cocktail, please.'

'Not in here, mate,' he laughs. Mate! Men who call you 'mate' ought to be shot.

'Glass of champagne, then, *pal*.'

'Me too,' says Louisa. 'Hi, Stella. You look fantastic.'

'Thanks. You too.'

'Hoegaarten for me,' says Frank. He is looking at me most curiously, almost as though he wanted to laugh.

People walk up and down past our table: it's a little like being at the zoo. They are extraordinary creatures. I see why Adrian chose this venue, though: he blends in perfectly. He occasionally detaches himself from the frankly lacklustre conversation – Frank oddly tense, until the drink kicks in, Louisa too gabby, Yungsta too patois, me too bemused by him – to high-five somebody, or throw those weird hand shapes at somebody else, or mumble nonsensical phrases. Frank seems to know a couple of people here and there too. Louisa and I sit admiringly, glad to have been allowed out, imagining a world not dominated by being by oneself.

'I'm hungry,' says Frank eventually. 'And I'm pretty sure, without having to ask, that Stella is too. What's the plan, mate?'

'Thought we'd chill for a while, mate, yeah?' says Adrian. 'And then maybe grab a bite down the road. I'm working at eleven.' He pulls a load of flyers out of his pocket. 'Here – you is all on the list. VIP room. All the extras, know what I mean?' He sniffs pointedly and grins.

Oh, no, not drugs. Oh, no no *no*. I can't stand drugs: they're number one on my list of Things People Shouldn't Do Past the Age of Twenty-five. (Top three: 1. Drugs. 2. Tantric sex. 3. Highlights/any hairstyle denoting generous use of 'product'. And that's just the tip of a very large iceberg.) All those middle-aged men in naff suits you see, running around Soho coked out of their heads, make me depressed. All those blokey blokes in their thirties, taking Ecstasy and dancing around their suburban living rooms, digging out their dungarees and waving their arms about and pretending that it's 1988 and that their hair didn't recede and that life didn't disappoint them . . . could anything be sadder or more piteous? Grimmer still are the ones who spent their adolescence swotting up and dissecting mammals (instead of taking drugs and bunking off school, which is the French way: we get it out of our system early), and who now stagger around coked up to the eyeballs, believing themselves to finally be 'cool' at the age of forty-two – aargh. I know loads of them through Dominic, who was not averse to the odd line himself and who'd spend the occasional blokes' night out with his male clients doing this kind of thing, usually involving dropping some Es. He'd always come back horny, too, and drool all over me, and when I'd finally be awake enough to respond to his drug-fuelled desires, I'd discover his penis had shrunk – Ecstasy does this – so that it looked like a little snail. A tiny, weeny little snaily. You don't want to start thinking of your partner's penis as a little snaily, believe me: thin end of the wedge.

I know this isn't a very tolerant way of thinking – I'm sure millions of perfectly charming people my age take drugs – but I do think there are some things which youth has a monopoly on and drugs are one of them. What's funny and wild and fun in a twenty-year-old just looks desperate and sad-beyond-tears in someone twice that age. Eurgh. And the bloody coke-fuelled inane chat that makes you want to tear your ears off and throw them on the floor in disgust . . . Oh, bugger. Drugs. On top of everything else, we're now to be the oldest swingers in town. I might have known. Cherry on the cake of my evening.

We move on to dinner, to one of those fur-coat-and-no-knickers restaurants that looks fabulous and serves disgusting food. Louisa and I slope off to the loo as soon as we've sat down.

'So,' she says from the cubicle next to mine.

'So,' I reply.

We both begin to pee, in perfect unison.

'It's going really well, I think.'

'Mmm.'

'Adrian really likes you.'

'That's nice.'

Rustle rustle with the paper, flush. A woman two cubicles down parps away like a trumpet. It always seems odd to me that people apparently store up their wind especially for visits to restaurants, the loos of which are always filled with women who seem to have considerable trouble with trapped wind until their buttocks hit the wooden lavatory seat of a public place.

Lou and I meet again by the sinks. My weird, sultry, pouty face greets me in the mirror, and gives me a shock. We catch each other's eye and smirk; the woman in the cubicle actually groans with pleasure, or perhaps relief: she sounds like she's just come. Lou and I start giggling as we wash our hands. Then she floofs out her blonde curls artlessly and opens her mouth wide, checking her teeth for spinach.

'Do you think Frank likes me?' she asks.

'Yes.'

'No, I mean, do you think he *likes* me, you know, in that way?'

'Yes.' I reapply a bit of blusher. 'I'm sure he does. You have a va . . . you have private parts, don't you?'

'Stella!'

'What? It's true.'

'Do you really think he likes me?'

'God, Lou, I've just said so twice, haven't I?'

'Are you sure,' she says, clutching my arm, 'that you don't mind? It's just you seem in a bit of a funny mood.'

'That's probably because I've spent the past hour listening to a lecture about hip-hop,' I smile. 'Sorry. That's cheered me up, though.' I gesture at the parpster's lair.

'Adrian really fancies you, I can tell.'

'We'd be a brilliant match if I were deaf.'

'So you're absolutely sure you don't mind? About Frankie?'

Frankie now, is it? I heave a giant, ultra-exasperated, couldn't-care-less sigh.

'Absolutely sure. Now stop bugging me about it, Lou.'

'He is just *so great*,' Louisa says with a beatific smile, much as a born-again Christian might say of the Lord Jesus.

'Mmm. He's not *that* great, Lou.' Do I tell her? Do I not? I am sorely tempted. But then I tell myself that Frank has never behaved badly to me, that his personal life is none of my business, and that I really shouldn't pick this moment to dump all over my friend's evening. Which isn't to say I am not tempted. But I resist.

'What happened yesterday?' I ask, unpinning my hair and then pinning it up again more messily for added sex-appeal. 'When you went to see his pictures?'

'His pictures are *great*, aren't they? Just great,' she gushes. 'I must say, I do love a bit of the old figurative art. A person who can actually draw. Or paint. Or both. Have you seen his sketches? They're beautiful. That lovely one of you . . .'

'Of me? He's never drawn me. He draws cows. As you'll have seen.'

'Yes, but there's that titchy one of you and Honey. You must have seen it, surely?'

'Oh, that,' I lie. Knowing that Frank has a secret drawing of me, with or without Honey, gives me a strange mini-thrill which I am unwilling to discuss with Lou. 'And then what?'

'When?'

'Yesterday. After you'd admired his cows, me included.'

'Oh,' she giggles. 'We had a cup of tea and I told him all about myself.'

'Including Alex's dad walking out on you?'

'Oh, yes. He was so sympathetic. One of the things – the many things – that I like about him is that he seems to be really kind-hearted. But butch with it, you know, not all sappy and sandally and horrible. Don't you think?'

'Up to a point.' I'm biting my tongue, though I must say Frank's hypocrisy could win awards. 'Superficially.'

'How do you mean?'

'Nothing.'

Lou shrugs and snaps her powder case shut.

'And then,' she says, 'he kissed me.'

Aargh. Aargh. On the other hand, if there's one thing I love it's having a song lyric thrown into the conversation.

'How did he kiss you?' I ask.

'With his mouth,' Louisa says, grinning. 'With his lips.'

'Hmm,' I say. 'A normal kiss? Because Frank strikes me as very possibly the kind of person who would wine-kiss you.'

'What's a wine-kiss?'

'You know, when men think it's incredibly sexy and fwoar-ish to slurp wine into your mouth as part of the kissing. People who think of themselves as sexually sophisticated do it, I've noticed.'

'Oh, God,' says Louisa. 'Does anyone really still go for that?'

'I think so. They think it's slick. Studly.'

'I had it done once with pear Thunderbird. When I was at school.'

'Well, quite. That's part of the problem – no one ever wine-kisses you with Château d'Yquem. I've had it with Blue Nun, and of course if the wine is revolting you just end up dribbling down yourself, and then the wine-kisser tries to lick the dribbled wine.'

'Like a dog.'

'Exactly. Actually, I'm rather surprised Dr Cooper didn't wine-kiss.'

'He's more of a naked-massage-with-oils type, judging by your description.'

'Oh, God! Naked massage with oils! And the oils always have a label that says "Sensual".'

'Sssenssual,' Louisa sniggers, sounding like Kenneth Williams.

Both of us are laughing out loud now. 'Sssenssual naked massage with oils,' Louisa honks. 'And the guy's always really rubbish at it, and keeps telling you to "relax" in a husky voice while he sort of kneads you, like dough. And the oil always goes into your bottom crack and feels horrible.'

'Bloody oils,' I say. 'So then you're wriggling around with an oily back bottom. And then you have to walk about – slide about – for two days smelling of hippie.'

Louisa nods in agreement. We both continue our make-up reapplications. I really love Louisa for understanding about the crapness of naked massage with oils.

'With tongues?' I ask nonchalantly, after a seemly pause. 'The Frank-kissing. Without wine – which I'm pleased to hear – but with tongues?'

'No, Stella,' she laughs. 'It was a friendly sort of kiss goodbye. On the mouth, though. Well, when I say "he kissed me" – I kissed him, and he kissed me back.'

'Right.'

'It was only quick, but he's a very good kisser.'

'Really.'

'Yeah,' she says. 'Experienced.'

'He's certainly that,' I say. 'Let's go back through, shall we?'

The woman comes out of the cubicle of shame as we pass by. 'Disgusting,' she sniffs. 'There's a time and a place for that kind of conversation.'

'The bean's a most extraordinary fruit,' says Louisa.

'The more you eat, the more you toot,' I complete.

We stagger out of the loo crippled with laughter at this infantilism. Despite myself, I'm cheering up.

I've noticed that people who spend a lot of time in very

noisy environments – night clubs, say – are extremely poor conversationalists. Adrian can barely speak in complete sentences, though by pudding time he has become very physically demonstrative (this possibly has something to do with his racing off to the loo a couple of times and coming back unusually animated). He starts off by pushing back a stray hair from my cheek, graduates to feeding me mouthfuls of his pudding (which sounds like a really *nasty* euphemism – 'Feed me mouthfuls of your pudding, babe' – but isn't) and concludes by engaging in a robust game of footsie, which I try and semi-resist as I worry about his giant trainers scuffing my boots. Frank, who has dropped a napkin, gets a close-up view of this, and re-emerges from under the table looking grumpy, which puts me in an excellent mood.

'So,' he says, putting his arm around Louisa so that his left hand is casually resting by her breast. 'Where to next?'

'Bangin',' says Adrian, trying the same trick with *his* arm. Unfortunately, my bosoms are considerably bigger than Lou's, though less pert, so he accidentally ends up with a handful of chest.

'Fuck! Sorry,' he says, but for some reason it takes a while for his motor skills to catch up with his thought process, so that, though appalled, he is still clutching, squashing, my entire left breast, holding it as though it were a fruit. Confused, he squeezes it neatly twice, rather too hard for my liking.

'Um,' I say, 'do you mind?'

'Sorry,' says Adrian helplessly, still inexplicably attached to my breast.

Frank reaches across and pulls his hand away.

'Fook's sake, mon,' he mutters, sounding more Geordie than he has done for ages. 'Aa'll cloot yor jaw.'

'I didn't mean . . .' says Adrian. 'Sorry, mate. Dropped an E, yeah?'

'It's OK,' I say, feeling a tremendous urge to laugh. I wink at Frank, my hero, who looks unamused, though Louisa is grinning as though she'd burst.

'Nice pair, missus,' she sniggers. She does it for slightly too long, so that her snigger turns into a horrible snort.

'Oh, my *God*,' she blushes. 'I can't believe I did that. Like a disgusting pig. I'm so, so sorry.'

'I thought it was sexy,' says Frank, giving me a look and slowly unfurling his wickedest smile.

'Shush, Frank. No one cares,' I say, but a giggling fit is building up in the pit of my stomach.

'Anyway,' I continue, grinning at Adrian like an imbecile who loves nothing more than having her breasts groped over the *tarte tatin*, 'you were saying?'

'Um, yeah. Bangin'. It's the club I'm at tonight. It'll be a bit quiet for a while but you can have free drinks.'

'Where are you from?' I ask Adrian. 'Because your accent is, ah, variable.'

'That would be telling, my love,' says Adrian, now sounding bizarrely like a West Country farmer. It must be the drugs talking.

'Let's go, shall we?' says Frank impatiently. 'I need another wee drink.'

He and Louisa walk down the street hand in hand. Not to be outdone, and very possibly crazed by the four glasses of red wine I've had with dinner, I squeeze Adrian's behind forcefully when the four of us are standing in the Great Eastern Road, looking for a cab.

'All righ,' says Adrian happily, turning his head so that our lips brush.

'Mmm,' I whisper hoarsely. 'Never better.'

But I still really, really want to laugh, especially when I catch Frank's face, staring at me impassively in the drizzling rain. Still, considering I was dreading the evening a mere couple of hours ago, this has got to be a turn up for the books.

Bangin' is the name of a night that happens at a huge gay nightclub called, sweetly, Fist. Yungsta – he most certainly stops being Adrian the second we approach the door – DJs in the big main, ground-floor bit, but there are apparently another couple of floors that play different (and hopefully more *sympathique*) kinds of music. What I'd really like is a little blast of Charles Aznavour, but never mind: I need to get to grips with the troubling issue of my grotesque musical taste, and what better way of broadening my outlook than a couple of happy hours spent listening to what I gather are technically known as 'bangin' choons'?

Yungsta settles us in at the ground-floor bar, orders us drinks and then departs to fiddle about behind his decks, planting a lingering, slightly slack-mouthed kiss on my lips and promising to return soon, yeah? He looks quite cool, now he's on home ground, and I am pleased I squeezed his bottom earlier. Well, pleased-ish. Hardly delirious with happiness, but, you know.

Louisa, Frank and I sit ourselves down – thigh to thigh, very cosy – and look around: the club is beginning to fill up, and more or less everyone in the room is a good ten years younger than us at the very least. Which is no wonder: I haven't been to a nightclub for years, and although Frank looks reasonably at home, I know he doesn't make a habit of going out clubbing either. Louisa can't believe her eyes: she is rubbernecking like mad, trying to take it all in, occasionally breaking off to murmur how it all makes something of a change from Happy Bunnies and sitting on your own with your cup of organic tea, trimming a hat, and how she feels really, really old.

'I don't even know what those drinks are,' she says, pointing to a group of young people carrying what look like beer bottles, filled with pastel-coloured liquid. 'I feel like my own granny.'

'Vodka and fruit juice,' says Frank. 'Or rum and a mixer. Don't you go to the pub?'

'Oh,' says Louisa. 'Right. No, I don't go to the pub. Don't have anyone to go with. Well, I didn't,' she simpers at him. 'Until now.' She resumes her eyeballing of our fellow clubbers. 'And why do all these people look so vacant? Are they all on drugs? I can't even understand what they're saying.'

'Some of them are on drugs,' Frank says. 'Not all. Most of them just look like that all the time.'

'People don't make much of an effort any more, do they?' she continues. 'I mean, in my day, when we used to go to a nightclub, we really, really glammed up – took us hours to get ready. Especially when I was a Goth.'

'What?' I say.

'Especially when I was a Goth.'

'You were a Goth?' asks Frank.

'Yes.' Lou shrugs impatiently. 'And it took ages to get ready, as I was saying – all that panstick, and then the hair. But all these girls are in jeans and T-shirts.'

'Glamorous jeans and T-shirts,' I say. 'And it's not like

they buy their trainers at Asda. I know what you mean, though. It's hardly an ocean of beauty and style, is it, that dance floor? Mind you, I wouldn't call an ocean of Goths a thing of beauty either.'

Frank laughs.

'I wasn't a Goth for very long,' says Louisa. 'Anyway, all I was saying was that a little sequin here or there wouldn't go amiss. Oh, but I did used to like dressing up. Nobody's properly dressed up in here. Except you, Stella.'

'By mistake,' I say. 'It stupidly didn't occur to me that we'd end up at a club. I'd have worn something more comfortable if I'd known. Like a long black coat and a pair of fangs to make you feel at home, Vampyra.'

Lou makes a face and sticks out her tongue.

I'm still in the belted pink velvet coat, and getting rather hot. But getting up and exposing half an acre of flesh would immediately mark me out as some tragic granny on the pull, I feel, in this environment, so the coat stays firmly on.

More drinks arrive, as does a discreet little paper wrap of cocaine, courtesy of Yungsta, slipped into my hand by an improbably wholesome-looking character in a hat.

'Gosh,' I say to Frank and Lou. 'We seem to have scored.'

Frank looks at my clenched hand in an I-can-take-it-or-leave-it sort of way. 'What is it?'

'Charlie,' I say, quoting the hatted man. 'Couple of grams, he said, which if I remember rightly is quite a lot. Do you want some?'

'You don't know where it's come from,' says Louisa. 'It could be bad stuff, and then you'd be dead or handicapped for life. I've never touched it, myself.'

'Don't be so melodramatic,' I tell her. 'I'm sure it's not bad. Presumably this is the resident dealer, and he seems to know Adrian. Well, what shall I do with it, if you don't want it? I don't take drugs either.'

'Come off it,' says Frank. 'I can't believe that.'

'When have you ever known me to take drugs?'

'Never, but that's because you're always at home.'

'Well, I have a theory about old people taking drugs. I think it sucks, and so I don't do it.'

'How long's it been?' asks Frank.

'About ten years. More, I think. Do you want some?'

'I'll have a line, yeah,' says Frank. 'Pass it over here. God, I can't believe I'm here with a couple of puritans.'

Louisa sips her champagne. 'I'm not a puritan,' she says, giving Frank a very smouldery, dirty look and putting her hand high up on his thigh.

'No?' says Frank casually.

'No,' I pipe up helpfully, not liking the look on either of their faces. 'She was a Goth.'

'No,' echoes Louisa, and then she grabs his head and kisses him. With tongues. For ages. In front of me. Tongue, tongue, tongue. He kisses her back, too. Lick, probe, lick, slowly, repeatedly, and then she starts sort of eating his face. It amazes me to watch this, but watch I do, gripped, appalled, horrified.

Then I snatch the little white envelope of coke off the table and stand up. Frank has the courtesy to look up and mutter, 'Where are you going?'

'To take drugs.'

Frank pulls back from Louisa for a second, to rest his tongue muscles. He has the horrible look on his face of a man with a stiffy. 'But you've just said you never take drugs.'

'I've changed my mind. Total U-turn. See you.'

And I wander off, the envelope in my hand, in search of a loo.

When I'm a safe distance away, I turn back and look at them. Louisa's head is cradled in Frank's arm. They're still at it hammer and, um, tongues.

15

The nightclub is enormous – disorientatingly so – and try as I might, I can't seem to locate a Ladies on the ground floor, though there must be one: I just go round and round in circles, feeling lost and rather panicky. The place is getting packed and the music is pounding louder than before: heavy insistent beats with no melody, bang bang bang, louder and louder, making your entire body vibrate. Adrian mentioned something called 'deep Belgian house' at dinner: perhaps this is it. If so, can't say I think much of it.

I decide to try upstairs and wind my way up a metal staircase. More crowds of people are on the first floor, leaning over a balcony area, looking down on the dance floor, on which everyone is dancing exactly as though they were monkeys. The number of people present, and the anxiety it provokes, make me wonder whether I am in fact suffering from an advanced form of claustrophobia: I'm not used to feeling like a sardine, and I don't like it – the Bains Douches, surely, was never this bad. I keep walking, if you can call squeezing past people 'walking', up another staircase leading to the second floor, where I find what I overhear being referred to as a 'chill room'. The music here is certainly kinder to my ears – it's a sort of poshed-up whale music that reminds me of natural childbirth and thus, unpleasantly, of playgroup – but there are still too many people, all of them seemingly paired off, all of them nearly young enough to be my children, all of them looking a) not entirely on the ball and b) at me as though I were a curiosity. Which I expect I am. And I still can't find a loo.

There is a third staircase, smaller, leading to the third floor, so I take it. Unfortunately, there's a bouncer at the top: a blonde drag queen, statuesque in her glittery heels, impossibly long-legged, with enormous, darkly outlined lips, silver false eyelashes and giant pink pointy nails. 'Yeeeess?' she growls.

'I'm looking for the Ladies.'

'Well, here I am, honey,' she smiles coldly.

'The loo, I mean. The lavs. The toilets.'

'Downstairs. Second floor. This bit's members only. Sorry, love,' she drawls, not looking sorry at all and already looking past me.

'Members?' I pun cringingly. 'You could have fooled me, dressed like that.'

She allows me one small, unamused smile.

'What happens up here, then?' I persevere. I have this very bad character trait: the minute someone tells me that something is forbidden to me, I want that something more than anything else. It's very childish.

'This bit's for homos,' she explains. 'Our tiny refuge. Seeing as your lot overrun the club every Friday night.'

'Those drongos? They're not my lot. Please let me in.'

'You,' says the drag queen, 'are not a homo. Go on,' she adds, but not unkindly now. She looks as bored as I am. 'Hop it.'

'Oh, please. I'm so bored down here. And I hate the music and the crowds. I think I may be claustrophobic. And my friends are snogging each other. At least you look about my age. And anyway,' I scramble wildly for something appropriate to say, 'I'm thinking of exploring lesbianism any day now.'

'You and some pierced bulldyke from Stokey?' she says, painted-on eyebrow arched, looking me up and down for the first time. 'I don't think so, love. Not in that faaabulous coat.'

'Well, it's just an idea,' I concede. 'But put that way, it doesn't sound wildly appealing, I must say.'

She actually laughs at this, so I continue, encouraged, 'Look, I'm telling you so that you feel some sense of gayness coming from me, and so that you let me in, please.'

'Hmm,' she says.

'Go on,' I say. 'I love drag. I love cabaret too. My father took me to see drag shows from the age of twelve onwards. In Paris. I loved them. I'll feel right at home. *Please* let me in.'

'Go on, then,' she sighs, smiling quite warmly. 'And the lav's on the left, all the way down.'

I beam happily. 'Thanks,' I say. 'Thank you so much.' I walk away, but then walk back to her. 'Would you like some cocaine?' I suggest, to show my appreciation. 'I've got heaps of it.'

'Heaven,' she says, now all smiles, 'must have sent down an angel. Don't mind if I do. I'm Regina Beaver, by the way. And I love your coat, Miss French.'

'Stella.'

Regina leads the way. The third floor is smaller, more compact than the previous two, and filled with squishy sofas and soft lighting. There aren't many people up here – not as many as downstairs, anyway – and it is actually, blissfully, possible to walk without bumping into anyone.

'Why are you in a place that you hate with a load of coke?' says Regina, gliding regally through the little crowd, issuing greetings left, right and centre.

'Well, my date is DJing downstairs and, as I was telling you, my other two friends are snogging each other.'

'Holy Virgin,' says Regina. 'Do you go out with Yungsta? So called. I happen to know he's at least forty-one.'

'Not go out, no. We had a date.'

'I can do all of that, you know,' Regina says. 'With the hands. Watch.'

There is a chandelier on her right, and an expanse of wall by her side. 'Look,' says Regina. She folds and bends her fingers, the light shining. The shadow of a dog appears on the wall. 'Yo! Homie! Don't fuck with ma bitch,' Regina says, voice-perfect.

I start giggling helplessly.

'I can do ducks, too,' Regina says, demonstrating. 'I reckon all that hand-signalling is really a very competitive way of letting your "crew" know you can do the tricky ones, like Da Antelope or Da Wolf.'

I am actually snorting with laughter as Regina continues her display, forgetting the shadow-play now and just concentrating on saying 'Yo' and turning her fingers into da rabbit and da fox. 'Come on, girlfriend,' says Regina, herself laughing like a drain. She has a really rough, raspy voice. 'We are toilet bound.'

'Do you know him, then?' I ask, trotting after her and feeling small to the point of midgethood – she must be at least six foot four in her heels.

'Oh, yes,' she says. 'Here's the toilet.' She looks me up and down. 'Wouldn't have thought he was your type.'

We wedge ourselves into a tiny, pee-scented cubicle.

'Line them up, girl,' says Regina.

'Could you? I haven't done this for ages.'

Regina does, expertly, with the help of my Sainsbury's Reward Card ('Oh, will you look at that. We're not in Kansas any more, are we, Toto?'). Regina snorts up a couple of fat lines, while I content myself with a smaller single one. Everything Regina says makes me die laughing: I honk like a seal every time she opens her filthy mouth. I must bring Papa here, I think to myself – he'd love it.

We trot back to the top of the stairs.

'Through there,' says Regina. 'That's the piano bar. I think you'll like it. I'm doing a turn myself in ten minutes, so I'll see you then. Tell Kevin behind the bar that you're with me.'

I part the dirty curtains – ooh! missus! – and sigh with pleasure. *This* is more like it. I'm in a smallish, square room, redly lit, with a mini-stage at the front, five or six tables in front of it and a general bar-cum-milling area at the back. There's a piano by the stage, a baby grand, which a balding, middle-aged man is playing. Another drag queen, this one in green sequins and a black beehive, is draped across the piano, singing. The words – some fabulous old torch-song about her man doing her wrong – send goosebumps racing down my arms. I am in heaven. If all nightclubs were like this, I'd be in one every night.

I actually beam with happiness, like a simpleton. Everyone else in the room – a mixture of all sorts of men, young, middle-aged, old, fat, thin, plain, lovely and a couple of women (female guests, presumably, are allowed) – seems to be beaming too. There's a friendly buzz of chatter and a sense of anticipation. I walk over to the bar and introduce myself to Kevin – an enormously fat, barrel-chested skinhead – who pours me a double gin and tonic and waves away my money.

A man appears on the stage. We're having half an hour of singing from 'our resident goddesses', after which we're all allowed a go. I down my G&T in two gulps. I briefly wonder about Adrian, and Frank, and Louisa downstairs, and then push them out of my mind. One's working, and the other two are making tongue sandwiches. It's no fun. This, though – now *this* is fun.

Regina reappears and introduces me to Miss Chastity Butt and the Hon. Fellatia Lipps, her fellow artistes (drag queens, I notice with some sorrow, seem to have the monopoly on amazing legs), and to a sweet man called Barry, who apparently comes here every night. I like them so much I offer them my coke too, and take a second line myself, and then a third. There's still masses left, and after an hour of listening to their singing – all my favourites, plus some I didn't know – I am in such a spectacularly good mood that I offer my coke to every other person I speak to, which is to say half a dozen people. In return, they buy me more of Kevin's giant G&Ts. By the time the floor show starts, I am hysterical with happiness. And, possibly, drugs and alcohol.

I must have been right about Regina being roughly my age, because the bulk of the floor show concerns itself with the Eighties. It's not really a 'show' as such, more a series of performers – the girls, and later on members of the audience – stepping up to the microphone and camply bellowing out a classic, accompanied by the man on the baby grand.

It would be fair to say that I am flying by this time, and

so when Regina nudges me and asks me to go up and do a duet with her, I want to kiss her. I love Regina, I love the piano bar at Fist, I love 'Prince Charming' by Adam Ant, which Fellatia has just performed magnificently, and I love, love, love my life at this moment.

'Come on, then, miss,' says Regina, taking my hand. 'Let's show them how it's done.'

'What shall we sing?'

Regina looks me up and down. 'You seem like the sort of girl who knows her Judy Garland,' she says. 'Are you?'

'Well, Regina, yes – *obviously*. By heart, actually. But isn't it, you know, a bit of a cliché? Sing Judy to the poofs? Follow it up with a bit of Barbra Streisand?'

'It may be a cliché, but, darling – who doesn't love a bit of Judy of an evening?'

'Not me,' I say happily. 'I love a bit of Judy three times a day.'

'Exactly,' says Regina. 'Let's go. Do you know "You Made Me Love You"?'

'Every word.'

'That's my girl,' Regina growls. 'Come on.'

We clamber up on to the side of the stage. 'Look at the knockers on that,' says the compere as I take off my coat.

I am, it must be said, looking a little the worse for wear. My hair, for instance, has collapsed: the *soigné* chignon of two hours ago is just a messy mass of curls, and my tits are indeed falling out somewhat.

'And here, ladies and gentlemen, for your delectation, are Miss Regina Beaver and friend.'

Since half the audience have sampled my drug wares, we get a rapturous reception. The audience, small as it is, whistles, stamps its feet, whoops.

'*You made me love you*,' Regina starts. '*I didn't wanna do it, I didn't wanna do it.*'

'*You made me love you*,' I continue, '*and all the time you knew it, I guess you always knew it.*'

I am a natural. I am a born entertainer, I think to myself. Suck my dick, Judy Garland, I think, except I say it out loud, much to the audience's delight. Haa! I love my time. Could anybody's time be better than this? Regina and I have got a crap dance routine perfected: we twirl around, pulling Judy-faces, camping it up for all it's worth. The bliss of not having to be cool in a nightclub! The fun of not pouting!

Oh, and look: Frankie. Frankie's here. This seems almost miraculous: I left him three floors down, in another world. There's Louisa, looking worried, following him. I see them before they see me. I decide to dedicate the rest of the song to Frank, who has sweetly come to join in my fun. What a pal. *What* a pal. He is weaving his way through the crowd, looking left and right, looking everywhere, in fact, except up at the stage.

'*You made me love you*,' Regina starts again.

We're nearing the end of the song: time to give it some welly. I join in with the end of the chorus, looking straight at Frank, who has finally clocked me and is shaking his head, smiling. I give it, as they say, all I've got. The rhythm changes, and I decide to go for a little shimmy from the hips as I sing to Frank.

> '*Gimme gimme gimme what I cry for*
> (leery wink – returned by Frank)
> *You know you've got the kind of kisses that I die for*
> (thrust – Frank blows kiss)

You know you made meeeeee love yooooooooo
(total collapse: I am hysterical with laughter).'

The crowd, who have been singing along, go mad. Regina and I drop into deep curtsies. Clap clap clap, whoop, go the audience, more. I really think I missed my vocation.

'We can do another later, if you like, after the disco,' says Regina. 'You can be my bitch for the night.' She high-fives me, gives Da Rabbit, and totters off to find her pals. I stand by the stage, drenched in sweat and feeling somewhat dizzy, but in a good way. I'd rather like Regina to be my mother, I think to myself. Pity she's a man. Still, there's always Papa.

'Stella!' says Louisa. 'We've been looking everywhere for you.'

'Have you? Well, here I am. Ta-daa!'

'We thought you might have gone home,' says Louisa reproachfully. 'We were worried.'

'Why on earth would I go home? I just got bored,' I tell them playfully, poking each in the tummy in turn, 'of watching the pair of you suck face. Suck suck suck. Yuck.'

'Adrian was looking for you too,' Lou continues. 'In the break between his sets.'

'I'm up here,' I tell her. 'Here I am. Spread the word. But don't spread your legs.' Oops. Where did that come from?

'My nan would love you,' says Frank. 'You'd be a laugh down the pub. I didn't have you down as a chantoose.'

'*Chanteuse*,' I correct. 'Well, you were wrong. I *chante* away. Will you *chante* with me, Frankie?' I curl an arm around his waist. 'Go on. You know you want to. Go on, Frankie,' I whisper in his ear. 'You're gagging for it, *gagging*.'

Frank smiles his cryptic smile at me again. We are standing extremely close.

'We are standing extremely close,' I tell Frank meaningfully.

'Hot lady,' he says, which breaks us up.

'Can we go back downstairs now?' says Louisa. 'It's better down there. What are you, Stella, some kind of fag hag?'

'Better than that, Lou. I am in fact a fag,' I bellow. 'I am trapped, trapped, *trapped* in this body, but really underneath I am 100 per cent pure poof. Like father like daughter. I am an homo.'

'You had the coke,' says Frank, grinning.

'Hey, Einstein. Do you know what? I did. And I have revised my opinion of drug taking. Want some?'

'Come on, babe,' says Louisa. 'Are you OK up here on your own, Stell?'

I don't like the 'babe'. The 'babe', I don't like.

'Stay, Frankie,' I tell him, looking straight into his eyes. 'Sing with me.'

'I think we'd better stay a while,' he tells Louisa. 'She's completely off her face.'

'I am *not*. I am a little bit cheerful, but you should be pleased. A little bit. *Une petite bite.* One day I'll tell you what that means in French. Come on, Frankie, don't stand there like my grandad. Let's dance.'

Frankie shrugs at Louisa, who stomps off to the bar, and allows himself to be led by the hand to the tiny, packed dance floor.

We dance to 'Enola Gay' by OMD, 'It Ain't What You Do' by Bananarama, 'You Spin Me Round' by Dead or Alive (which I especially love: *watch out, here I come*, I explain to Frank, could be a lyric made for him), 'Don't Go' by Yazoo and 'The Look of Love' by ABC. We dance our arses off, in stitches half the time as one or the other of us remembers some long-forgotten little dance routine. And then it's a slowie – 'True' by Spandau Ballet – and suddenly here is Louisa, snaking herself around Frank, while I slink back to the bar.

Only one slowie, though. And then, oh joy – and do please forgive me my exaggerated sense of kitsch – it is, grotesquely, splendidly, fabulously, Agadoo time. Clearly, much of the assembled crowd considers this one irony too far, but I leap across the room and back on to the dance floor, grabbing Barry-who-comes-here-every-night on the way. Barry, in turn, grabs the Hon. Fellatia Lipps, and the three of us tumble on to the dance floor.

And that is how Yungsta finds me: I am pushing pine-apple, shaking tree with a fat middle-aged man and a seen-better-days drag queen, pouring with sweat, more or less hysterical with laughter.

'Stella?' he says.

'Yo,' I say. 'King kickin' in da area.' I howl with laughter at my own joke. My time downstairs wasn't entirely wasted: these things clearly seep into your head by osmosis.

'I bin lookin' for ya, man,' Yungsta says. He is standing by the edge of the dance floor. I am still *on* the dance floor, because I need to shake the tree one more time before the song ends.

I smile pleasantly at Yungsta, who's come all this way to get me – bless – and snog me, probably. Unfortunately, maintaining eye contact with him, I notice he's not looking too chirpy: incandescent would be a better description, also disgusted. I also notice that, clothing-wise, he looks *absolutely absurd*. I've noticed it before, obviously, but not so violently. Looking at him now, Mr Forty-one-year-old DJ Yungsta, it becomes as clear as glass that there is no point whatsoever in pretending to myself that I fancy him, because I simply don't. Not unless he were to ditch all the clobber, and the facial hair, and the faux-accent. Not until, basically, he'd had a complete makeover, personality included, and how likely is that? And then he'd have to learn the art of conversation. So, no.

The song finishes.

'What da fuck are you doin', man?' asks Yungsta.

'Dancing.'

'That ain't dancin',' he spits.

'It is to me,' I reply politely, though I don't think much of his tone.

'I came lookin for ya,' he says.

'Well, you found me.'

'You look mingin',' he says.

I don't know what this means, but I don't like the sound of it.

'And what's with da battyboys?'

'So sorry. Was having a good time.'

'Where da snow?' Yungsta demands. 'Where da snow, man?'

'In the cold clouds in the sky,' I reply.

'My coke,' he hisses.

'Oh. I thought it was *my* coke, so I shared it.'

'Where is it?'

'Up these nice people's noses. There's a tiny bit left, I

think. Sorry. I didn't realize it wasn't mine. Have some money, and then you can get some more.'

'Man,' says Yungsta. 'You is dumped.'

'MC Yungsta on da wheels of steel,' bellows Regina, who has arrived by my side. 'Make some noiiiise.' She does Da Fox at me, and nearly sets me off again.

'Gerroff, man,' says Yungsta.

'Adrian's a homophobe,' explains Regina. 'Never comes up here. Thinks he might get diseases.'

'I is not goin' out with a lady that does that,' Yungsta explains to me. 'I is a top DJ.'

'Cut the crap, will you,' I say, 'and speak normally, Adrian.'

'You are so dumped,' he says, looking at me as though I were a poo on the sole of his shoe. 'You have no class. You have no taste. I can't *possibly* go out with you. I have my reputation . . .'

'To maintain,' says Regina, in an incredibly posh comedy voice. 'That's right, Aidey, you do. Now leave, before I kiss you.'

'Don't worry, freak. I'm outta here,' Adrian, my nearly-man, says nastily. And off he goes.

'I think,' says Frank, 'that this is probably quite a good time to go home.'

16

As soon as I am capable of thought the next morning – which takes a while, since at first I am only capable of sickness – my thoughts are as follows.

My first thought is, obviously, that I feel incredibly crap, especially around the jaw and sinuses, and that I am too old for this. My second, more troubling, thought is that I am an unfit parent. My third thought – the thought that makes me sit bolt upright, and then sink down again when I realize its full implications – is to wonder whether Louisa is here. Whether Louisa slept here. With Frank. In bed. Make fucky. Jiggy-jig. Humpty-hump. Oh, God.

It's funny how it is possible to have moments of absolute lucid clarity when your head and your body are such poor, befuddled things. And I have such a moment right now: I know, crystal-clearly, that I don't want Louisa to have slept with Frank. No no no: I don't want it.

I groan, and slide back under the covers to think. Ten minutes later, I'm no less troubled, but at least I know what I have to do. It's time to get up.

I can't quite remember how the night ended. I just about remember falling through the front door, and then Frank half carrying, half pulling me up the stairs. I think I remember Frank putting me to bed; at least, I remember him looking down at me, for ages. Did he undress me? Somebody did: Louisa, perhaps – I'm wearing a T-shirt, not the little black dress. And then I don't remember anything: for once, I didn't fall asleep listening to Frank having sex.

But that doesn't mean he didn't have any. Did he have sex? I must know. It's urgent.

I heave my shaky legs out of the bed and sit, feeling queasy. There's a bottle of Evian on the little bedside table and I drink half a litre. What's the time? Where are Honey and Mary? Did Frank get laid, did Lou?

Maybe she went home. She was looking pretty pissed off when we were dancing. Maybe she came back here, undressed me and went home. She must have gone home, because what about her baby-sitter? Or did her baby-sitter stay the night, like Mary?

I manage to stand upright without hurling, find and pull on a pair of red flannel pyjama bottoms and a clean T-shirt, and stagger into the bathroom to brush my teeth. No sleazeball condoms floating in the lav, which is a good sign. I realize that the T-shirt I slept in was Frank's – what does *that* mean? Did he take it off there and then, kindly, or were he and Louisa so busy getting sexy that they started taking their clothes off the minute we got back home? Did they get half-naked *before* he helped me upstairs? Did they pre-shag gruntily while I was lying there in a comatose heap? Not that I remember, granted, but I don't quite trust my memory this morning: there are huge gaps, like the journey home.

I blow my nose, and blow again, and still it doesn't feel better. The house is absolutely quiet. I splash some cold water on to my face and go downstairs. Quiet, quiet. No Honey, no Mary, no no one.

'Morning,' says Frank. He is sitting at the kitchen table

eating a piece of toast and wearing a clean grey T-shirt with arms, and a purple T-shirt on top of that. I look around the room for Louisa – everywhere, even in the broom cupboard – and when I don't find her, I scan the garden through the French doors.

'Lost something?' says Frank. 'And do you want some tea?'

'Where's Lou?' I croak.

'Lou? Search me. Home, I expect.'

Oh, thank God. Oh, thank Mary and Joseph and all the saints and you, lovely lovely baby Jesus. Thank you. *Thank you.*

'And Honey?'

'On the Heath with Mary. They're having lunch at Kenwood House and then Mary's taking her to the party of some kid from playgroup – Perdita, is it?'

'What's the time?'

'Just after twelve.'

'My head. Been up long?'

'A while. Some evening, eh?'

I nod, and pad over to the fridge for the milk.

'I always had you down as a sophisticated type,' says Frank.

'I have hidden depths. Hidden shallows, rather.'

'You were great,' he laughs. 'I love all of that myself. Oh, and I'm sorry it didn't work out with the DJ.'

'Don't be.'

I take a sip of tea; it hurts me to swallow.

'Are you really sorry?' I ask him.

'Yeah, of course.'

I put my cup down, spilling Earl Grey everywhere.

'Really, Frank? Really? Why?'

'What?'

'Why are you so, *so* sorry?'

'I'm not so, *so* sorry,' he smiles. 'But if you liked him, then I'm sorry, you know, that it didn't work out.'

'Frankie,' I say, 'we need to talk.'

'Talk away.'

Time seems to be of the essence. I don't really have time to beat about the bush, and besides, my chronic hangover means I can't think of a delicate way of phrasing what I need to say.

'I think,' I tell him, holding my head in my hands, 'that I fancy you.'

Frankie spits out a great big splurt of tea.

'*What?*' he says, looking at me hard. 'What did you say?'

'I said, I think that I fancy you. Amazing, but true. Take me, Frankie.'

'Don't bugger about,' says Frank irritably. 'Christ's sake, Stell.'

'I am not buggering about,' I protest. 'I mean it. I fancy you. I don't know why. So take me.'

'Stop saying "take me", will you?' says Frank.

'This is wrong,' I say, feeling a bit huffy. 'You're supposed to leap over the table and tongue me.'

'Stella! Will you stop pissing about, you mardy cow?'

'Look, I'm not feeling very articulate this morning. But it's been building up for a while. I didn't see it coming – it's taken me by surprise too. But I really, really like you. I have the best time with you. You make me laugh. And never mind about the rest. I'm not saying, let's get married, Frank. But I *am* saying, let's go to bed.'

'What do you mean, "never mind about the rest"?'

'I think we both know what I'm talking about. And you

see, I must really like you a lot, because to me that kind of thing is unoverlookable.'

'I don't know what you're talking about, Stell,' says Frank, looking bewildered. 'None of it. I don't understand a word.'

'Forget the other thing. I'm saying, do you think we could go out? Have a proper date and then, you know, go to bed? Tonight, maybe? Or, um, now?'

Frank sighs, and runs his hands through his hair.

'No,' he says. He has really beautiful eyes, and he is looking at me all softly and sadly. 'Stell, is this one of your jokes? Tell me.'

'I am completely serious.'

'Then I am very flattered, but the answer's no.'

'No?'

'No. I can't.' He reaches over and strokes my face, just once, with his thumb.

'I thought maybe you fancied me a bit too,' I say. I try and give a casual laugh. 'On account of me having a vagina. And secondary sexual characteristics.'

'I . . .' says Frank, sounding strangled.

'But never mind,' I lie grossly. 'I think I'll go and have a bath now. And then maybe ring Lou. Meet up for lunch. Or something.' My voice fades away. I need to get out of the kitchen, because I'm going to cry.

'Stella,' says Frank. 'Don't go.'

'I feel all grubby,' I say. 'Need a bath.' I clear my throat. 'Sorry about that. Guess I misread everything. Sorry, Frankie. I didn't mean to embarrass you.'

'Lou's coming over,' he says.

'Oh. When?'

'She just went home to change. I said I'd take her to

lunch.' He is looking straight at me, and his face is white. He shrugs helplessly.

I actually feel weak about the knees, like in an old film. I feel faint.

'You . . . you slept together?'

'Yeah,' says Frank.

'Was she a dirty ride?' My eyes are welling up like a baby's. I have to get out of here.

'Don't, Stella.' He reaches for my arm. 'Come here.'

'Don't touch me,' I yell, like a maniac. And I run upstairs.

Well, that was magnificently handled, was it not? Well done, Stella. Bravo. Now what? Oh, God, how embarrassing. How *excruciating*. How desperate.

Bloody Louisa. I know Frank is so feeble that he can't say no (except, evidently, to me), but she should have known better. She's my friend. My only friend, really. How could she go and jeopardize a thing like our new, lovely, happy friendship for a bloody shag from bloody Frank, who is bloody ginger and has a bloody family buried away somewhere and fucks everything that moves, not including me? And it's not as though I didn't warn her.

Of course, she did ask me if I minded a couple of times . . . Well, she should have known. If she's my friend, she should have known that I was hardly likely to turn around and say, 'Actually, I do mind.' Of course you say you don't mind, just as in England you say, 'I couldn't possibly,' before helping yourself to thirds of pudding. It doesn't mean it's true. A proper friend would have recognized that. Which means she isn't a proper friend. Which means I am friendless and alone, alone, all all alone. If this bath were a sea, I'd swim away from all this with Honey on my back, like a sea-cow or manatee. I'd swim to kinder shores. Oh, fuck. What's going to happen now?

There goes the door. I can't skulk up here, hiding, in my own house. I get out of the bath, reluctantly, and throw on my clothes again. I have to go and face them now, otherwise I might as well hole myself up here for ever.

It takes all the courage I can muster, though. Frank and Louisa are standing in the middle of the living room, by the yellow sofa. She looks blissfully, deliriously happy, and I realize I can't really be angry with her; he's looking at her sort of quizzically, as though he can't quite believe that she exists.

'Stella!' she beams. 'Have you slept it off yet?'

I grunt a greeting and nod.

'What a night! *What* a night! We're just off to lunch now.'

I grunt again, and bend down to pick up bits of Honey's tea-set off the floor.

'I saw Adrian as I was leaving the flat. He wasn't looking too happy.'

'I is fed up with him,' I say. 'I is not wantin' to be his bitch.'

This elicits a wan smile from Frank, which makes a nice change, as ever since I came downstairs he has been looking at me as though I were ill, with a puzzled expression that really sticks in the craw and makes me furious.

'Will you join us?' asks Louisa. 'We're just going down the road, to the pub that Frankie says does nice food. The Duke of something.'

'Cambridge,' says Frank. 'Stell?'

'No thanks,' I say. 'Can't quite face it.'

'Well, you know where we are if you change your mind,'

says Louisa, who is bouncing around the room like Tigger, so happy that she doesn't seem to notice my somewhat surly, offhand manner. Frank goes off into the hall to find his jacket, and she suddenly hurls herself at me, raising two thumbs right into my face.

'What, Lou? Fandabidozi?'

'Well, yes,' she whispers. 'You said I wouldn't get a second date, but look, here I am.'

'I'm very pleased for you.'

'Not as pleased as me, Stell. Last night was . . . well, it was just *fantastic*. He . . .'

'Spare me the details, Lou.'

'But he was so amazing. He . . .'

'Better than Thomas the Tank?'

'Yeah,' she grins. 'You could say that.'

'Probably more practised,' I nod. 'Though who knows?'

'Come on,' says Frank. 'Let's go. See you later, Stell. Will you be OK?'

'Why shouldn't I be? I'm not ill, Frank. I just feel a bit crap. It'll pass.'

'Yeah,' says Frank. 'It will. See you later.'

I go back to bed for the rest of the afternoon and emerge at tea time feeling mighty refreshed. I cover Honey, not seen since last night, with tickly kisses, give her her bath, play tea-parties with her at enormous length, read her an extra-long bedtime story about a blue kangaroo, and tuck her up at seven o'clock. My baby. I love her more than anything.

'Fwankie?' she says, just before settling down. I promise he'll come and kiss her later.

Fwankie reappears about an hour later, alone. I am, as

usual, eating – a small, lonely bowl of noodles, in this instance – and he comes into the kitchen just as I am slurping up a particularly long tangle of strands. There's miso broth all down my chin.

'Do you want a drink?' says Frank, who doesn't look all that sober himself, interestingly. 'Hair of the dog. Might help you. Helps me. Here, have a napkin.' He tosses a piece of kitchen roll at me.

The idea of a drink makes me want to gag, but he has a point. I could drink myself into a stupor, like the tragic abandoned housewife I am, and then fall into bed and into a dreamless, Frankless sleep. I wipe my chin.

'Why not? A glass of red, maybe. Where have you been?'

'In the pub,' says Frank.

'With your girlfriend.'

Frank doesn't smile; his jaw perceptibly tightens.

'Whatever,' he says. 'Something like that.'

'With your girlfriend of love,' I say sadly, except it comes out more facetious.

Frank sighs, does the thing with his jaw again and stares at me greyly.

'Don't look at me like that, please. You look like a wife-beater.' And you probably are, I add to myself. 'Like you might raise your hand to me.'

'Here's your wine.'

'I'm going to drink it on the sofa. Are you coming? As the Louisa said to the Frankie.'

'I am,' says Frank, allowing himself one unamused little smile.

I curl up on the sofa, pulling a fleecy throw off the back to cover myself in and rearranging the cushions for maximum nestiness. The sofa is one of those outsize numbers, so that although Frank joins me on it, our limbs don't touch: there's a good couple of feet between us. He perches a massive tumbler of neat whisky on the sofa arm and reaches for the television remote.

'Where's Louisa, then?' I ask, like a broken record. I can't help myself.

'At home with Alexander. What do you want to watch? A movie?'

'Anything soothing. Why aren't you there with her?'

'Because I'm here with you. Can you shut up about it now, Stell?'

'Not really,' I say, hoping he'll admire my honesty – slim chance of this, though, looking at his thunderous face: he looks almost scary. I take a sip of wine, he takes a massive gulp of Scotch and flicks through the channels, looking angry. 'I need to know, Frank. I need to make plans.'

'Why?'

'I just do. I need to prepare myself mentally. Is she going to be here all the time?'

Frank rubs his face. 'I don't know. How the fuck would I know? Bloody hell,' he says. 'Look at that.'

'What?' I look up at the television: we're on Cartoon Network. 'It's just Betty Boop.'

'You missed the title. Guess what it's called?'

'Don't know.'

'*The Bum Bandit*. Does that count?'

'Rispeck, Frankie,' I say. 'I didn't know about that one. Very good.'

Frank laughs and presses the 'I' for Information button on the satellite remote. '1931,' he says. 'It's about a train robbery.'

'That goes straight into the top ten, though I still think

Unlawful Entry occupies the number-one slot, don't you?'

'Definitely *Dark Passage*, for me.'

'Speaking of which . . .'

'Leave it.'

'Speaking of which . . .'

'I said, leave it.'

'I'm not asking for a blow by blow account, Frank. I just want to know if . . . if your intentions are honourable.'

'What are you now, the father of the bride as well as the matchmaker?' He takes another huge glug of whisky.

'What do you mean, the bride? Are, are, are you planning on *marrying* her?' I feel as though I've been punched in the stomach.

'Don't be thick, Stell. I was joking.'

'Are you going to keep on living here?' I'm so relieved by the non-marriage news that I finish my wine and stretch out a bit. 'Do you mind if my feet are on you?'

'Live here? Yeah. Unless you don't want me to,' Frank says, which seems a bit melodramatic to me.

'Look, I just offered you a shag. And you turned me down. Fair enough. Mad of you, but fair enough. It doesn't mean I am carrying an enormous torch and am going to stagger around the house weeping, you know.' I won't have Frank walking about coatlessly, on his long legs, pitying me. 'So living here is probably safe,' I say sarcastically. 'I might just be able to control myself. Just.'

'I know,' says Frank.

'I wasn't planning on proposing to you.'

'I know,' says Frank.

'Or on having ginger children with you.'

'I get the picture,' says Frank, raising a hand.

'I just wondered what it would be like if we shagged.'

'*OK*,' says Frank. 'Shut it. I understand.'

We sit in silence for five minutes: is it my imagination, or has the air thickened?

'Why did you really want me to shag you?' says Frank.

''Scuse me?'

'Why did you want a fuck from me?' He sounds much more northern than he did five minutes ago, and it's not just the air that's thickened, it's his voice, too.

'Why not?' I reply breezily. 'Everybody else has had one. I feel a bit left out.'

Frank tuts exasperatedly.

'Well, it's true,' I lie.

'Don't you see,' says Frank, 'that it would ruin everything?'

'I don't, actually,' I reply, still keeping my voice airy and carefree. 'As I say, I wasn't planning on marrying you.'

Frank is facing me, sucking in his cheeks and looking flintier than ever. I meet his eyes for a second, and then look down again, because – sorry to be crude – the look in them practically makes me come. Frank drains his glass and wipes his mouth with the back of his hand.

'Go on, then,' he says.

'Go on, what?'

'Let's go.'

'Where?'

'Upstairs,' he says, getting up. 'To fuck.'

'No thanks,' I say, with extraordinary restraint. 'I don't want a pity-fuck.'

'It's not a pity-fuck. Come on.'

'Well, if it's not a pity-fuck, then judging by the look on your face, it's a hate-fuck. So thanks, but, you know, no thanks.'

'What the fuck's a hate-fuck?'

'When you hate the person so much you have to sleep with them. It's fucked up. I used to do it quite often at university.'

'Oh, yeah, I've had those,' says Frank. 'Terrible. But often quite good at the time. The sex, I mean.'

'Exactly. Awkward to share one's house with the hate-fuckee, though, so as I was saying, no thanks.'

'I've always fancied you,' says Frank. 'Since the day I met you. Since Paris. It wouldn't be a hate-fuck. Come on.'

'No.'

'I don't fucking *believe* you,' says Frank. 'What are you, some fucking schizo?'

'What about Lou?'

Frank sighs. 'What about her, Stell?'

'She wouldn't like it.'

'No, I don't expect she would. Will you tell her, or shall I?'

'You, Frank, are a pig bastard.'

'I am *not* a pig bastard,' he says. 'I am offering you the shag you claim you want.'

'Poor Louisa. She's going out with a pig bastard.' I really like saying 'pig bastard' to Frank.

'We're not "going out". She threw herself at me. And you stood there and pushed her into my bed, more or less. What did you expect me to do?'

'Fuck her,' I shrug.

'Exactly. Which is what I did. And then she bugged me to take her out to lunch, so I did that too. Because she's your mate. So don't take the moral high ground with me. I'm not the one that flirted with me all last night to annoy her friend.'

He has a point, even though annoying my friend was only the half of it. There's only one thing left to say, really.

'OK,' I say, draining my glass. 'You win. Let's go.'

17

We get up in silence and go up the stairs in a mini-Indian file, with no physical contact whatsoever.

'Condoms?' I say.

'By the bed.' He opens the door to his bedroom, which he keeps very nice, I must say: all white and clean and stripped back, with – natch – a giant, outsize oak bed with cream linen sheets. One of the walls is pinned haphazardly with sketches of wild flowers.

'Are these sheets clean?' I ask conversationally, standing by the bed fully clothed.

'No.'

'I'm just going to brush my teeth,' I say. 'And take my clothes off.'

Frank holds his bedroom door open for me. He isn't smiling.

'Missing you already,' he drawls, which makes me laugh on the inside.

I brush, strip, put on an only vaguely sexy old kimono, and go back to Frank's bedroom. He is lying on the bed, stark naked. Very nice body, but I knew that already. Ginger hair: no problem. Hasn't been for some time, actually. He has a massive erection.

I stand by the edge of the bed, looking at him. He looks back.

'I feel this situation lacks romance,' I say.

'Come here,' says Frank, pulling me down.

*

Frank is very good at sex. Well, obviously: practice is supposed to make perfect. And his has. It *is* perfect, in a very hard, dirty, sweaty, explosive kind of way: we have the kind of sex that people usually describe as 'animal' but which I always think of to myself as more mammalian. We are mammals. He whispers a torrent of absolute filth in my ear: of what he would like to do to me, how he's going to do it, how long he's wanted to do it for, and so on. Unusually, this is incredibly horny-making. And all the while, he's doing it. Bang, bang, bang. This way, that way. I don't know about me, but he is certainly the dirtiest ride I've ever encountered.

I come twice; I see white dots of light; I shout, I think, at one point. He calls out my name – clever of him to remember – and presses his face into my hair as he comes.

And then we're lying there, panting, with all the lights on, at about nine o'clock on a Saturday night, in silence.

'Marry me,' says Frank. He sits up and reaches for a cigarette.

'Can you imagine? But we'd have a very happy sex life.'

'Yeah, we would.'

'You're very talented.'

'Cheers. You're not bad yourself.'

I brace myself. I roll on to my stomach and put my head on his stomach.

'Was I,' I ask, 'a dirty ride?'

Frank laughs. 'Not this again.'

'Come on, Frank. Was I? I was, wasn't I? I thought I might be. A filthy ride, probably. That's right, isn't it?'

'Here, do you want a drag?'

'Yes.'

'No, Stella, you weren't a dirty ride.'

I sit upright. I am outraged. *Outraged.*

'What are you, some kind of sicko? What more could I possibly have done to make myself dirtier? Bloody hell, Frank, you cunt. Give me that fag.'

Frank strokes my hair and laughs.

'I obviously didn't explain it properly that time. A dirty ride's a one-off. You know, a girl that's gagging for it and loves doing it. But you don't want to see her again. You don't want to dwell on her, really. She's just a dirty ride.'

'What am I, then? What does that make me?'

'You,' says Frank, taking the cigarette from my mouth, 'are a ride.'

'Is that a compliment?'

'Yeah.'

'Oh, good.' That's that settled. 'What shall we do now?'

'Don't tell me: I can guess. You're starving,' he laughs.

'How did you know? I am, actually. Famished. And don't say, "Do you like chicken? Suck this, it's fowl."'

Frank rolls his eyes. 'Let's go downstairs. I'll feed you.'

And he leans over and kisses me, very sweetly, on the forehead.

18

We ate cheese omelettes and drank more wine and then went to bed again. And then I fell asleep and woke up in Frank's arms, much to Honey's astonished delight the next morning. And then we got up on Sunday, wheeled the pushchair up to Primrose Hill, and had a brisk, red-nosed walk, the three of us, giggling at everything and nothing. I roasted a leg of lamb, and after lunch we lay on the sofa watching a video of *South Pacific*. And after Honey'd gone to bed on Sunday night, we did it again.

So that's all really romantic and charming, isn't it? Ad-o-rable. Like teddies and clouds and robins. We are those round-faced, round-bodied teddies you get on greeting cards. Boing boing, we go, bumping tummies, rosy-cheeked. I am wearing a little pink ribbon, and he a pale blue one. The robins are our friends. Come, robins, we cry. Perch on our teddy arms.

Except that things look dramatically different on a cold, rainy Monday morning when you wake up in your own bed (by mutual agreement: we were both really tired). There are problems, frankly. There are issues.

One, poor old Louisa has left three messages for Frank and one for me, and none of these have been returned.

Two, it's all very well to sit here musing about teddyhood and love's young dream, but one needs to be realistic: I had a fabulous time in bed with Frank, but that's just what Frank *does* – when he's not painting cows, he's giving people fabulous times in bed. And then he buggers off. Louisa's unanswered phone messages are merely the most recent in a long, tiresome line of plaintive voices wailing out of the answering machine. And so am I, the latest in a long line, though I am not wailing yet. That's because I am not deluded, or rather, because I am trying my hardest not to be deluded. I am the latest willing notch on the bedpost, I keep telling myself. I am a notch. A girl can dream, though . . .

No, she can't. And besides, I'm not a girl. I am a thirty-eight-year-old woman and I need to be realistic. I *am* a notch. All women are notches to Frankie. I need to think of him as a notch too – a notch on *my* bedpost. A lovely, wonderful, funny, clever, best-sex-ever notch who made cheese omelettes as though he were French and licked the toast crumbs off my lips, laughing, and then stopped laughing and . . .

But imagine, I tell myself, ignoring the stomach-ache of longing that the toast memory introduces. Imagine the gradual reintroduction of strange girls at breakfast. The awkwardnesses. The pretending not to mind.

I am a notch. I shall remain a notch. I need to make contingency notch plans, sharpish. And I wonder whether it would be really bad to do it one more time with Frank before, as they say, closure.

Frank's at the studio when the phone rings. I know it's Louisa. I pick it up, feeling a sort of terror.

'Stella! Where have you *been*?'

'Sorry I didn't ring you back. We, I, we, er, I had a busy kind of weekend.'

'Are you fully recovered?'

'From Friday night? Oh, yes.'

'Well, what are you up to?'

'Oh, this and that, you know.'

'I'm on my way to a client, but we could have a coffee, if you liked? Do you know the cottagey place in England's Lane?'

'The place that looks like it should be called Mrs Tiggy-winkle's?'

'Yes. See you there noon-ish?'

'OK. Bye, then.'

'Stella?' says Lou. 'How's Frank?'

This is a nightmare. What am I going to tell her?

'Fine, I think.'

'It's just, he hasn't phoned me.'

'No. Um. I haven't seen him today.'

'Oh, shit – I'm about to go into a tunnel. I have to go. We can talk about it later. See you at twelve.'

She hangs up, and I hang my head.

Louisa bounds into the coffee shop like a Labrador, shakes her blonde mane, boings herself down, beams, and asks me how it's going. *Oh, you know, fine, but (wince) bit sore when I sit down. Because I've spent the weekend in bed with the man you've set your sights on.*

'Fine.' I smile. I'm aware of the smile being strange, as though someone had betted me that I could show all my teeth. 'How about you?'

'A shop in South Molton Street is taking my hats, so I couldn't be better.'

'Where's Alex?'

'With his dad all week. Which means,' she beams, 'that the mouse is away. And that the cat will play.'

'Oh, right,' I say, taking a sip of my latte. 'What did you have in mind?'

'You know,' she giggles. 'Your resident dish. I haven't stopped thinking about him. Fwoaar,' she says, poking me with her arm. 'I can't tell you what it was like . . .'

I know what I'm going to do now. I've worked out my plan.

'Spare me the details, Lou.' I try and laugh. It comes out like a strange, yelpy little bark. 'You said he hadn't called. I did warn you.'

'No, but with men like that you need to do a bit of chivvying,' she says, not looking too troubled by the idea. 'It's not like he was exactly begging to take me out to lunch, either. I just sort of . . . bent his arm.'

'What, and you'll bend it again?'

'You'd better believe it,' she grins. 'All the way up the aisle.'

'Lou, there's something I have to tell you.'

'I didn't *literally* mean all the way up the aisle,' she says. 'Not that I don't think it'd be a good idea. The sex, Stella. The sex was amazing.'

I quite want to know what she means. Her sex can't have been as amazing as mine. It just can't. Her sex can have been good, or very good, or hot, but it can't have been – what's the word – *revolutionary*, like mine. Or perhaps it can.

Do I really want to know? No. I'm not brave enough.

'Anyway,' says Lou, 'sorry to witter on. You were saying you had something to tell me?'

'It can wait. Carry on.'

'I really think we're made for each other,' sighs Louisa. 'It wasn't just one of those meaningless shags. It was fantastic.'

'You should bear in mind,' I remind her gently, 'that pretty much any shag was going to be fantastic after two years.'

'Yes, but not fantastic like that. I really felt – and this is going to sound so corny – that we were, you know, as one. Perfectly in tune. And then when we went to lunch the next day, he was looking at me in that dazed sort of way that men have when they're beginning to fall for you despite themselves. Has he said anything about me?'

'I haven't really spoken to him about it. He's a big boy now.'

'He most certainly is,' says Louisa, blushing slightly. 'But it wasn't just the sex. I like the way he doesn't talk much – he's more of an action man. He doesn't really chat or do jokes – he's more the strong, silent type, and sexy as hell with it.'

The waitress arrives. 'Anything else?'

'Two more coffees, please,' says Lou. 'Do you want anything to eat, Stella?'

'No, just coffee. Shall I say my thing now?'

'Do,' says Lou. 'And then I can tell you my masterplan.'

'What masterplan?'

'My gentle, arm-bending masterplan.'

'Resulting in?'

'Matrimony,' she laughs, in the way that people laugh when they actually mean the embarrassing thing they've just said. 'Cohabitation, at the very least.'

'He cohabits with me.'

'You wouldn't miss him. You're not very nice about him.'

'Look. What I was going to say was this. Frank is a sack artist. It's what he does, in the same way as you and I do,

I don't know, eating, or coffee drinking, or tooth brushing. I don't think you really understand about men like Frank, Lou. It's just how they are. There's no point in thinking they're going to reform, because they're not. They do it because they can and because it gives them pleasure.'

'They're not the only ones. To get pleasure, I mean.'

'No,' I sigh. 'They're not. Which is why men like Frank are a great idea if that's all you're after – pleasure. If you're really on the same wavelength, and you really want absolutely the same thing: fabulous sex, no strings. But that's not what *you* want, Lou. You've got it into your head that if you chivvy him enough, he'll fall down on one knee and propose to you. It doesn't work like that. It just doesn't.'

'Why are you being such a downer? You know nothing about it. OK, you live with him. But you weren't there the other night. You don't know how he looked at me.'

'Louisa, try and listen to what I'm saying. God, I really fancy a cigarette. Do you have any?' She pushes a packet across the table. 'Thanks. I know quite enough about him, thank you. I know that there's some strange woman . . . that there's some strange woman in his bed two or three times a week – never the same one twice, as far as I can make out. I know that the answering machine is filled with messages like the ones you left this weekend. And I know that he doesn't give a fuck. He wipes them off. Erases them, Lou, and never thinks about them again. He thinks that he's honest, that he goes into these things honestly, that he never pretends to be more interested than he is, and never makes promises he can't keep. And so he thinks that if some woman wants to misinterpret that "honesty", as he'd see it, then that's her problem.'

Louisa is looking at me, not very lovingly.

'Are you saying that he's never, ever fallen in love, or ever had a long-term relationship?'

'No. I know that he has.'

'Well, then!' she says triumphantly. 'If he's capable of falling in love, why shouldn't he fall in love with me?'

I'm just not getting across – and perhaps that's because I don't really want to. Everything I am telling Louisa, after all, could apply equally to me, which fact sickens me a little bit. My heart isn't in this conversation, and I'm achingly aware that my motives are lacking somewhat on the nobility front. Perhaps I'd be better off just coming out with it, just telling her – but I don't have the stomach for that, either. I make a superhuman effort to persevere with Plan A.

'You know that look that people get when they're in bed with you, that look in their eyes?'

'Yes,' says Louisa dreamily.

'Frank had it, right? The look that says, "You are a goddess and I love you madly."'

'Yes,' says Louisa, looking me straight in the eyes. 'He had that look.'

I swallow. 'Well, Lou, here's the thing, here's some news. All men get that look. They could be in bed with a, a donkey, and for a few seconds they'd still give that look.'

'You are very cynical,' says Louisa. 'That's not true.'

'No,' I concede. 'Sometimes the look is for real. But maybe a handful of times in a lifetime.'

'I don't understand what your problem is,' says Louisa, but is it my imagination, or is she sounding a tiny bit less convinced? 'I *know* that he and I are right for each other, even if he doesn't. Yet. And really, Stella, you ought to be happy for me. What's the matter with you? I thought you were my friend. What's with the prophet of doom stuff?'

'I'm just warning you, that's all. You were a notch on his bedpost.'

'Yes? Well, maybe the bedpost is full up and there was only space for one more notch, and I was it. The last notch. Why are you looking at me like that?'

'Nothing,' I shrug. 'Maybe. Maybe you're right.'

'I've got to go,' says Lou, looking at her watch. 'Could you send him my love? My best love?'

'Sure.'

'And see you at playgroup, yes?' She gets up. 'Thanks for all your advice, Stella. We'll see. You do probably have a point, you know.'

'I know.'

'Maybe I'm jumping the gun a bit.'

'Maybe.'

Louisa laughs. 'There's just something about him . . . Still, I'm going to go home and have a think.' She bends down to kiss me. 'I'll ring you. Bye, darling.'

I think that possibly, possibly the penny has dropped. It'll be a long descent, but the penny has dropped. I really hope it has, because I don't know what I'd do otherwise. If I thought about it for too long, I'd feel so sickened by myself, I'd have to take to my bed for six months. But I'm not going to think about it any more. Not today. Tomorrow, as Ms O'Hara so correctly said. Tomorrow.

Honey and I are wrapped in a quilt, watching Maisy videos, when he comes home.

'Hey,' he says, touching my face. 'Hot lady. Grrr.'

'Oi girl,' says Honey, whose vocabulary is slowly

expanding. 'Oi mouse,' she adds, just to confuse me. 'Loike Maisy.'

'Hello, Maisy,' says Frank, stroking her hair.

'Nice day at the office, dear?'

'Excellent day. Brilliant day. Spoke to Dom, and guess what? Guess what, Stell? He's only bloody gone and got me a show in New York next April.'

'Frank, that's brilliant. I'm so pleased. *So* pleased for you. Will you, er . . . Nothing. Do you want a drink?'

'Will I what? Yes, do you? I'll get you one.' He goes into the kitchen humming 'Hey, Big Spender' and reappears two seconds later with two glasses of red. We're turning into alcoholics. 'Top gallery,' he says, naming one.

'Cheers,' I say. 'Chin-chin. Bottoms up. Very many congratulations. That's fabulous, it really is.'

'It is, you know. It's just the best thing.'

'How is Dom?'

'Asked after you, actually. Well, he always does.'

'You didn't tell him. . . .'

'No. I had the feeling he might not like it.'

'I'm sure he wouldn't mind. It's just that . . . well, too much information, really.'

'Yeah.'

'So, will you go to New York?'

'Yeah, in the spring.'

'What . . . to live?'

'Just for a couple of months.'

'Oh, right.'

Frank looks at me. I look at Frank. Nobody says anything.

'I had a coffee with Louisa today.'

'Yeah?'

'I was going to tell her, and then I changed my mind. It made me feel sick, Frank. So I told her you were a sort of priapic monster, and that she shouldn't bother with you.'

Frank laughs. 'A priapic monster?'

'Yes. Permanently, you know, ready. For it. With anyone.'

Frank smiles. I wish he wouldn't smile at me like that. It would really help.

'You sacrificed my reputation, you mean,' he says, still smiling.

'I sullied your pristine name. Yes. I'm sorry. I didn't know what else to do. And besides, I wasn't exactly lying.'

He shrugs. 'So, what did she say? Louisa.'

'She really likes you. She thinks you're her boyfriend.'

'Yeah? Why's that, then?'

'Because you slept with her, maybe, idiot-head.'

'I vass only obeyink orrders,' he says.

'What orders?'

'Yours, love.'

'*I* didn't order you to sleep with her!'

'Funny,' says Frank. 'I thought that was exactly what you did. Pushed us together. Bit baffling, Stell.'

'Anyway, now she thinks you're an item.'

He looks completely uninterested. This is awful, obviously, but it makes me very, very happy.

'Frankie, you might at least pretend to care. For God's sake. You did *sleep* with her.'

'Sleepies,' says Honey.

'I do care. I care that you're still friends. You are, I hope?'

'I don't know, Frank. I can't imagine she's exactly going to whoop with joy and crack open the champagne when she finds out what really went on. And it's going to have to come from me – I'm going to have to tell her, sooner or later. Sooner, probably. I feel like such a bitch.'

'Let's not think about it now,' says Frank. 'And stop wincing. She's a big girl. She'll get over it.'

'She was imagining herself more or less engaged to you.'

'Silly her, then,' says Frank. 'I went out of my way to give her the very opposite of that impression. I always do.'

I sigh massively. 'Anyway. Do you want some food? I couldn't be bothered to cook. I was going to get a takeaway. Or are you going out?'

'Out?' says Frank.

'Yes, you know. Outside. The great outdoors. The outside world. *Là-bas.*'

'No,' says Frank. 'No, I wasn't going out.'

We watch Maisy at the swimming baths. Her swimming costume is stripy, with a hole for the tail.

'Do you want me to go out?' says Frank.

'If you like.'

'Would you *rather* I went out?'

'It's up to you. I meant, don't stay on my account. If you want to go out, then go out.'

'I see,' says Frank. 'OK.'

'About last night . . .'

'And the night before,' he says. I wish he wouldn't give me those looks – they make me die.

'I . . . we . . . I'm not expecting . . . you don't have to . . . You're a free man, Frankie.'

'When's Honey going to bed?' Frank asks.

'In a minute.'

'Shall I take her up?'

'No, let her finish watching this one.'

'OK. You were saying?'

'Oh, for heaven's sake. I was trying to be *subtle*, Frank. What I was trying to say is, it's OK. I don't expect us to start going out. It was really great, but I don't want it to feel awkward between us, and so I was saying, if you want to go out, then go out. With everything that implies.'

'You want me to bring strange girls home?'

'If you want to.' *No no no.*

'What, as in threesomes?' he laughs. 'Blimey.'

'No! Not as in threesomes. As in sexual partners for you.' I can hear my voice, and it sounds very hard. I don't mean it to. But I can't lie in my real voice.

'For you,' says Honey.

'But . . .' Frank has stopped laughing. His face is pale and tight.

'That's all I was saying. Come on, Honey, bed. Sleepies.'

'Stella!'

'In a minute,' I say, already halfway up the stairs. Now, I think to myself as I tuck Honey in. Now. I'm going to ask him now, about his daughter and his daughter's mother and why his loveliness doesn't extend to them. Now.

But when I come back down, he's gone.

19

Twenty minutes later, the door goes. He must have forgotten his keys.

'Thank God,' I say as I open the door.

'Hello,' says Mary. 'Am I late, pet?'

'Hello, Mary. Er, no. You're not late at all. In fact . . .' What's she doing here?

Mary scoots past me and takes off her coat.

'Brass monkeys,' she shivers. 'Now, is my Honey still up?'

'She's asleep. Er, Mary?'

'Look at you,' says Mary. 'Still in your scruffy old house clothes. It's already quarter to nine – you should really go and get ready. I've brought my things in case you wanted me to stay the night again.'

'I . . . I think you made a mistake, Mary. No baby-sitting tonight.'

'Oh, yes,' says Mary. 'Francis said. Rang this afternoon. About five-ish. Taking you to dinner, to some French place, to celebrate something or other, he said. I know it's not really any of my business,' she continues, 'but are you . . .'

'No,' I reply, rather dazed. 'We're not.' Oh, no, *no*. Frank was taking me out to dinner to celebrate his American exhibition and I basically took down my trousers, bent over and crapped all over his evening. Oh, God. I swallow hard. It stings behind my eyes.

'Only his mam asks after him such a lot, and I like to keep her up to date. You and Francis seem to get on so well . . .'

'Yes,' I murmur. 'Yes, we do.'

'It's just he's a grown man now, thirty-five, and she frets about him having a family, you know. Finding the time for it, what with all the fuss they make of him down here. I don't like those cows much, though, do you? Now the dolphin, there's a nice animal.'

'Mary, he's not here,' I say. I feel dazed; I can't think straight. 'I'm so sorry. I think you'd better go home.'

'Aah, he'll turn up. Men are always late,' she says cosily, heading for the kitchen. 'Cup of tea, Mrs Midhurst?'

'No thanks. Look, I really don't think he's coming. I'll call you a taxi to take you home.'

'Don't be so silly. I'll just settle myself down here, and you go and have a nice hot bath. Go on! Off with you.'

'I, er, OK.' Mary in capable mode can be very persuasive.

I've no sooner got into the bath, like an obedient child, than I get out again, spraying slidey water everywhere and practically breaking my leg in the process. What was all that business about Frank's mother worrying that Frank was forgetting about having a family? What was that?

'Mary,' I shout, racing down the stairs in my kimono.

'Mrs Midhurst!' she says, coming into the hall. 'You'll catch your death.'

'Stella, please. I've asked you a thousand times.'

'You're a bad girl, Stella. What is it, pet?'

'Frank. Francis.'

'Yes?' she says, blinking helpfully.

'How well do you know him?'

'Francis? Oh, I've known him since he was a child.'

'Yes, yes, of course. I knew that.'

'I'll tell you all about it one day, if you like. Only – ' she looks at her watch – 'you're going to be very late if you don't get a move on.'

'Now, Mary, tell me now.'

'Well, all right. But you'll catch . . .'

'Never mind about that.'

'What would you like to know?' asks Mary, with the true gossip lover's glint in her eye.

'How? How do you know him?'

'His mam and I are old, old friends,' she says. 'Back home. We were at school together. And my eldest, Andrew, was at school with Francis. Isn't that nice?'

'Yes, yes, that's lovely.'

'It is,' agrees Mary. 'Was there anything else? Only I'm watching such an interesting programme. About fish, you know. Strange beasts, they are, this lot, with huge teeth. I didn't think a fish could have very big teeth, did you? Or a hen,' she adds pensively.

'Hens? No. Fish, I'm not sure. Look, I know this sounds odd, but what I really need to know – please, Mary, it's important – is whether Frankie – Francis – was . . . well behaved. Before he came to London. Was he good, Mary? Did he . . .'

'Oh, no,' says Mary, shaking her head sadly. 'He was a very bad boy. Broke his mam's heart.'

That feeling comes again – that empty, drained, I've-been-weeping-for-days feeling. I push it away and sit down on the stairs.

'He was always naughty,' she says. 'Always. From child-hood. Always in trouble. But kind, you know, to his mam and to his brothers and sisters. Do you know,' she says, 'I probably shouldn't be telling you this, but he sends money home every month.'

'That's very sweet,' I agree. I feel like there's a wasp buzzing about inside my head. 'But you said he broke his mother's heart.'

'Oh, yes,' says Mary cheerily. 'She was very upset when he said he was moving to London. She relied on him, you see. For everything. What with her husband dead. So she was in pieces. She cried for days and begged him not to go. She's all right now, though. Never happier. She does make a fuss,' Mary chuckles affectionately. 'Loves a drama, that one.'

'What about girls?'

'Oh,' Mary laughs – ho ho ho – 'well, *yes*. He was always a one for the girls, that's for sure. And they were a one for him too. Can't say I blame them. Lovely lad. Lovely head of hair.'

'Quite. Was there ever, you know, any *trouble*?'

Mary's round blue eyes gaze up at me, appalled.

'Oh, *no*,' she cries, 'Mrs Midhurst, no. Nothing like that. Goodness me, no. Francis is a gent, always has been. Lovely manners. He has charm, you know, I'll grant you. He's a bobby-dazzler. And he did make the girls cry sometimes – they all wanted to marry him. It's a small place, Mrs . . . Stella, you see. He was the pick of the crop.'

'But nothing bad? Nothing *really* bad?'

'No!' she cries, scandalized at the very idea. 'Heavens, no. Nothing like that.'

'OK. Sorry about the interrogation, Mary. Sorry. And thank you. Thank you.'

'Can I go back to my fish now?' asks Mary.

'Yes, please do.'

I fly back up the stairs, heart pounding, and fall on to the phone. I need to have a little chat with Dominic. Now.

'Do we really have to do this now?' says Dominic sleepily. 'It's half past six in the bloody morning.'

'Too fucking right we do,' I reply.

'OK,' yawns Dominic. 'I lied.'

'*What?*'

'I lied,' his disembodied voice says, sounding bored. 'OK? I'm hanging up now. I'll call you later.'

'What do you mean, you lied? Why did you lie?'

'I mean I made it up. Invented it. Span a falsehood. *J'ai menti.* Do you understand?'

'But why, Dom?'

Dominic laughs. 'I've got nothing against Francis. Did you hear about the exhibition, by the way? Fan-fucking-tastic.' He pauses. 'Not least because it'll get him away from you. I think your set-up is overly cosy.'

'Why did you lie?'

'Why are you asking?'

'Dominic, I am about two seconds away from really, really losing my temper. Just answer me, will you?' I roar down the phone.

Dom seems to find my rage deeply entertaining: he allows himself another slow, lazy laugh.

'Got the hots for Frankie, have we? Christ, Stella.'

'*Dominic.*'

'OK, OK. It's very simple, Stella. I have these people in my working life. I'm surrounded by them: bloody provincials with two O-levels and a way with a brush. They can't talk, Stella, in case you hadn't noticed. They can't hold a knife as though it weren't a pen. And that's one thing. But the oiks spreading into my personal life – well, that's quite another thing. I don't want you shacked up with some Geordie yobbo. So I just told you something that I thought would encourage you to keep your distance. And,' he adds languidly, 'it worked.'

'What are you talking about, Dom?' I whisper. 'You know Frank lives here.' I could pass out with shock.

'Well, if you must have the Geordie yobbo as a lodger, fine,' Dominic says generously. 'What I meant was, I'm not warmed by the prospect of having the Geordie yobbo in your bed. In our bed, to be technically accurate. Not that I have any wish to return to it, you understand. "Our" bed means the bed that I paid for. In my house. With the mother of my child. Which leads me to Honey.'

'What about her?'

Dominic sniggers. 'Do you really think, Stella, that I want my daughter to have some peasant for a stepfather? Some uneducated, inarticulate oik like Frank? As for his legendary promiscuity . . .'

'Leave it.'

'*The fog on the Tyne is all mine, all mine,*' Dominic sings down the line, his voice echoing over the oceans, his accent grotesquely, cartoonishly distorted. 'At least that wimp Rupert went to public school.'

'You make me sick, Dominic,' I tell him. 'You make me vomit.'

'See you,' says Dom, the smile still in his voice. 'Love to Honey.'

I throw the phone across the room.

And then I run, *run* to the bathroom.

*

'That's better,' says Mary approvingly. 'I love that dress.'

'Did Francis tell you the name of the restaurant, Mary? Please, try and remember.'

'Restaurant, restaurant . . . Oh, yes. He said something about the French place around the corner, if I remember rightly.'

'Did he say what time he'd booked for?'

'Nine o'clock, I think.'

'What's it now?'

'Ooh,' she says pulling up her woollen sleeve incredibly slowly. 'Quarter to ten.'

'Stay here, Mary, OK? Is that OK? Just please stay here.' I grab my coat and keys and fly out of the door.

'Have fun, pet,' says Mary. 'I hope you find him.'

Odette's. He must have meant Odette's, where Rupert took Cressida. It's on Regent's Park Road, where Louisa lives. Surely he can't have asked . . .

No. I run out of the door, springing on my trainers, and keep running, like Forrest Gump. How can I have been so thick? I'm Forrest Gump myself, from my thick head to my bu-ttocks.

Five minutes later, panting like a dog, I push open the door of the restaurant. There he is, eating, at a table set for two, a bottle of wine in front of him. The silver on the table glitters in the candlelight.

'Frank.'

He looks up; I register his surprise.

'Stella.'

'So bloody like you to deprive me of my dinner. Why didn't you say?'

'Nice to see you. I was going to. But then you kicked me out.'

'Don't be wanky, Frankie.'

'Could we have another menu, please?' Frank asks the waiter. 'Here, have some wine.' He passes me his glass.

I raise it. 'Congratulations, Frank. Well done. I am very proud of you.'

'Cheers.'

'What are you eating?'

'Onion *tarte tatin*. Want some?'

'Yes, please.'

He puts a forkful into my mouth. I fleetingly wonder whether it would be bad form to hintfully fellate the fork.

'So,' says Frank.

'So,' I say.

'Here we are.'

'Yes.'

'Want me to give you more pulling tips? Point out the dirty rides?'

'Have you been casing the joint?'

Frank gives me an especially Frank look.

'No, Stella. I've been eating my dinner.'

'I must order mine.'

'Naturally.'

'I'm sorry about earlier, Frankie,' I say thickly, addressing the menu. 'I got this weird idea into my head. I . . .'

'It's OK, love,' he says, raising his hand. 'I understand. What are you eating?'

'Steak. You don't understand, actually . . .'

'Don't spoil it,' he says gently, looking at me hard. 'I like having my dinner with you.'

'What I mean to say, Frankie – no, please listen – is, do

you think you could not point out the dirty rides any more?'

'OK,' says Frank slowly, still fixing me with his eyes.

'Would you mind?'

'No,' he smiles, filling the glass the waiter has just brought.

'I wouldn't love it any more. And I wouldn't love it if you brought strange girls home,' I add. 'I wouldn't love strange girls in pants. In the bathroom. Frankly.'

'Really?' smiles Frank, and with his lovely smile an entire ocean of complications and what ifs and oh my Gods just seems to float away. 'Mmm. I was getting kind of tired of them myself.'

'Look,' I say, a grin splitting my face from ear to ear, 'I don't know what'll happen in the end. But after we've finished eating, could we just go home and . . .'

Frank looks down at his plate and then flicks his eyes at me. 'Yes,' he says, in his low voice, with his grey eyes, with his hard mouth that make me d-r-o-o-l. He smiles a smile that manages to be dirty and sweet at the same time. 'Let's eat our dinner and go home and go to bed and not come out till Christmas.'

We look at each other and carry on eating, probably faster than is seemly. 'I don't want pudding,' I say, with my mouth full.

'Bloody hell, Stella,' he laughs. 'Know what you mean, though. D'you think they'll put the cork back in the wine for us?'

'Corky shmorky. Let's go home.'

We pay the bill and I get my coat and suddenly we're out in the street. My hand's in his hand and it stays there this time and it's really sexy – SEXUS MAXIMUS, is what it is, SEXUS VOLCANICUS, is what I want to scream – but I have to tell you, and I might be going mad, that sexy is not the only thing it is.

I turn to Frank and am about to speak, but then I think, No, I've said enough. He looks at me.

'*Be*,' he says. 'Let's go home, Stella, and just . . . be.'

Acknowledgements

'Fog on the Tyne', written by Alan Hull; reproduced by kind permission of The Charisma Music Publishing Co. Ltd/EMI Music Publishing.

'You Made Me Love You', words by Joseph McCarthy, music by James Monaco, © 1913 Broadway Music Corp., USA. (50%) Redwood Music Ltd, London NW1 8BD; reproduced by permission of International Music Publications Ltd. (50%) Francis Day & Hunter Ltd, London WC2H 0QY; reproduced by permission. All rights reserved.

'You Spin Me Round (Like a Record)', words and music by Peter Burns, Stephen Coy, Michael Percy and Tim Lever, © 1985 Burning Music Ltd and Mat Music. (73.33%) Warner/Chappell Music Ltd, London W6 8BS; (26.66%) Westbury Music Ltd, London SW9 8DA; reproduced by permission of International Music Publications Ltd and Westbury Music Ltd. All rights reserved.

'Kiss Me Kate', words and music by Cole Porter, © 1948 Buxton Hill Music Corp., USA. Warner/Chappell Music Ltd, London W6 8BS; reproduced by permission of International Music Publications Ltd. All rights reserved.

INDIA KNIGHT

MY LIFE ON A PLATE

Does secretly fantasizing about buying slut shoes and see-through tops make you a Bad Mother? What about wearing pyjama bottoms on the school run?

Clare Hutt (known to herself as Jabba the) has put her foxy single days very much behind her (rather like her cellulite), and has Got Her Man.

She has a nice house, adorable children who only annoy her 90 per cent of the time, a large, eccentric and charming family, and an attractive (but increasingly mysterious) husband. And she gets to have regular sex . . . well, ish. Anyway, what the hell, it's only loins . . .

Everyone wants to be married – don't they?

India Knight will make you weep with laughter in this hilarious and moving novel, which proves that you can still be Married and Minxy; or possibly just that Solid Torso Action Man, MAC make-up, pumpkin ravioli and Manolo shoes do have something in common.

'Made me laugh out loud. Does for divorcees what *Bridget Jones's Diary* did for singletons' Lynn Barber, *Daily Telegraph*

'Brilliantly funny' *Vogue*

INDIA KNIGHT

COMFORT AND JOY

'I'd say Christmas was about hope. Yeah. Hope. And optimism. It's like the fairy tales in the window: for families, every Christmas is a new opportunity for Happy Ever After. No pressure, then . . .'

Oxford Street, two shopping days left to Christmas, and wife and mum Clara Dunphy is desperately, madly trying to make everything, not perfect, but just right for her extended family on the greatest day of the year. But then she gets distracted . . .

'Brilliant. As healing as a champagne cocktail' *The Times*

'A hilarious, bawdy yet touching portrait of Christmas' Jilly Cooper

'Riotously high in laughs and glamour' *Independent* Books of the Year

'Will make you laugh, maybe make you cry and keep you reading past bedtime' *Grazia*